It was a nut of lichen-gray leaves woven onto a wicker framework. Something shifted across the opening from within.

This has to be a boulder, humped and gray and rolling out through the doorway toward me. . . .

The humped thing straightened onto two of its six legs. Its eyes were faceted red glints. The remainder of the body was gray and yellowish and fish-belly white.

The creature was alive and half again as tall as Dennis. Its jointed legs had spikes and knife-sharp edges of chitin. They glittered as the creature flexed them with scissoring clicks.

"It's time and past time," the creature said, "that Conall remembered that he owes more than beef to feed Malbawn."

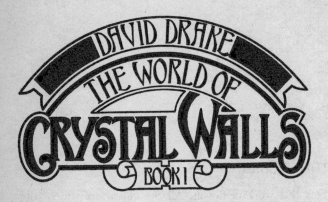

DAVID DRAKE

THE WORLD OF

CRYSTAL WALLS

BOOK 1

THE SEA HAG

BAEN
BOOKS

THE SEA HAG

This is a work of fiction. All the characters and events portrayed in this book are fictional, and any resemblance to real people or incidents is purely coincidental.

A Baen Books Original

Baen Publishing Enterprises
260 Fifth Avenue
New York, N.Y. 10001

First printing, August 1988

ISBN: 0-671-65424-1

Cover art by Larry Elmore

Printed in the United States of America

Distributed by
SIMON & SCHUSTER
1230 Avenue of the Americas
New York, N.Y. 10020

DEDICATION

**To my folks
Who read me fairy tales
before I could read myself.**

DRAMATIS PERSONAE

DENNIS

He'd been born a prince; it was time for him to prove that he was a man.

CHESTER

His wisdom was the vain mumbling of the past— but his steadfast courage would never be out of date.

ARIA

Her life had been a round of pleasure and privilege; now she learned that it all had a price.

THE SEA HAG

It was willing to wait for payment, but it would never forgive the debts men owed it.

CHAPTER 1

The tower quivered when the dragons roared at the village perimeter, where they guarded the community of Emath from the jungle beyond and the things in it.

The noise startled Dennis. He didn't much like heights, and he was holding onto the railing of the highest of the palace's crystalline spires. He'd thought maybe he could see his father's boat from up here.

He'd been wrong. There was no sign of King Hale or the net-tending skiff which the king had rowed to sea alone this morning and every other morning for the past week. Far out on the horizon, the glittering needle of Banned Island pinned the dense gray-green sea to the blue-white sky . . . but there were no sails, and no little rowboat either.

"The heart which worries," said Chester, "makes its owner ill."

"Do you *have* to keep saying things like that, Chester?" Dennis snapped to his companion.

"Indeed I must say them, Dennis," Chester replied smugly. "It is to speak such wisdom that I was fashioned."

1

The lilting voice came from somewhere in the featureless forty-pound metal egg that served Chester as head and body combined. Dennis knew his companion well enough to read Chester's tones as clearly as the facial expressions of a human speaking . . . but Chester had a right to be smug; and anyway, it didn't do any good to get angry with him.

"Well, talk then if it satisfies you," Dennis replied, half resigned and half sulky. "But I don't see that it's ever done me any good, your wisdom."

He turned from the sea to watch the dragons. It was market day, so the Wizard Parol was opening a path for visitors through the concourse which the great beasts prowled—ready to tear and devour anyone who tried to enter Emath unbidden from the jungle.

Dennis craned his neck, but even so he could barely peer past the new houses of stone, wood, and tile built right up to the perimeter's inner edge. Emath was growing, had been growing fast for as long as Dennis was old enough to notice. He could remember when the village was only a straggle of shanties against the walls of his father's great crystalline palace. . . .

Or he thought he could remember that; but memory was a funny thing. The present bustling community didn't have much to do with that dim past, when he'd walked clutching the hands of his parents and looking up in wonder at a new world.

Emath had changed. Her fishing boats were richly successful. The magnificent harbor—the only good one on a coast wracked by storms—made her the center of exchange between human traders and the tribes of lizardfolk from the jungle of the interior.

And Dennis had changed even more. At sixteen—in three days more—he was as big as a grown man; as strong as most; and quicker than anyone else in Emath.

He was Prince Dennis, who wished his father didn't row out to sea alone—and that Hale didn't when he was home snarl as savagely as the dragons on guard.

"The man who sold me to your father on the day of your birth, Dennis," Chester said, "had intended to keep me for himself forever; saying that I was a great marvel."

"And indeed you are a very great marvel, Chester," the boy agreed, reaching down to stroke the smooth metal of the little creature's case.

He was suddenly glad to have a friend who stayed a friend: who didn't glare at him with unexplained anger, like Hale; or cling and cry like Queen Selda, and neither of them able to say what was wrong.

Or even admit that something was badly wrong. It was the uncertainty. . . .

Chester reached up to Dennis with one of his eight ropy limbs, legs when he walked and hands when he chose they should be. "He said to me, 'Can you not silence your silly wisdom, Chester?' And I told him, 'The fault of every character comes from not listening, master.' And he sold me to your father, saying that I was just the thing for a child babbling nonsense."

"If you had fur, Chester, I would rumple it," Dennis said as his fingers scrabbled against the metal. "Since you do not, I will only tell you that indeed I have gained from your wisdom—if that wisdom made you become mine."

Chester's tentacle squeezed the boy's waist gently, then released him.

Again a dragon roared. The beast lurched up on its hind legs, lifting its great-toothed snout a full twenty feet in the air. Its short forelegs were flailing at an invisible barrier, the passage that Parol's magic had armored across the beasts' concourse.

Lizardmen waited at the edge of the jungle. Distance made their features impassive to Dennis, but their heads darted from one side to the other to watch each of the pair of dragons. When Parol signaled, the lizardfolk would sprint across the perimeter into Emath with their trade goods.

Not so long ago, the native traders would have crossed with stately pomp. Some of them would have rolled clumsy great-wheeled carts laden with fruits and pelts and timbers, gems washed from the flanks of distant mountains and items still more wonderful dug from the ruins of incredibly ancient cities. But that was when the Wizard Serdic controlled the perimeter he had established when first he came to Emath—

And when Parol was only Serdic's most recent apprentice.

Parol was a plump, ill-favored youth, much like the others in previous years whom Serdic had hired—or bought—from trading vessels. The apprentices helped with spells so complex they required two voices, and they did the physical drudgery in the separate wing of the palace that formed the wizard's quarters—sweeping the floors, cleaning the equipment, and carrying meals to Serdic's sanctum, which ordinary servants of the palace were never permitted to enter.

Then, after each few years, Serdic brought in a new apprentice and disposed of the old one. Put the boy on an outbound trader with a warning never to return, King Hale said; or darker things, as others whispered, but they never spoke where Serdic might be listening— and where might not so great a wizard find a way to listen if he wished to?

Serdic talked little of himself; talked little to anyone except when he had to, as when he tutored Dennis in reading and mathematics and astronomy because the king had set that among his wizard's duties. Serdic had been cold with Dennis and utterly disdainful of Hale— but he'd obeyed Hale, in that as in all things which the king ordered.

Rumor—manufactured in the parlors and taverns of Emath, or brought in with traders like other exotic cargoes—said that there was no wizard in the world more powerful than Serdic, and that Serdic was three hundred years old. Everyone had been certain that in a few weeks or a month, Parol would go whichever way the earlier apprentices had gone, before they learned enough to pose a danger to their master—who was as cautious as he was terrifying.

But instead, the Wizard Serdic had died.

"It is a son's good and blessed portion," said Chester, "to receive instruction."

"I wish my dad would come back," said Dennis.

He twisted his head around abruptly as if he could trick fate into giving him a glimpse of what he wanted to see. A pair of fishing boats were headed in early. Either good fortune had filled their holds or bad luck had left them in need of repairs. Facts were facts; what they meant was in the hands of time or the gods.

King Hale's skiff was not in sight.

"You can't see him, can you, Chester?" the boy asked in sudden hopefulness.

"From here I cannot see him, Dennis," Chester replied. The robot had no more eyes than mouth, so Dennis had never been sure how he went about seeing. "If he were to row back over the horizon, I would see him."

"Doesn't matter," the boy lied.

The dragons snarled and lunged from either side against the magical barrier which restrained them from the scampering lizardmen. The lithe, gray-scaled traders from the interior carried their packs over their flat heads as they crossed, partly as a feeble protection in case the guard beasts broke through the barrier—and partly so that if the worst occurred, the victims would be blindfolded by their loads and wouldn't see what had happened until the great teeth ended their fear.

"Parol isn't very good, is he?" Dennis said. His mind could spin for only so long on uncertainties before it settled back to practical problems. "We're going to have to get a real wizard to replace him."

Serdic's death—Serdic no longer a lowering, sneering presence in the palace—had exhilarated Dennis as surely as the clear, cool sky that follows a storm.

If Serdic really was dead. No one had believed it at first.

The wizard had been speaking to Hale in the throne room of the palace in front of a score of people—including Dennis. "But raising the port duties from one percent to two *won't* cut trade, your majesty," the wizard said. "Majesty" when Serdic's tongue wrapped around it rubbed Dennis like a handful of nettles. "They have no other port that—"

Serdic stopped. Everyone watched him, waiting for some particularly waspish concluding statement.

The wizard fell forward. His forehead clunked hollowly against a crystal floor so hard that years of use had not even dulled its polish.

"It is true, Dennis, that Parol can barely bridge the barrier for the traders to come and go," Chester was saying. "He will not be able to expand the perimeter again, as surely it must be expanded lest the folk of Emath all be stacked upon one another."

It took Dennis an instant of shock to remember they were talking about Parol, not the Wizard Serdic who was terrible even in memory.

Any thought that the apprentice might know more than an innocent man should about his master's death was put to rest when they summoned Parol to the audience hall immediately—and Parol fell on his knees in horror and disbelief.

For three days, King Hale kept the wizard's body on a bier in the audience hall, dressed in its richest robes. Parol insisted that the Wizard Serdic couldn't have died, not truly. Everyone else believed that this was some sort of sardonic trick with dire implications for those who acted as if Serdic were really gone.

Then the body began to decay, and they had to bury it—with honor, near the Founder's Tomb on the spit of land across the harbor entrance.

It was still hard to believe Serdic was dead, but watching Parol bumble through a simple task cast a pinch of dust over his master's memory.

"Of course," Chester went on, "it may be that Parol will learn if he applies himself. He who is thoughtful and persevering, that man is chosen among the people."

"How can Parol learn?" Dennis said. "Serdic isn't around to teach him any more."

He frowned. "Is he?"

"Serdic is not here to teach him, Dennis," Chester replied. "But Serdic's books and the equipment Serdic brought here to your father's palace, those are here for Parol to use. Only . . ."

The robot paused thoughtfully. Dennis looked down at him and raised an eyebrow.

"Only," Chester said, "the teaching that comes to the fool, Dennis, is as weightless as the wind."

In the same tone, so that it was a moment before the boy understood the words, the robot added, "Your father is returning now."

The skiff was a dot on the horizon, scarcely distinguishable to Dennis' eyes from the mast tips of the dozen or so trawlers sailing in for the evening also. Dennis blinked back tears.

"Well," he said, "let's go down and meet him. Maybe he'll be in a . . . better mood than he's been for a time."

And maybe Hale would even tell his son what was wrong; but the boy didn't believe either of those things would happen.

CHAPTER 2

Chester could probably see in the darkness, but nobody else could; there was nobody else around this angle of the palace roof anyway; and anyway, Dennis wasn't going to break out in a gush of tears again.

"Does he want me to hit him?" the boy whispered to his hands, flat on the backs of his thighs. "I'm bigger than he is, now."

Chester murmured, "It does not kill a son to be punished by his father."

"He shouldn't *say* things like that! He told me I could never go out in a boat and *that's* crazy enough, isn't it, with him spending all day in a skiff if it's so dangerous? But he *never* told me not to come down to the dock to, to *welcome* him!"

Hale's face had been black with sun and fury as he hunched his way up the wooden ladder to the quay. Dennis bigger than his father? Probably, but . . . Hale had shoulders like a troll's, and watching him climb had exaggerated the strength of the older man's back and arms besides.

Dennis had a right to be frightened by someone as powerful as Hale in a boiling rage; but that wasn't why the tears had started to bubble up when he ran from his father.

Chester stroked Dennis' shoulder with a tentacle.

"It's just so frustrating," the boy said. "I must be doing something wrong, but he won't tell me what. I don't know what to do, and nobody will tell me."

He wasn't angry any more, just mentally tired from spinning between anger and emptiness.

The air was so clear that the stars glittered in reflection on the palace roof. Dennis looked at the sky and wished that he could draw himself up into it, to cover himself in a fluffy stellar mist like a feather quilt and hide from all the uncertainties on Earth.

Men came from the stars. At least all the books said they did, though not even the Wizard Serdic could explain *how* they had come here to Earth. The founder of Dennis' family had come from the stars in times so ancient that even his name was lost. He was buried on the headland opposite the palace and his sword of star metal was carried from his hulking rock tomb in the Founder's Day parade every year.

It wasn't Earth that Dennis wanted to leave; just the business of living on it just now.

"A time in misfortune, Dennis, does not make a good man give up," Chester said quietly.

"Maybe there's nobody who *could* tell me what's wrong," Dennis said. He was still morose, but he was thinking about the problem again instead of dreaming it would be nice not to have problems. "I'm not sure Dad even knows. It's just that he's afraid of something bad."

In sudden suspicion, the boy said, "*You* don't know what's wrong, do you, Chester? You aren't just waiting for me to ask, the way you do?"

"I do not know, Dennis," the robot said. "But it may be that old friends of your father know."

"Ramos!" Dennis blurted as he jumped to his feet. "Why didn't I think of that?"

"Why indeed did you not, Dennis?" Chester replied primly. His limbs tick-*whished* as he followed the boy's swift strides toward the window they'd climbed out to hide here.

CHAPTER 3

The palace walls carried light the way a wick carried lamp-oil: along their crystal courses, with only the least seepage across the surface. Dennis was so used to the effect that he walked the long corridors at a normal pace, though they were outlined only in the blue shimmer of starlight which the clear night transmitted.

The palace was huge, far larger than the needs of King Hale and his household. Most of the monocrystalline building was empty. Though the village of Emath was crowded—more so every day with immigrants and the birthrate normal to a peaceful, prosperous environment—there were no squatters lurking in the glittering back-corridors. Only those who'd been welcomed into the palace felt . . . welcome.

Nothing unpleasant happened to interlopers, mostly newcomers to Emath who slipped in through a window or an unguarded entrance with their bindles and ragged offspring. They just didn't feel comfortable in their new surroundings, and they soon left.

Ramos belonged in the palace, but . . .

11

From the bottom of the stairs leading to Ramos' tower room, Dennis could hear the old man singing in a hoarse voice. At first the boy thought the song was a chantey of some sort with a refrain. As he and Chester climbed the tight, dizzying spiral Dennis began to make out the words.

Ramos was singing, "Many the ships that sail right in. . . ." Over and over, the same words each time, trailing off into a repetition as unmusical as the one before.

Unmusical and angry. There could be no doubt of the anger in the cracked, hopeless voice.

The doors of the palace varied. The panel standing ajar at the top of the staircase was layered in pastels and creamy richness like the interior of a shell—but the material formed a flat sheet broad enough to cover the portal without join marks.

Dennis knocked diffidently on the jamb.

"Many the ships that sail right in—"

He knocked louder, on the door itself. The lustrous panel quivered a little farther open.

"—and they never sail out a'tall!"

"Uncle Ramos?" Dennis called. "May I come in? It's Dennis."

"What's stopping you?" the voice demanded. Glass shattered within the room, then tinkled as the larger pieces fell to the floor and broke further.

Dennis opened the door wide with his arm before he stepped through it.

Chester said, "It is the great glory of the wise man to be controlled in the manner of his life."

The windows of the tower room looked out over the harbor and sea in three-quarters of a circle. The water glowed with tiny life. Froth lifted by the breezes traced ghostly arcs above the surface.

The purity and vibrant motion of the water beyond was in shocking contrast to the squalor of Ramos' room.

A lamp hung from the bracket just inside the door. Its wick was turned low. The rush mats that softened the floor hadn't been changed in months, perhaps years. Scavenging insects, startled by the newcomers, sank within the woven rushes like oil being absorbed in filthy sand.

Plates—fine porcelain decorated with gilded rims and the palace crest—were scattered on the floor. On some of them, the food appeared not to have been touched.

"Uncle Ramos. . . ?" whispered Dennis. The stench of the room made him jump as though he'd been slapped in the face.

"What's the matter, kid?" Ramos said with heavy irony. "You don't like my singing?"

He hawked and spat. "For many the ships—" he repeated, but his voice broke in a fit of coughing.

Ramos was a big man, tall where Dennis' father was broad. He was shockingly gaunt now, but even so his heavy bones made him look a giant as he sprawled on the bed. He was wearing his state robes, scarlet and cloth-of-gold; but they were as stained and foul as the floor mats.

There were plates on the bed; but mostly there were bottles, squat green quarts of fortified wine from Bredabrug far down the south coast. The mats beneath the open windows sparkled with bottles that had smashed on the casements instead of flying out of the room.

"Hob-nobbing with the common folk, are you, kid?" Ramos asked.

He'd turned his head to the door when Dennis entered, but now he let his eyes rock back to an empty window—or to nothing. Glass clicked as Ramos rummaged with one arm among the bottles beside him.

Dennis swallowed hard. "Uncle Ramos," he said as he walked toward the bed, pretending he didn't feel the way the rushes wriggled beneath his boots. "Are you sick? And why haven't the servants. . . ? Why have they—"

Ramos had found a full bottle among the empties quivering as the bed moved. "Have a drink with nobody, your Royal Crown-Princeness, sir," he said, still lying flat on the bed.

He had a folding sailor's knife in his right hand. The knot-breaking marlinspike blade was open. He began worrying at the cork—without effect, because he was using the wrong end of the knife.

Dennis forgot his horror. When he was a child, Ramos had carried him perched on one shoulder like a pet lizard. He'd felt taller than the ships' masts then—and perfectly safe, because Ramos steadied him with a hand as solid as carven stone.

Dennis swept bottles away and sat down on the bed. The mattress squelched; more debris rolled down the coverlet in response to his weight. Dennis took the bottle and knife from Ramos, whose fingers didn't resist.

"I'll get some servants up here at once," the boy said quietly.

"No guts, these servants, you know that?" Ramos said, glaring truculently for a moment before closing his eyes and letting his body settle back onto the mattress. "No sporting instinct. They stick their heads in, and if they don't have more wine, I throw empties at 'em. That's sporting enough, ain't it, Royal Crown Princeling?"

"What's the matter, Uncle Ramos?" Dennis asked softly. The horn-scaled knife clicked against the bottle when he switched both objects to his right hand. He twined the fingers of his free hand with those of Ramos, marveling at how near to a size he was with the man he remembered as a giant.

Ramos opened his eyes again. "I'm not your uncle, boy," he said; but without the anger that had edged every word he'd spoken thus far tonight.

"I've always called you that, Uncle Ramos," Dennis said.

Ramos made a mighty effort to sit up, but the mattress was too soft and Dennis didn't realize what the older man was trying to do until it was too late to help.

Ramos let himself flop back. He smiled and said, with something between bitterness and affection, "I didn't always call your father 'king,' you know, boy."

"Is my father angry with you?" Dennis asked. "Is that why . . ." He started to gesture to complete the question, then realized that he didn't need—or want—to call attention to the filth in which the old man was living.

"Hale angry with me?" Ramos said. The bed rocked with laughter which became a paroxysm of coughing without a perceptible transition. He pounded himself on the chest, then rolled onto his side.

With Dennis' help this time, Ramos levered himself into a sitting position. He crossed his long legs beneath him like a sailor mending nets on shipboard.

Ramos started to spit, then caught himself and fumbled for a moment till he found a napkin on the bed. He cleared the phlegm from his throat into the linen, which he folded neatly and tucked into a pocket.

"Your father doesn't care enough about me to be angry, Dennis," he said. His eyes were pale blue, winking from beneath his bushy eyebrows like aquamarines in a matrix of granite. "All Hale wants is for me to keep out of sight and not remind him of what he is."

"What is my father?" Dennis said with almost no inflection. By summoning all his concentration, he was able to keep his eyes meeting the older man's.

"Oh, nothing so very bad, boy," the older man said. There was no mockery in his voice, nothing but mild sadness. "Do you know what I am?"

"You're the Captain of the Guard, Uncle Ramos."

Ramos ruffled the boy's hair. His fingers moved slowly, as if his joints were sticking. "What kind of guard do we need here in Emath, Dennis?" he chided. "I was a soldier once; but mostly I'm just a fisherman."

His expression hardened, his voice taking on the strength and timbre Dennis remembered from childhood. "And I would to god," Ramos continued, "that I'd realized that years ago and not pretended to be what I'm not."

His blue eyes held Dennis like pincers. "And I would to god that Hale did the same: told the world he was a fisherman and not pretend to be a king!"

"But—" said Dennis. The bottle and knife in his right hand rang together as instinct made him jerk back. "But he *is* king, Ramos. Look at the palace."

Dennis made a circular gesture which freed his hand from the older man's without him drawing it away quite deliberately. "We've always ruled in Emath, as long as there've been men on Earth. Look at the—" he gestured again, toward the window facing the other spit of the harbor "—Founder's Tomb."

"Oh, aye," said Ramos ironically. He squinted at Chester and said, "Here, you. Give me a hand up and we'll look at the tomb, we will."

"Help him, Chester," Dennis said, for Chester took orders only from his owner—and even then, the little robot had a tendency to respond literally rather than according to Dennis' broader intent.

"The fool who does not help others," said Chester equably—he braced himself with four tentacles while the tips of the remaining four eased beneath Ramos' elbows and the points of his jutting hip bones "—loses all he has."

Ramos got up from the bed, unfolding like a jack-knife. A bottle turned under his foot. He kicked it aside violently; plates and more bottles clashed in its skittering path.

Dennis moved in front of the older man and swept a track to the window clear with the side of his own boot. Ramos followed him, his second step steadier than the first and the third as firm as that of the laughing, sober giant he'd been in Dennis' earliest memories.

"There, I'm all right," he said, running his fingers down the edge of the window casement—not for support, but for reassurance that the support was there should he need it suddenly.

Chester released the old man, but two silvery tentacles quivered just short of touching: Dennis, not Ramos, had ordered him to help.

The Founder's Tomb was of local rock, the porous laterite limestone used for pillars and thresholds in the houses below the palace's crystal walls. By day it was a hulking thing whose red color was as dull and angry as coals banked in a furnace; but at night, it disappeared into darkness like the jungle beyond. Only when a wave of some size washed the headland did the tomb appear, in silhouette against the glowing sea.

"Look at my hands, boy," Ramos said, raising them beside his shoulders with the palms out. They trembled, and the calluses that had sheathed them once had sloughed away; but the scars from decades of brutal work still remained. Dennis remembered with a shock that his father had hands like that also.

"I *built* your 'Founder's Tomb' with these hands, boy," Ramos said. Instead of bitterness, his hoarse voice glowed with pride: pride in a piece of craftsmanship, and pride as well in the physical labor the job had entailed.

"*I* did it, and your father beside me. Cut the stone, sledged it to the headland, and hoisted it into place."

Ramos paused, looking out into the night. "Wasn't easy, boy, but we did it. Hale thought he needed it, that nobody'd take *him* for a king if he didn't have ancestors back to the Landing. But I don't know . . ."—*now* the voice was bitter— "It seems to me that they never doubted, not a one; and him no more than a fisherman who owned a boat in shares with me as grew up with him Downcoast."

"But the palace. . . ?" Dennis whispered.

He couldn't believe what Ramos was telling him—but neither did he doubt it. Dennis' mind reviewed the vision of his father rowing out to sea every day of the past weeks: the practiced motions, the flat arcs his oars cut above the surface, the minimum of froth and fuss as they bit and drove him forward on the swell. Another old fisherman, going out on the sea that was his livelihood. . . .

Ramos began to shake. Dennis reached to support him, but the older man said, "Wait, no. I'm all right." He leaned over the casement and vomited into the night.

"Oh!" Dennis said. "Let me—"

One of Chester's tentacles touched the boy's lips. "Do not let your tongue go where it was not summoned," the robot quoted as his touch turned Dennis aside.

"There," Ramos murmured after the third spasm had wracked him. He lowered himself carefully to sit on the window ledge. "There, I'm all right." He smiled ruefully at Dennis.

The boy sat down on the other side of the broad ledge. Shards of green glass twinkled jealously on the ground forty feet below.

Ramos reached over and squeezed the boy's knee gently. "Don't look so stricken, lad. Hale's a good man, always has been. I spoke out of place. It was the liquor talking, not your Uncle Ramos."

"Tell me about the palace," Dennis said. "Please, Ramos."

Smiling—toward the sea, not his young questioner—and pinching a curl into a lock of hair that should have been cut long since, Ramos said, "We owned the boat together—built her together, near enough, lad, as bad a shape as she was in when we bought her from old Kilkraus. We named her *The Partners*. Would have liked to call her the *Selda*, both of us; but we didn't dare, because we didn't know which of us she'd pick when the time came for that."

"My mother?" Dennis said.

His body was growing cold. He felt a sort of creepy disorientation. It was as if the ledge on which he sat had tilted up 30 degrees while he continued to talk in seeming normalcy.

It was just that everything looked different from the angle at which he was viewing them since he'd entered Ramos' room.

"Oh, aye, your mother, lad," Ramos said with his smile for the night. "Old Kilkraus' daughter, and a fine woman for all she chose Hale and not me . . . but that was later."

As Ramos talked, his mind sharpened and his tongue gained flexibility. He pointed into the harbor, leaning forward with an easy certainty of his balance that made Dennis queasy to watch. "She was a little craft, *The Partners*, not like those down there at the docks. There were no safe harbors on the coast, so we had to drag her ashore every night."

"But there's a harbor here—" Dennis protested, his sense of skewed reality increasing.

Chester touched the boy's cheek with a tentacle. "Do not let yourself be known as the prattler, Dennis," the robot said, "because your tongue is everywhere."

"There was no harbor at Emath," said Ramos with a flat voice and a flat smile for the boy. "Nothing but rough red cliffs—and the Banned Island to seaward, where any boat swamped if it tried to land."

He waited a moment in grim silence, waiting to see if Dennis would object again.

The boy nodded, agreeing that he had heard the words. He was slipping into a reality different from the one in which he'd lived for almost sixteen years. It was as frightening as if the ground had fallen away from him in the darkness; but if he waited and listened, maybe it would all make sense. . . .

"A little craft, as I say," Ramos continued, a touch of humor in his grin at last, "and a sweet one. We worked her together for choice, but either of us could handle her alone in fine weather, and the weather couldn't have been more fine the day Hale took her out while I lay on my cot, raving with fever while Selda sponged my forehead."

Ramos leaned out into the night, turning toward the sea rather than the harbor he faced when looking at Dennis. "Not so very long ago," he said musingly. "But a lifetime naytheless."

"Before I was born," Dennis said, afraid to give the words even enough inflection to make them a question.

"A year before you were born, lad," Ramos said to the phosphorescent sea. "Exactly a year."

He turned sharply, hard eyes in a hard face—glaring at the bottle Dennis still held. Then the granite lines of Ramos' visage softened and he smiled again. "Not your fault, lad," he said. He was answering a question that Dennis couldn't guess, much less ask.

Firmly again but without anger, the older man continued, "That was in the morning. By noon, my fever had broken and the sky was black with the storm that had blown up. Boats from our village were flying back, those who'd sailed south; but Hale had taken *The Partners* north, up the coast, and she didn't come home in the face of the storm that shook the shutters and lifted roof slates from our huts."

"At Emath," Dennis said, forced by his confusion to spike down at least the physical setting of the new reality Ramos forced him into.

"There *was* no Emath," the older man said harshly. "Only cliffs, boy, bare teeth of rock with raw jungle above them."

He glared. Dennis nodded, and Dennis' fingers wrapped themselves into knots as complex as those of sea-worms breeding.

"Not your fault," Ramos repeated softly. He cleared his throat and swallowed instead of spitting.

"We lost boats that day," he continued. "Fully crewed boats. And I'll tell you something you'll understand some day soon, I'd judge, from the size of you: I cursed myself, lad; because I'd lost my boat and a friend closer nor ever a brother was to me—and I was glad in my heart, for it meant that Selda was mine."

Ramos bent forward, his eyes fixed on Dennis' eyes. The boy did not flinch, even when Ramos reached out and took Dennis' jaw between a thumb and forefinger so gnarled with sinew that they looked like net supports roped in brown seaweed.

Ramos lifted the boy's chin slightly, then turned it to look at the fuzz-downed face from an angle. "Not yet," he muttered to himself. "But you'll understand soon."

"What happened to my father?" Dennis said, trying not to choke on his awareness that Ramos' light touch could crack his neck if a fit of madness took the big old man. The world was going mad already, it seemed. . . .

Ramos jerked his hand back into his lap as if the same thought had danced through *his* head—and he found it more horrifying than even the boy did.

"Nothing happened to Hale," he said harshly. "*The Partners* sailed back with the next dawn, clean and as shipshape as if she'd just been careened. And your father Hale took me and took Selda aboard, and he told us that he was a king now in a crystal palace."

He looked into the darkness while his hand stroked Dennis' knee with the affection of an old man for something he's known and loved for years. "We thought he was mad, Dennis; but we went with him because we loved him, both of us. And he sailed us up the coast to here, to Emath, and it was as you see it—harbor and palace, all perfect, and nothing but rock and danger three days before when we fished the same coast together."

Ramos' hand curved up and gripped Dennis, as gently as could be without the least doubt that he meant the boy to meet his eyes for what he said next: "I will not lie to you, lad. If all the gods stood here before me, I would tell them the same thing. There was nothing—and when your father came back, there was Emath. And he was king of it."

The ledge on which Dennis sat was as solid as all portions of the palace—beyond wear and apparently beyond destruction. He felt as if he were sitting instead on a scrap of timber in a maelstrom, whirling downward toward an end as horrifying as the ride.

"Chester?" Dennis said, turning to his robot companion. "Is this so?"

In his need for the information, he ignored the insult he was offering the man beside him; but Ramos only nodded in haughty assurance.

"It may be so, Dennis," said Chester.

"The people?"

It wasn't clear—even to Dennis—who the boy expected to answer. Chester rested silently on his eight limbs, the tips slightly raised so that not they but the metallic curves beneath the tips took the robot's weight.

"Not the people, lad," Ramos said. "The people came after, when I took out word that the harbor was here. I sailed *The Partners* up-coast and down."

Talk of that past prodded the older man into motion again. He stood up, rising slowly to his full height instead of the stoop in which he had shuffled across the room initially. He said, "I went to every little settlement: where they dragged their boats up a creek-mouth and where they scraped their keels on a shingle shore. I told them—"

Ramos was sixteen years and a lifetime younger now. His voice boomed in the open room and out across the water.

"—there was harborage that would keep them safe in

the worst of storms! Fishing boats and great high-decked traders, it was all one. They could shelter beneath the crystal walls of a palace like none they ever dreamed of, beneath the protection of King Hale."

Ramos sagged as though his hamstrings had been cut. The collapse was utterly unexpected. Dennis jumped up, but far too late to have kept the older man from falling—

Except that Chester had already caught Ramos and was supporting him with four flexible limbs, because Dennis had told him to help Ramos, and the robot never forgot an instruction.

"No, no, I'm all right," said Ramos softly; and perhaps he was, but Chester didn't let go until he'd lowered his charge to the ledge again. Dennis settled back, afraid to appear too concerned about the older man's sudden collapse.

Ramos met his eyes. With a firmness that was a matter of present will rather than past memory, Ramos said, "I told them they would be under the protection of King Hale and Queen Selda."

His pause was only to prove that he was in control of his words and his emotions. "And so they have been, all who came then at my urging or later as the word spread of its own accord."

Dennis swallowed. He couldn't absorb all he had been told, much less accept it. But in this moment—when the world was shifting around him, and the ageless crystal palace in which he'd been born was suddenly a construct younger than many of the fishing boats in the harbor—Dennis couldn't doubt the story either.

But while Emath might have been built recently, it had not been built by men.

"Where did the palace come from, Uncle Ramos?" Dennis asked.

The older man shook his head sadly. "A god, a sea demon. There are plenty of demons out on the water, lad. Besides the ones we men bring with us."

His hand played with the window frame as if it were the shroud of a sailing vessel . . . and slipped away because it was not, because it was only slick stone with no life or meaning to him. "Nobody doubted, Dennis. People we'd known all our lives came to Emath—boys we'd played with, girls we'd met at night beneath the shelter of the sail spread as a tarpaulin. And it was all King Hale this and Queen Selda that. . . ."

"But surely somebody would have remembered," Dennis said, letting the doubt he wanted to feel enter his voice.

Ramos smiled. "I think at first they all remembered," he said. "But they didn't want to, because they wouldn't be able to understand it. *I* didn't want to remember, lad. But I built the tomb with these hands—"

He raised them. They no longer shook.

"—and nothing can change that."

Ramos glared at the floor and the filth in which he had been living these weeks, these months; longer. "Not even the liquor!"

Dennis made his decision as he stood up. He didn't know what his new knowledge meant, but he was certain of what he owed Ramos—for himself and for his father—in the immediate present.

"You can't stay here," he said briskly, now the prince that he'd been raised to be. "Come on, Uncle Ramos. We'll help you to my room for now. You can bathe and sleep there tonight while I have the servants clean—" he caught the disgust that had almost broken out into words "—clean up."

Ramos stood obediently. He looked tired, but he was in no need of help Chester and the boy were ready to give. The drink had burned out of him; and so had the emotion that had staggered Ramos with memories of the woman he'd loved—and had lost when his world shifted, as he'd now shifted the world of the boy who called him "Uncle."

"I think . . ." said Dennis wonderingly. He put his arm around the older man's in affection, not for need as they shuffled together through the debris to the door. "I think that you can wear some of my clothes, Uncle Ramos. Until we see what kind of shape yours are in."

As Chester opened the door ahead of them unbidden, Dennis realized that—whatever might be the full truth—the world was no longer the place it had been when he entered Ramos' room.

And in many ways, it was better.

CHAPTER 4

Dennis stretched luxuriantly in the sunlight that flooded the spare bedroom of his suite—and leaped up, shouting, "Oh!" when he realized that it was three hours later in the morning than he had intended to rise.

Hale had rowed out to sea before Dennis could demand an explanation—or a denial—of Ramos' story.

"Chester," the boy said angrily. "You knew I wanted to talk to Dad. Why didn't you wake me up when you saw I was sleeping late?"

"Gentleness in all behavior gains the praise of a wise man, Dennis," said the robot.

"But why didn't you—" Dennis started to repeat . . . and caught sight of his multiple images, reflected in the prismatic walls of the unfamiliar room . . . and laughed instead. He *had* to laugh to see dozens of himself, wearing pajamas and furiously waggling fingers against an equal number of impassive Chesters.

"All right, Chester," he said ruefully, patting his companion's smooth carapace. "You didn't wake me because I didn't tell you to wake me. That was my fault."

"You did not tell me to wake you," Chester said. "And you were sleeping soundly, Dennis, as you have not slept in some weeks past. I am glad that you have slept."

Dennis had snatched an armload of clothes from the wardrobe when he turned over his usual room to Ramos the night before. He'd gotten several blouses, but the only trousers were a pair that had grown too tight for comfort in the past six months.

It would've been simpler to keep his usual room, the larger one of the suite, and give his guest the spare; but—Dennis didn't need Chester spouting a tag like "Do not take precedence over an older man," to know that he owed honor as well as help to Ramos.

Dennis had been raised to be a prince.

Whether or not his parents were really a king and queen.

The dragons were bellowing again. Parol must have decided to start earlier today. Lizardfolk weren't permitted to stay overnight within the perimeter of Emath. Almost no daylight had been available for trading yesterday, by the time the guard beasts were finally contained.

The apprentice wizard would gain skills quickly—or he'd have to be replaced. Unless the perimeter were expanded within a matter of months, people would have to start building on the headland opposite the palace, displacing the graves there. Even another Serdic looked preferable to that.

King Hale would probably have acted already . . . except that he'd spent the past three weeks with the sea and his own grim thoughts for company, instead of taking care of the business of his kingdom.

Dennis pulled his trousers on, then paused. "I still want to talk to him," he said harshly to Chester, glaring at the argument he expected to hear from the little robot.

"Do not be so impatient when you ask," Chester said, "that you then become angry when you listen."

"I . . ." Dennis began.

He began doing up the buttons of his blouse so that he didn't have to look at his companion when he continued, "Look, Chester. Dad doesn't want to talk to me. He'd have talked already if he did. So he's going to get angry—"

The boy raised his eyes to the robot, poised motionlessly on the curves of its eight limbs. "Chester, I'm going to make him tell me no matter what. Because I've got to know what happened before I was born. And from what Uncle Ramos says, there's no other way I can learn."

Chester swayed slightly from side to side. Dennis' reflection in the robot's dull silver finish seemed to be shaking its head.

"*Is* there another way I can learn?" the boy demanded.

"There is another way you can learn, Dennis," Chester said with self-satisfied calm. The robot never exactly volunteered information, but there were times he was more forthcoming than others. When Dennis was pushy or hostile with his little companion, he could expect to be given time to consider his behavior.

When Dennis calmed down, as he'd learned to do immediately by now, he knew *that* was for his own good too.

"Please Chester," Dennis said with polite formality. "What is the way that I can learn how Emath came to be—without asking my father?" He bowed.

"The Wizard Serdic had a device that could tell us, Dennis," Chester replied with equal formality. "The wizard is gone, but the device is not gone from the rooms in which he worked."

"Oh," said Dennis, trying to process the information

he'd just been given. "Oh. But will Parol help us, Chester?"

The robot raised one tentacle in a delicate gesture that indicated to the boy his ill-temper had been forgiven. "Parol cannot help us, Dennis," he said, "for Serdic did not teach him the use of the apparatus."

Chester paused. Instead of flaring up angrily again, Dennis smiled to show that he knew Chester was trying to trap him.

"I know the use of the apparatus, Dennis," Chester said, the approving smile in his voice matching the boy's reflected expression.

"Then let us see what the apparatus will tell us, my friend," Dennis said, squeezing the raised tentacle as he led the way to the door. "If Parol can't help us, we'll look into his rooms while he's occupied with the dragons."

Dennis kept a cheerful lilt in his voice, while his quivering stomach was all too aware that "Parol's rooms" had been the Wizard Serdic's rooms not long before.

But the feeling of doom that lay over Emath frightened Dennis more than memory of Serdic could.

CHAPTER 5

Serdic had appropriated a ground-floor wing of the palace. It extended along the seacoast rather than the harbor which the suites of the royal family overlooked, so Dennis and Chester had most of the building's convoluted length to traverse.

When they started out, the boy felt furtive: he was going to sneak into somebody else's private rooms. Then Dennis noticed that the servants he met jumped and bowed to him with more than their normal courtesy.

There wasn't a great deal of work to do about the palace except on special occasions like the Founder's Day ceremonies. The servants he ran into in these sprawling corridors where neither he nor his family had much reason to walk—were here to avoid notice. They didn't expect to be bothered by their superiors while they ate, chatted, or diced in desultory games.

Dennis didn't expect to find Rifkin, the butler, among the idlers, though.

The butler's voice, loud and demanding in its timbre, came from what should have been an empty room.

30

There was a woman speaking also, but her words were scarcely a breathless whisper beneath the butler's insistence.

The boy paused and cocked an eyebrow at Chester.

"Do not hesitate to do what is right, Dennis," the robot said tartly.

Dennis rapped on the door with his knuckles.

"Go away, fool, or I'll have you flayed!" Rifkin bellowed from within.

"Rifkin!"

There was a silence as palpable as an indrawn breath. The door flew open. The butler was tugging the ends of his sash together with one hand and holding the doorknob with the other. He was a big man but soft, a moon-shaped head above a pear-shaped body, and at the moment his pale fingers had the look of uncooked sausages.

"Your highness!" he said in amazement. His voice had its usual rounded dignity, but the look in his eyes awaited the garrote.

There was a rustle within the room. One of the maids—a young girl, younger than Dennis—pushed out between Rifkin and the doorframe with a gasp. She sprinted down the hall and around a corner, trailing sobs.

Dennis stared at the butler. "Has Councilor Ramos' room been cleared yet, Rifkin?" he said without emotion.

Rifkin made a little bow. "It will be seen to immediately," he said.

"I woke you last night and asked you to take care of it at once!" Dennis said.

Instead of thundering with command, Dennis' voice was getting high. His skin became prickly-hot all over. He was frustrated and angry—and those emotions threw him back to other moments of anger and frustration, the times he'd tried to talk as a man with his father and had been slapped verbally as a child.

He was afraid he was going to cry.

"Yes, of course, highness," Rifkin replied as his hands did up his sash and his face pretended it had never been untied. The first panic had passed, and the butler was in full control of the situation again. "And I'll see to it at once. Even in such a—if I may say—humiliating circumstance as that one, your highness' word is our law."

"Why didn't you—"

"Perhaps your highness might wish to consult his father now that your highness has had time to reflect on the matter?" Rifkin continued smoothly. He smiled.

"Do as you're ordered!" Dennis shouted as he turned away. Shouting because at any lesser volume his voice might have choked, turning because he wasn't sure what his eyes were going to do.

"Yes, of course, your highness," the butler murmured unctuously to Dennis' back as the boy stumbled toward a staircase to the ground floor.

"Chester, why can't I. . . ?" Dennis said with his teeth clenched against his own emotions. "Why won't anybody. . . ?"

Instead of spouting some scrap of the wisdom programmed into him in a far time on a distant planet, Chester wrapped a tentacle around Dennis' waist with a touch as delicate as that of a spiderweb.

CHAPTER 6

The entrance to what had been Serdic's wing of the palace was off a small rotunda at the base of this staircase. The rotunda was empty except for litter and a vague smell. There was regular traffic to the wizard's quarters, meal-trays being brought and removed—but the adjacent part of the palace didn't get cleaned.

Despite that, the circular room had a striking beauty at this hour. Sunlight wicked through twisted prisms in the high ceiling and framed the western half of the circumference with columns of pure colors.

In the center of the insubstantial colonnade was a tall door of black pearl. It was ajar.

"Why isn't it closed, Chester?" Dennis asked as he walked closer. "Isn't Parol down at the other end of town with the dragons?"

"Parol is with the dragons, Dennis," said the robot. "And he has wedged the door open so that he can enter again when he returns this evening."

Dennis stared at the door. Over the threshold had been shoved a heavy foot-bath. It was a malachite. The stone's hideous green color clashed with the pure columns of light—and would have looked equally ugly in almost any other setting as well. Dennis could imagine why Parol used the piece as a doorstop.

But he couldn't imagine why a doorstop was needed.

"Can't he open the door to his own rooms?" he asked wonderingly.

"He cannot open the door to the Wizard Serdic's suite from the outside, Dennis," Chester explained. "There is a spell on the panel that Serdic placed, and it is not within Parol's power to work or change it."

Dennis' face set at the reminder of Serdic—and that Serdic's death did not necessarily end the wizard's power. "All right," he said. "Let's go in and, and do what we must do."

He pushed the panel open against the natural tendency to close which all the doors in the palace shared. The black pearl was vaguely warm and had a waxy slickness.

Dennis was frightened to enter the wizard's suite, but it was a fear he could face and accept. The feeling that his father's anger struck into him was fear also—but it was a child's fear of ultimate power.

Even though Dennis knew that Hale's shouting rage could not itself hurt him—that physically the two of them were at least a near match by now, father and son—Dennis reacted to his father's moods as unreasoningly as he had done when he was an infant.

The wizard's apartments were unfamiliar, and they might be dangerous; but Dennis could face them as the man he was growing to be.

There was nothing in the anteroom of the suite except an oil lamp burning on a cast-bronze pedestal. The open flame was backed and doubled by a round silver mirror, but even so its gutterings as the door swung open were almost invisible in the flood of light through the crystal walls and ceiling.

Dennis frowned at the lamp. "Does he expect to come back after dark then, Chester?" he asked.

"He may or may not, Dennis," said the robot. Chester curved a tentacle almost to touching the stand. While the lamp was very plain, the pedestal on which it stood was a delicate tracery of cast insects clinging to one another. "The lamp, though, is only the watchman Serdic left to tell him what happened in his suite while he was gone."

"What?" said Dennis, the word a way to gain time while his mind worked on the implications of what he'd just been told. "Will the lamp talk to Parol when *he* comes back?"

Two of Chester's limbs moved in a shrug. "That I do not know, Dennis," he admitted.

"Anyway," said Dennis, "it doesn't matter because we're here now."

He nodded curtly to the quivering flame and strode further into the apartments, his thumbs hooked arrogantly in his belt.

The design of the palace had no fixed floor-plan. This wing consisted of rooms opening directly off one another instead of lying along a corridor.

Only the oil flame furnished the anteroom. The following chamber was larger with a ceiling vaulted into five sections. The pentacle formed by the crystal groins might have had something to do with why Serdic appropriated this set of rooms, but the room formed a museum of sorts instead of a magical workroom.

Along the crystal walls stood bubbles of human-blown glass. In any background but that of the palace, they would have been amazing for their size and the skill of their manufacture.

From the largest bubble glared the lifelike mummy of one of the lizardfolk: his gray scales bore a healthy luster, and there was a glint in his yellow eyes. Dennis couldn't imagine how anyone could have blown a bottle so large and nearly perfect . . . but swatches of the glass had a milky sheen, and variations in thickness distorted the lines of the specimen within.

The crystal room was perfect and in its perfection denied any possibility that Emath Palace had been built by men.

There were scores of other containers—perhaps hundreds, because most of them were tiny and contained six- and eight- and many-limbed creatures. Dennis glanced around, curious and suddenly aware that he didn't know what precisely he and Chester were looking for.

He recognized most of the larger exhibits—birds and the lizards of various shapes that skittered into Emath across the perimeter, unhindered by the dragons on guard. There was one creature, though, that was so unfamiliar that Dennis didn't remember ever having seen anything like it.

Except perhaps for a human being.

Only the face was man-like—and that in a wizened, sneeringly-angry way. Its muzzle was broad and flat. Muzzle, lips, and the palms of the creature's hands were bare black skin. The remainder of the little body—it could have weighed no more than a few pounds in life—was covered with coarse hair that seemed either red or blond depending on how the light struck it.

It was unique and uniquely unpleasant—though Dennis couldn't have explained why it bothered him more than, say, one of the long-fanged lizards he knew to be poisonous. He turned away, his face wrinkling into a grimace like the creature's own, and said, "Chester, what are we looking for?"

"It is in the next room that we must look, Dennis," the little robot said nonchalantly as he led the way through an open doorway decorated with crystal arabesques.

The walls and ceiling were swathed in black velvet so

that even now, at mid-morning, the sun penetrated only through the door. A further drape, pinned back at the moment, could be swung to close that opening as well.

The circumference of the room was filled with machines—things of metal and glass and dull ceramic. Dennis couldn't imagine a use for any of them.

The velvet was solid black, as nighttime in Emath never was. The darkness pressed in on Dennis and added to the discomfort he'd felt since pushing open the black pearl doorpanel.

The air within the wizard's quarters was as musty as the atmosphere of a deep cave. It wasn't poisonous or even actively unpleasant; it just hadn't moved very much in all the time Emath existed. The anteroom smelled of hot oil; around the glass bubbles hung a chlorine tang vaguely reminiscent of the sea.

In this third room, the odor of velvet slowly decaying struggled against a sharpness that was less a smell than a rasp at the back of Dennis' throat.

It reminded him of the night lightning had struck a dozen times on the highest towers of Emath. After the last stroke, a hissing orange globe had floated down a corridor and into the center of the throne room before exploding. The ball of lightning left behind a miasma like the one which emanated from the wizard's machines.

"Chester," Dennis said.

He took a deep breath and looked around with a haughty expression that protected him from the fear that would otherwise make him shiver. "Well, get on with it. Are we going to stay here until Parol gets back?"

Chester leaned his egg-shaped body back at an angle and said, "The man whose good character makes him gentle, creates his own fate, Dennis."

The boy's nostrils flared in anger—and he caught himself. "Little friend," he said, smiling and reaching for the tentacle which the robot raised to meet the offered hand. "I don't like it here. Forgive me my irritability."

"One does not know a friend's heart until one sees him anxious," Chester said with approval. Even as he gripped Dennis' hand, three more of his limbs were playing over the case of the nearest machine.

The device had a broad, flat surface like that of a draftsman's easel. For the moment it was tilted up at 45 degrees, but the slender arms supporting the easel seemed to be as capable of movement as Chester's own limbs.

When they'd entered the room, the pedestal and easel were of the same dull black material. At the robot's touch, faint colors—too angry to be called pastels; the shades that metal takes as it heats and cools in a forge—began to streak what had seemed the pedestal's solid interior.

The room began to quiver at a frequency too low for sound. There was a fresh whiff of lightning-born harshness.

"What is it that you wish to know, Dennis?" the robot asked.

"I—" the boy said. "I—Chester, ask it what it was that my father did in the storm the night—the storm Ramos told us about."

Instead of speaking, Chester shifted the delicate tips of three tentacles. Colors richened and merged with one another. Dennis leaned over the flat surface, wondering if he would see letters form there. The blackness of the easel was a palpable thing that sucked in the dim light. It had no reflection.

The illumination within the chamber increased and changed quality with a suddenness that made Dennis whirl. He expected to see the drapes sliding back and someone—Parol, rationally; but momentary terror filled his mind with a vision of the corpse of Serdic—standing in the door that was the only way to escape from this complex of rooms.

Instead, he didn't see the room at all.

Where the velvet and squatting machines had been, the sea tossed under a sky of terrifying gray-green translucence. Lightning spat from point to point on the wall of encircling clouds; waves shot straight upward from the sea's surface, although there was no wind.

Dennis had never been permitted to board a ship, but he was looking from the deck of one now: an open fishing boat, single-masted and tiny against the lowering circle of clouds. Chester had vanished. Dennis' own body had vanished.

His father clung with corded muscles, the tiller in one hand and a mast stay in the other. Rags of sailcloth snapped from the spar every time the open boat pitched.

Hale's hair was black and his face younger than that of the father Dennis knew in life. His mouth was open, but he was no longer trying to shout against the tumult.

The sea became as still as the dead air within the eye of the storm. The water began to change color beside the boat's starboard rail. Streaks of brown, waving in sinuous ripples; coalescing, spreading wider and sharpening into burnished purple. . . .

The ripples of color formed a circle forty feet across. A living thing rose in the center of the tendrils that were the fringe of its body.

"A sea hag . . ." Dennis whispered to Chester; but the boy had no companion to hear in this place of storm.

The sea hag had the face of a beautiful woman floating in the swirl of her lustrous hair, but the skin was gray and the expression was still as marble. Beneath the face and seeming hair was a greasy hugeness over which the ocean shimmered like the surface of a wading pool. The fishing boat steadied.

Nothing moved but the sea hag's hair and the wall of storm beyond.

"What is it that you want?" Hale shouted at the

creature which gripped the keel of his boat. His voice was clear and strong; fear had raised it an octave above its normal pitch.

Dennis had heard of the sea hag as he had heard of a score of other bogeys from his nurse's imagination or the ancient past of Earth before men came here from the stars. Imagination surely, but—

The thing floating in the water opened a mouth that split the woman-face and crossed the "hair" floating a yard to either side. The creature's gullet was arched with bone and otherwise as red as heart's blood. From corner to corner, the mouth was wider than Dennis was tall.

The sea hag said in a cavernous voice, "King Hale, I would bargain with you."

The huge lips closed and their edges merged. The female features reformed as if they had never been split and distorted across the head of a monster as great as the boat beside which it floated. The ridges of brown and purple scales that counterfeited hair trembled again to complete the illusion.

"Let me go!" Hale cried. "You have the wrong man. *I'm* no king!"

"Would you be a king, Fisherman Hale?" rumbled the sea hag, smearing its human countenance again.

Dennis would have closed his eyes, but he had no eyes in this time, and no sound came when he tried to scream.

"Or would you be a drowned corpse that my sea casts up when the fish are done with it?"

The white-red throat growled like the storm. The lightning-shot circle squeezed closer to the motionless boat.

"What will you bargain, sea hag?" Hale demanded with shrill courage that calmed his son to hear. Hale was frightened, facing death and a monster more shocking than death; but he was facing them as best he could.

Dennis, safe behind a veil of time and magic, had his father as a model of how a man should act in the final crisis. Hale's son could do no less than control his feelings now, when he was only a phantom of sense and feelings.

"I will make you king of this shore, fisherman," the sea hag said. "King of Emath."

"Dead man on dead rocks, is that what you mean?" Hale cried. "Begone, sea-bitch—the storm will bargain me *that*."

"I will make you king in a crystal palace if you bargain with me, fisherman," said the sea hag. "I will raise a harbor safe in any storm, and all who use the harbor will be yours to command under our bargain. All this . . . or the rocks and the fish and the birds to peck your bones."

"You're toying with me," Hale said, no longer shouting or angry. He let go of the tiller and stay; the boat was as firm as if it were dragged its length onto shore. "Why do you talk of bargains, sea hag? I haven't anything but my clothes and this boat—and only a half share in the boat."

The sea hag closed its lips. Its woman-face smiled at Hale with the icy visage of a castle courtesan.

"Give me your firstborn son, King Hale," said the terrible real mouth.

"I haven't a wife, I haven't a son," said Hale, wringing his hands at the false hope. "I *haven't* a son!"

"Give me your firstborn son when he is a year of age, King Hale," said the sea hag. "And I will give you Emath and your life."

"You can't really do that," Hale said. "You can't make me king. . . ."

His voice had fallen almost to a whisper. Dennis heard it, and the woman-face smiled again.

The wrack of storm clouds was clearing, blowing away in tatters in every direction. The sun was low in the west. Its light streamed in crimson fingers through the remnants of the storm.

"Bargain with me, King Hale," said the sea hag.

Hale closed his eyes. His hands gripped one another so harshly that the blunt nails drew blood.

"Have your bargain then!" he shouted to the creature.

"I have your word, King Hale," said the sea hag. "And when the time comes, I will have our bargain."

The creature began to sink. The boat trembled as a fresh breeze shook its mast and furled sail.

When the cloud curtain rose, it displayed the shore half a mile to leeward. The rocks of the corniche were dulled by the horizon's shadow, but sunlight still lit the jungle canopy and the rare bright flowers there.

Hale muttered a thankful curse. He slipped a loop of rope over the tiller preparatory to shaking out enough sail to tack clear of the cliffs.

It was as if neither storm nor sea hag had ever existed. Dennis was suddenly sure that he was a wraith in a time that had never existed: that his father would sail off into a future of fish and—

Water began to surge at the shoreline.

First a rumble, then a double spout that threw mist high into rainbow diffraction. The breeze that had followed the storm now failed, but the boat began to pitch with the violence of the sea roaring in the near distance.

Ropes of glowing rock lifted high enough above the sea that the steam of creation no longer hid the angry glare. The lava was fiercely orange at the moment it appeared, black the instant it cooled below liquescence. As the double headlands rose into a firm barrier against the might of any storm, their sea-washed roots took on the same dull red as the corniche from which they now extended.

A vagrant puff of air blew from the land. It felt hot and smelled of sulphur. Fish floated belly-up on the surface of the sea. Dennis' father held a sheet reeved through the three-fall block at the masthead, ready to raise the sail; but he hadn't moved since the shore began to boil into a harbor.

For a moment it looked as though steam and mineral-rich vapors were growing thicker over the south headland. Something like a vortex reached out of the clouded land, climbing higher—

And exploding into brilliant crystalline radiance as it rose into the plane of the sunset. Emath Palace was growing while Hale and his unseen son watched and wondered and thought about the bargain which the sea hag had sealed in crystal.

For a moment, the light on the sprouting towers was as dazzling as the heart of a ruby. Then the light faded; the world faded; and Dennis stood in a dim, musty room, looking at Chester and shivering.

Dennis started to speak and found he had to cough to clear his throat of dust from the velvet. "Did it really happen?" he asked quietly.

When Dennis entered the wizard's chamber, he'd thought he was a man whose father treated him like a boy. Now that he'd seen what it might mean to be a man, he was no longer sure what he was.

But he knew what he would try to be.

"The device shows only what has happened, Dennis," Chester said, waggling a tentacle over the machine that was again cold and dark. "It shows that or nothing."

"Then—" Dennis' mind struggled out of the memories that enmeshed it like tendrils of brown and purple hair gaping into red terror.

"Then," he repeated firmly, "did I have an elder brother who was traded for the kingship?"

"I do not know if you had an elder brother."

Dennis grimaced toward the doorway, steeling himself for what he must do next. He had to demand an explanation from his mother, despite the tears and waves of guilt with which she would flood him.

"But," the little robot volunteered unexpectedly, "you became my master at your birth, Dennis; and that was a year to the day from when the sea hag bargained with your father, as we saw."

Dennis found that his hands were stiff because he'd been clenching them since . . . he wasn't sure how long he'd been doing that, trying to control his emotions by keeping a tight grip on all his muscles. He stretched deliberately, knowing that he couldn't relax but he *could* keep his tension from hurting him.

"Chester," he said, "you showed me how my father became king. Can you show me what happened wh-wh-when his son grew to a year old?"

"I will show you, Dennis," said the robot, his tentacles waking the pedestal to colored life again. Their motion paused.

"Dennis," he said, "the man who does not resent his fate has a good life."

"I . . ." said Dennis. "Please show me how Hale met his bargain, friend."

"I will show you, Dennis."

There were rooms beyond this one in the wizard's suite—a bedchamber; surely a library; and whatever else only gods or devils knew, and Dennis had no desire to learn. The youth rubbed his palms together to work off nervousness without clenching them again.

The room faded into a sky as thick as velvet and almost as black.

Dennis was on/in/over a vessel again on a stormy sea, but this time the boat was even smaller than *The Partners*. It was an open net-tending skiff like the one—perhaps the very one—in which Hale had rowed to sea these three weeks past.

Hale sat on the midship's thwart, resting his oars on the gunwales and looking toward the horizon with a face as grim as the encirling storm.

Hale was not yet the man Dennis remembered as his

father, but neither was he quite the fisherman standing transfixed by horror on the deck of *The Partners*. Instead of homespun linen, Hale wore a silk tunic next to his body and covered that with blue-black wool from the Islands of Hispalia.

Around Hale's neck was a triple chain of heavy gold. Though the chain's lower curve was hidden beneath the garments, Dennis knew that the royal seal of Emath hung there as it always did when his father was awake.

Hale's face was fleshier than it had been when he was a fisherman, but emotions pulled it into a rictus almost as inhuman as the visage of the little creature next door in a bubble of glass.

The storm was a brutal thing, as savage as any tempest that lashed the seas of Hell; but Hale rode in the eye of it, where the sky shone green and grim and the leaping water was disorienting but not dangerous.

No vessel could have survived the wall of wind and lightning which encircled the boat. Even the greatest of the trading ships which anchored in Emath Harbor during Dennis' present would have been torn to bits by the ravaging weather. Hale was alone except for his boat, his son's wraith, and the gelatinous shape of the sea hag, rising from the deep as the sea stilled.

The human head broke the calm surface, smiling and making enticing gestures with the arms that lay in the circle of hair. Hale stared at the creature fiercely without speaking.

The sea hag's real mouth gaped open. The arms deformed into barbels at either corner of the jaw. The smile smeared itself unrecognizably into scaly horror.

"Welcome, King Hale," said the sea hag. Dennis could hear the amusement in the booming voice. "Have you brought me the price of our bargain two years past?"

When the creature spoke, the air stank of fish and death.

"Make me another bargain," Hale blurted. His hands clenched together, releasing the oars. The blades slipped only an inch or two into the sea, where they rested on something beneath the surface. "I'll give you anything you want. Anything!"

"You're a rich man, King Hale," chuckled the sea hag. "You have everything that trade and power can bring a man . . . and everything you have is a thing that I have given you—except one. Pay me the price of our bargain, King Hale."

"Take my *life*, damn you!" shouted Dennis' father as he lurched upright in the boat. "Take *me!*"

"The storm had your life two years past, fisherman," said the creature. "As I saved you then, so I will have our bargain now. Bring me your firstborn."

"Oh god," said Hale as he sank back onto the thwart. It was prayer or curse or a despairing ejaculation, and perhaps all three at once in his voice. Though he sat down heavily, the boat barely shuddered.

"What would you have, King Hale?" said the sea hag in a voice that rumbled like the bellies of the dragons— but much louder.

"He's so . . ." Hale tried to say between the net of fingers with which he covered his face. By an effort of will, he jerked his hands down and looked at the monster which taunted him. Tears were dripping down his weathered cheeks.

Dennis reached out to put his arm around his father's shoulders. He touched nothing, because he had no body in this place.

"I can't let you have Dennis," Hale said simply. "When his mother holds him, she looks . . . looks like an angel, sea hag. Are you woman enough to understand that? Take me. I can't give you my son."

No one could doubt the quiet determination behind the words. Hale's tears continued to stream down his face. He didn't bother to brush them away.

Dennis tried again to clasp him. If he'd had eyes, Dennis would have been crying also.

The sea hag laughed. "You think you love your son because he is still an infant," the creature said. "Shall I give you until his fourth birthday, King Hale? Would you find that merciful?"

Its laughter boomed and stank around the boat as Hale gaped at the creature's shuddering maw.

"Do you mean that?" he pleaded.

"I will keep my bargain, Hale," said the sea hag. Its mouth closed so that the woman-face smiled momentarily once again.

The sea hag seemed to be sinking. Hale relaxed, and Dennis looked out over the sea to note the storm breaking as the magical image of an earlier storm had broken minutes before.

But before the creature disappeared, it chuckled again and added, "I will keep my bargain, Hale. And you will keep your bargain too. In good time . . ."

And as the sea hag finally disappeared, the velvet drapes and the darkened palace closed Dennis in the embrace of reality.

Dennis flexed his arms, then offered a smile to his companion. "It's hard to do that," he said. "Hard to—to be there and not be able to, to really be there."

"Shall we go then, Dennis?" Chester replied, shifting his body doorward on the four of his limbs that now supported him.

"No, I—" He stopped and put on a calm expression, as if the robot's featureless case had eyes which a man could catch and hold. "Chester, will the machine show the future?"

"It will not show the future, Dennis," Chester said. Then, tartly, he added, "Fate does not look forward—and its blows do not fall wrongfully."

Dennis hugged his shoulders to remind himself that he had a body now . . . and to make sure that memory was fresh in a few moments, when he re-entered the past through magic.

"I want to see what happened next," he said. "When . . . wh-when I was four years old."

Chester's tentacles did not move on the pedestal at once. He twisted to face the door as if he heard someone coming.

"Parol!" Dennis shouted, resting his knuckles on his hips so that he stood arms akimbo. "Are you there?"

"He is not here yet, Dennis," Chester said, easing back on his limbs at his master's unexpected reaction to his hint.

"It doesn't matter where he is," Dennis said. "I want to know what happened on my fourth birthday—if this won't tell me what's going to happen on my sixteenth."

"The fool builds a fire and burns himself on it, Dennis."

"Chester, I am your *master*!" Dennis said, letting fear and uncertainty come out in his voice as anger. "I have the right to order you to do this thing!"

The little robot must have made allowances for the emotions that ruled Dennis at this moment. Instead of the silent insolence that Dennis expected even as the words left his mouth, Chester said, "I will do this thing, Dennis. . . ."

His tentacles played on the controls, three of them touching the surface of what seemed metal until it lighted in its interior and the fourth poised, waiting for some stimulus that did not come before Dennis again sank into a dream of storm and darkness.

Hale's face was a younger version of the one Dennis had seen the evening before, ruddy with good living— and frightened gray beneath that patina of success. He was daubing at his palms as he waited within the circuit of the protective storm.

Hale's hands had grown soft and he'd lost his calluses in the three years since his son's image had watched him. The oar-looms had raised blisters and then torn them open as the king—no longer a fisherman—stroked his way out of Emath Harbor.

To bargain with the creature who had given that harbor to him—for a price.

When the sea hag rose, its mouth was already open. Water streamed back through hidden gills. There was no hint of humanity in the creature, and little enough of hope.

The fishing boat didn't pitch, because the sea hag's mass already gripped its keel and held it steady; but water thrown by the creature's upward rush slapped the wooden sides and filled the air with mist.

Hale very deliberately reached over the gunwales and skimmed his hands through the water, cleaning his blisters in its salty bitterness. "I have come, sea hag," he said formally.

"You have come alone, little man-thing," said the sea hag.

A lightning bolt wove its instant sinuosities across the storm wheel. The blade of blue-white light threw the boat into harsh relief and momentarily illuminated the monster beneath the water's gray surface. Dennis, looking down from standing height, saw not one mouth but a score of mouths gaping and grinning from a glode even huger than his nightmares.

The sea hag was nothing that had been born on a world that bore men.

The thunderclap pounded the ship and Dennis' father. The shattering cascade of sound provided the scream that Dennis had no mouth to utter.

He was not present in this past; his body could not be harmed here. But memory of the blue-lit sea hag would never leave his dreams. . . .

"I have not brought my Dennis," said Hale, forcing the truth as he knew it out in a voice that threatened to break.

"Goodlady—" Hale hadn't looked down into the water as his son did when the lightning illuminated it. No one who'd seen the sea hag's full reality could have used the polite human greeting, even now when the beautiful woman-face smiled out of the waves again.

"—I beg you, ask for something else. Anything I can give you. My—my ships, they bring cargoes from every port the sea bounds."

"Salt water is my kingdom," rumbled the creature in its great stinking voice. "Every shore the sea bounds is mine to travel more swiftly than you or your ships can dream, King Hale."

"Caravans from the interior bring me jewels and wonders that the seas have never known!" Hale said with desperate brightness. "Things from ancient times, marvelous things. Ask me for anything, goodlady, anything!"

He was rubbing his hands unconsciously. They jerked apart every time pain brought the open blisters to his attention—and then began washing one another again, because nothing in Hale's immediate physical reality could stay in his mind very long.

"Nothing . . ." said the sea hag—though Dennis thought there was for the first time a hesitation in the voice that had been all arrogant certainty before.

"Nothing, King Hale—" the hesitation was gone "—but the price of our bargain, your firstborn. Bring me the price agreed!"

"G-g-g—" Hale stuttered into the cavern of blood-rich tissues and bone. He covered his eyes with his hands. "Goodlady, I beg you—a delay, please. Not my son. Not *now*."

The sea hag's booming laughter shook the vessel almost as the thunder had done moments before. "Ah, shall I show you mercy again, King Hale? Is that what you think?"

"*Please.*"

"Then I will give you twelve years more with your

son," said the creature, "to see how much less you love him after you know him the longer. But Hale. . . ?"

"Please. Please."

"I will have the price of my bargain the next time we meet. Depend on it."

As the creature sank, a further bolt of lightning raked the sky, making Hale's hair stand out and reopening to view depths that should have remained hidden.

The sight and echoing thunder left Dennis shivering when the velvet room closed in around him and he had a body again.

Dennis' skin was hot and his head buzzed. He felt as though he were about to faint, so he squatted down on the cold crystal floor and put his head between his knees.

Chester looped a limb over his master's shoulders and hugged gently.

"What can I do, Chester?" Dennis whispered. He didn't open his eyes, but his hand reached out to embrace Chester's smooth carapace. "I'll have to go t-to it."

"Your father will not give you up, Dennis," said the robot.

Dennis rose to his feet, bracing his hand on Chester's body and partly supported by another of the robot's tentacles. The moment of real collapse had passed, but he didn't trust the strength of his knees just yet.

"He has to give me up, Chester," he said quietly. "Everything we have—everything we *are*—comes from the sea hag. If she takes back . . . Emath, the harbor, the palace . . . there's nothing. Everyone here will starve. And we're responsible for them b-because we're the rulers."

He squeezed his lips tightly together to keep them from quivering. His eyes looked unblinkingly at his companion, but he could not prevent the tears from dribbling down because of what he had seen—and was sure he must go to join.

"Now I know why Dad wouldn't let me go out in the boats," Dennis said. "He beat me when I sneaked aboard one of the big trading ships when I was little."

"The man who spoils his son, spoils himself," commented the robot.

"But that didn't *matter*!" Dennis shouted in sudden anger at the memory. "He can't save me from the sea hag because he can't save Emath!"

"Parol is here, Dennis," said Chester without any sign of emotion in the words.

CHAPTER 7

A man-sized cloud of light, mauve and blue and angry orange, danced through the opening in the velvet-shrouded room. "Prepare to meet your doom, interlopers!" it cried.

The cloud's voice was understandable but not *right*. Its words were speeded up a trifle beyond human speech, turning them into bird-like chirps.

Under normal circumstances the situation would have been startling—even fearful, despite the way the threat was twittered instead of being boomed. But the doom Dennis had seen in the lightning-lit depths of the sea had wrung him too thoroughly for anything with the apprentice magician behind it to arouse fear.

"Parol!" he shouted, hands braced on his hips again. "What do you mean talking to your prince that way?"

The vaguely-humanoid cloud quivered, turning a dull gray with only a hint of color. Then it shrank in on itself like a pricked bladder, drooling momentarily along the crystal floor before it vanished completely. Parol, his mouth open in surprise, stood in the doorway.

"W-what are you doing here?" blurted the apprentice wizard.

Parol had black hair, a pasty complexion, and eyes of different colors—blue-green on the left, muddy brown on the right. He was almost as tall as Dennis, but the shapeless black robe he invariably wore made his soft body blur into the background while his face hung in the air like the full moon at dusk.

All the Wizard Serdic's apprentices had the look and personality of creatures that entered Emath hidden in baskets of jungle fruit or dredged from the deep sea. Parol was no better than his predecessors—perhaps even a little slimier, a trifle more weakly vicious, than the others whom Dennis had been old enough to remember as persons.

Recollection of how frightened he had been of Serdic added cruel pleasure to confronting the dead wizard's flunky this way. "How *dare* you question me? Get down on your knees, you little toad!"

"Luck leaves the harsh man because of his brutality!" Chester said sharply.

Dennis, keyed up from the present confrontation on top of days of strain, whirled with his hand lifting to slap. His mouth dropped open in horror when his mind realized what his body was doing. "Oh," he said. "Oh Chester."

Parol had dropped to his knees at the haughty order. He was bowing his forehead to the crystal floor. "Pardon me, Prince," he babbled. "Oh, pardon my surprise, only my surprise—never disrespect to *you*, most noble prince."

Dennis felt awful. He'd invaded Parol's privacy—sneaked in, knowing the owner was gone and hoping to leave before Parol returned. And then, because he was caught . . . and frightened; and disturbed . . . Dennis had covered his wrongdoing with the sort of angry arrogance that bothered him so much when he saw his father do the same thing.

Worst of all, Parol was fawningly willing to accept that awful behavior.

"Ah, Wizard Parol. . . ?" Dennis said.

"*Pardon*, Prince," mumbled the other man—the other youth; he was a few years older than Dennis, but the only sign of color on his face were acne pocks. He was speaking to the floor.

"For pity's sake, get *up*," Dennis said.

He was disgusted with his own behavior a moment before, but Parol's behavior would have been disgusting at any time. The last thing Dennis wanted to do was to let his feelings about the pasty apprentice explode into fresh anger again—but if Parol didn't stop acting like a whining worm, it would be very hard not to treat him as one.

Parol didn't react for a moment, but his eyes scanned the reflection of Dennis' face in the crystal. He cautiously lifted himself, pausing for a moment on all fours while he watched the prince directly—looking like a dog ready to scuttle backward from a stranger who may kick.

"Wizard Parol," Dennis repeated formally as the apprentice at last stood like a man again. "I want to apologize for troubling you this way. Chester and I had some business here that didn't affect you, but we should have told you we were coming as, as a courtesy."

"Oh, your highness needn't speak to *me*," Parol said, bobbing his head. Either it was just the way he was standing or his left shoulder was higher than the right one. "Only—"

Parol had a disconcerting way of holding his head so that Dennis could see only one of his eyes at a time; now it was the brown orb, and both anger and fear glinted on its muddy surface "—some of the, ah, the devices . . . can be dangerous. But perhaps—"

Parol's head snapped around like that of a bird. "Your highness of course studied at length th-th-th. . . ."

His face lost everything but a glaze of stark terror.

"My predecessor taught you, your highness," Parol continued with his eyes both focused on an empty upper corner of the draperies. "No doubt he taught your highness the proper use of his devices?"

"We're here for our own reasons," said Dennis curtly. "Not wizard reasons."

He had to spit the words out harshly to convince himself that what he was saying was true . . . as it was almost true, if you viewed what he and Chester had done in the right way. They *weren't* wizards, so they couldn't have wizard reasons—

Except when they were using magic to watch the past.

"Yes, yes, of course, your highness," said Parol, his voice as false as the hatred in his hidden, winking glances was real. But—

Parol was something that could have been found under a rock; but this was his cork, and he had a right to be angry when somebody moved it and prodded at him needlessly.

Parol was moving backward, into the room of glass-cased exhibits. Dennis thought the apprentice was trying to speed their departure—and there may have been something in that, but there was a ring of truth in Parol's voice as he explained, "Whatever your highness wishes, of course, but—I don't spend much time here myself. I, my sleeping room is through there and the, the library, but this—these devices. I don't—"

He stopped and looked Dennis directly in the eyes for the first time since he'd confronted the intruders. "There are dangers in these devices," Parol said, speaking as closely to blunt honesty as it was in his character to manage.

He winced away into his normal cringing slyness. "Even for those of us who've been carefully trained in their use," he added, the implied lie an obvious one.

"Yes, well," said Dennis. "Well, I won't trouble you further, Parol. Sorry for the inconvenience."

He stepped forward, brushing back the velvet hangings —glad to be back in the normal diffracted brightness of daytime in the palace, but shocked again by the creatures displayed in glass bubbles.

Dennis' skin crawled, feeling the pressure of hundreds—thousands—of dead eyes glaring at him. Chester laid a tentacle on Dennis' hip bone, a firm, familiar pressure to remind him that even here he had a friend.

As they strode past the apprentice wizard, Dennis controlled the impulse to twitch his shirt close to his body lest its hem touch the fabric of Parol's robe.

"Ah, your highness?" Parol said from behind the two companions as they reached the anteroom.

Dennis turned his head. "Yes?"

"If your highness wouldn't mind perhaps telling me what it was that he visited these chambers for," Parol said with a smarmy smile, "then perhaps I could hel—"

The apprentice's words trailed off. He scuttled back out of sight, looking as fearful as he had when he tried to speak Serdic's name.

Dennis didn't understand the reaction until he caught sight of his own face in the reflector of the lamp beside him in the anteroom. Parol couldn't know that Dennis' expression came not from being asked an impertinent question but rather from being reminded of the sea hag.

And her bargain.

Chester swung open the black pearl door. The draft of air drawn from the rotunda was as enticing as summer flowers after the peculiar miasma of the wizard's suite.

"Ah, Chester?" the youth said when they had climbed stairs to the second floor and were no longer in sight of even the black door. "The little—furry animal in a case back there?"

"The tarsier, Dennis?"

Dennis shrugged. "If that's what it's called. When I looked back, I thought—" He sucked in his lips and chewed on them for a moment. "I thought I saw its head turn."

Chester said nothing.

"But I guess that's crazy."

They strode down the disused hallway together. The whicker of the youth's trouser legs brushing together merged with the swish-click! of the robot's limbs on the crystal.

"Parol does not wish you well, Dennis," said Chester unexpectedly. "It would be wise for you to watch yourself with him."

Dennis shuddered despite himself. "But it isn't going to matter very long, is it?" he said bitterly. "Not after tomorrow, when I'm sixteen and my father has to keep his bargain."

He spoke quietly, but for minutes afterward he could hear his words echo in the emptiness of his mind.

CHAPTER 8

The notes of a Pan pipe rose in utter purity from one of the palace courtyards. Air trembled in each wax-stopped tube of the set, achieving a resonance and precision of harmony possible only to a genius with an open-ended flute.

Pan pipes were a little too sweet and insistent for Dennis' taste; but the servants liked them, and somebody was always ready to play in the evening after chores were done, while a few danced and others listened and relaxed.

In the evening. But—

"Chester, how long were we in Parol's quarters?" Dennis demanded. Because of the shrouded gloom of the chamber holding the machines, he hadn't noticed earlier that the light shifting through the crystal palace wasn't the bright noon he expected but rather twilight.

"Seven hours, forty-nine minutes and a half, Dennis," said the little robot.

"But—" Dennis said.

Well, of course they'd spent that long. The light said

it was evening; the servants' music said it was evening; and Dennis' muscles all ached with the effort of holding him upright for eight hours without a break. So the question was—

"Where did the time go, Chester? Was it a trap of, of one of the wizards—to hold us there?"

"It was not a trap, Dennis. You wished to see certain things, and to show you those things required time. The time to see them, and the longer time to journey to where they were to be seen."

Dennis remembered the way his companion had urged him to leave the room of the machines—and how Dennis had masterfully insisted on watching Hale's third meeting with the sea hag. "I didn't know that," he said.

"You did not ask that, Dennis," Chester said primly.

One of the walls of the corridor where they were pausing was a true window, a plate of perfect clarity with neither facets nor filaments to diffuse the view beyond it. That view was of the open sky to seaward, sulphurous now as the sun set with no clouds to turn the event into a spectacular.

There would be a storm tomorrow, though. Of that, Dennis was certain.

"I would have stayed even if I'd known how—how long it was taking," he said. "But I thought it was just a few minutes we were there."

"That is so, Dennis," Chester agreed with the same tone of cool disapproval as before.

Dennis began walking again. The robot fell in beside him.

"Chester?" the youth asked without looking at his companion. "If I didn't ask you a question, and it was— really important that I know the answer anyway. . . . Would you let me—hurt myself anyway because I was too stupid to ask?"

Chester slipped a tentacle into the youth's right hand, brushing the palm gently with the hair-fine tip. "Some-times the guide," he said in a more diffident tone than he usually used for his pedantic catch-phrases, "is not himself a wise man."

Dennis squeezed the tentacle. "So long as he's a friend," he said.

CHAPTER 9

Three places were laid for dinner on the balcony which opened from the anteroom of the royal suite. Liveried servants waited there in feral nervousness— for diners; for orders; for *anything*, even a chewing-out, because that would be better than frightened uncertainty. Nobody knew what was wrong in Emath Palace; but everyone knew something was wrong.

Nobody knew but King Hale; and now, his son.

The servants leaped to attention when Dennis and Chester entered the suite. "Your highness," said the carver, bowing with a watery shimmer of the blue and silver flounces of her dress.

"Your highness-ighness-ness," echoed the three placemen—bobbing like birds and slightly out of synchronous in their haste to do the right thing.

"Will you be dining now, your highness?" asked the carver.

"Not—" Dennis began. He realized that he hadn't eaten since the night before. He ought to feel starved—

and probably he would, if his stomach weren't so knotted up with fear.

He wasn't afraid yet of the sea hag—because before he confronted her, he had to face his father.

"Not yet, thank you," he said, marveling that, though his face burned with the emotions he felt, his voice remained steady. "Ah—do you know if the King has returned as yet?"

The servants darted quick, side-long glances at one another. A placeman bowed and said, "Your highness, I believe one of the cooks did mention that King Hale had entered the suite by the back stairs."

Dennis realized that he was still limb-in-limb with Chester. He released the tentacle and said, "Thank you. I can't give you much direction on dinner, I'm afraid."

Terribly afraid. And what did it *matter* to them that the prince clung to a mechanical toy the way infants do a blanket or a fuzzy doll?

Dennis reached out as he stalked toward his parents' suite. His friend's looping grip was waiting for his hand.

Hale's chamberlain was outside the room Dennis' parents shared. "Your highness," he said, bowing.

The door was crystal with the look of water in the depths of the sea, dense and an indigo blue scarcely removed from black. It was as solid as the walls around it, but Dennis could still hear the angry shouting from within—Hale's deep, booming drumbeats punctuated by Selda's shrill insistence.

The chamberlain stepped aside, looking off down the corridor as if oblivious to the sounds. Dennis opened the door, held it for Chester, and closed it behind him on the sudden stillness with which his parents greeted his entry.

"Father, Mother," he said, bowing formally. "I need to talk to you about tomorrow."

Selda's face was still contorted with the angry words

she'd been ready to hurl at her husband. She remained poised for a moment, staring at her son and his companion. Then she collapsed into a chair carved delicately from a single giant fishbone and began to cry with her hands over her face.

Selda was a plump woman; but on those rare occasions when Dennis could think of his mother as a human being instead of a fixture in his life, he could see that she was good-looking.

When Dennis was very young, Selda's hair had been a sandy, pleasant red; for the past while, however, her locks had a harsh vibrancy that nature had intended only for the preparation of crushed leaves that she used to dye it. She wore increasingly more make-up as well. Now it was running from beneath her fingers in streaks of black and scarlet and bleached-flour white.

"Mom," Dennis said, striding to her. He felt her shoulders quake beneath his hands as she cried.

"I don't have anything to talk to you about," Hale grunted as he reached to a lacquered sideboard. "Neither of you!"

The cabinet stuck. Hale's great shoulder muscles bunched and jerked out the brass latchplate in a shower of splinters.

The sideboard held an assortment of liquors. Hale took out a square green bottle like the ones Ramos had been guzzling down. He unstoppered it by pinching the end of the cork with his fingernails.

"I've seen the sea hag," Dennis said. "Tomorrow I'll go to her as agreed."

Hale shifted his hand on the bottle, gripping it by the neck.

"What does he mean, Hale?" Selda asked, looking up fearfully like a startled nestling.

Hale smashed the bottle against the edge of the sideboard. Lustrously veneered wood shattered instead of the thick glass.

Hale swung the bottle at the wall. Fortified wine streamed from the spout as his arm moved, exploding in bubbles and aroma among the fragments of glass.

He turned to his son. The bottle had broken just below the neck. It winked from the clenched fist like a lamphrey's mouth of jagged, translucent teeth—a fisherman's weapon in a madman's hand.

"You will not do that thing," Hale said in a voice of absolute certainty.

For a moment, Dennis thought his father was about to kill him. It was just a thought, a fact, like the weather or the hour of the day. If Hale killed him, then Dennis wouldn't have to see in life the creature whose lightning-lit image had been terror to watch. . . .

"H-hale?" Selda said. She got up shakily and faced her husband, standing between the two men in the room. "Put that down. Please put that down."

Hale brushed her aside with his left arm—not a blow, but forceful enough to have pushed the woman out of the way no matter how willing she was to have resisted. Selda caught herself on the chair back, then slid with it to the floor and her sobbing.

Hale threw down the bottleneck. It broke further and skittered in a dozen directions. He stared at Dennis; Dennis met his father's eyes.

"You don't think you're a boy any more, is that it?" Hale said softly. "Well, maybe you're not. . . . But you're still my son, laddy. And I say you'll not do this—d'ye hear?"

Dennis felt his expression tremble. He could face anger, now that he knew what the anger hid; but his father had undermined his composure by treating him for the first time as an adult. "Father, if I don't go—"

Hale shook his shaggy head. "It doesn't matter to you. It's my bargain, and my decision."

"But—"

"It's *my* decision!"

Dennis spun to the door and jerked it open. It took all his remaining strength of will to plunge into the anteroom again before his own tears joined those of his mother.

This time, the cause was more complex than anger and frustration, though; and he half thought he heard his father start to cry also as the thick panel slammed shut.

CHAPTER 10

"I always used to like the night, Chester," Dennis said as he watched the sea surge and glow. "Remember? We'd lie out here and wonder which star men really came from?"

His back was supported by one of the smooth-contoured crenelations that decorated this roofline. The crystal was slightly chilly—it remained cool even in the direct glare of the summer sun.

The metal of the robot's case was warm and reassuring as Dennis reached out to his companion.

"Well, I still like it," the youth admitted aloud. "It's just that I haven't been having a good time at nights recently. I— "

He paused and looked at Chester, a dull blur against the vague light retained by the structure of the palace. "I don't know what to do, Chester. My father's been a good ruler, a really great one, even if he. . . ."

It was hard for a boy who's been raised a prince to find that he is both a man—and a fisherman's son. Though a prince as well, of course.

67

And Dennis was still a boy, too, unless he was careful about the way he reacted to danger and frustration.

"If you listen to the judgment of your heart," the robot said with the pompous weight of wisdom in his voice, "you will sleep untroubled."

As a friend in the darkness, Chester added, "What is it that you *would* do, Dennis?"

"I'd go out to the sea hag," Dennis said simply. Stated that way, he could forget all the doubts and terrors that the decision implied. "But I can't go against Dad."

"Do not leave a fool to rule the people," Chester said; but that was the program talking and not the friend Dennis had made during their sixteen years together.

Hale *was* being foolish in this.

". . . all will be yours to command . . ." the sea hag had bargained as Hale stood on the deck of *The Partners*. Knowing that, Dennis couldn't be sure how much of the way he obeyed his father was a result of the sea hag's magic. . . .

Chester would ask what Dennis wanted to do if he couldn't do the right thing—and even in his princely willingness to be sacrificed, Dennis felt an underlying joy that he *didn't* have to hurl himself into that waiting, stinking maw. But if he couldn't do that—

"Chester, I can't stay in Emath," Dennis said in sudden resolution. "My father never told me not to go out into the jungle. I'll do that tonight. I'll find—some other place to live."

He couldn't live in Emath and watch it be destroyed because of something he hadn't done, something his father wouldn't permit him to do. Perhaps if he left, the sea hag would spare the village.

And perhaps one of the jungle's hidden monsters would gobble Dennis down; and then he could stop worrying about what he ought to do.

"Oh—" Dennis said. Death was something he knew

only from books, where it seemed noble and heroic. Being alone was a fear of a much more serious order.

"C-chester, would you go with me if I leave Emath?" he asked.

A tentacle looped his shoulders and tickled the back of his left ear. "I will go with you wherever you wish, Master Dennis," the robot said softly.

Dennis jumped to his feet, speaking quickly so that emotion wouldn't choke him. "Right," he said, "great. I'll need food—I'll get some bread and sausages from the cooks."

He frowned. "That's the sort of food people take when they go out in the jungle, isn't it, Chester?"

Everything Dennis knew about the jungle was from books or the little he saw across the dragon-guarded perimeter. No human beings left the village for the lowering back-country. Occasionally, men straggled in wearing rags and a look of fear, but they weren't the sort who got invited to the palace. All the inland trade was in the scaly hands of the lizardmen.

"People might well take bread and sausage when they went out into the jungle, Dennis," the robot said. Dennis couldn't be sure from the tone whether Chester was agreeing with, warning—or gently mocking his human companion.

"Right, well," the youth said, deciding to take the words at face value. "And I'll take a fishing line too, so that we can catch our own food. Ah—"

He looked down at Chester. Dennis' first enthusiastic movement had left him still on the roof, poised by the casement of the window opening to his personal suite. "Ah, there's water in the jungle, isn't there? I mean, pools and streams?"

It struck him suddenly that Chester might be as ignorant of this business as Dennis was himself. After all, the little robot had been brought to Emath by sea and hadn't left the perimeter since.

"There are pools and streams in the jungle, Dennis,"

said Chester, calming *that* momentary fear. "And there is also rain."

"Sure, but I'm not going to walk around with my mouth turned up," the youth said while his mind concentrated on things he thought were more important.

He pursed his lips, squeezed the cool crystal of the transom with both hands, and added, "And I'll need a sword. Chester, I'm going to take the Founder's Sword from his tomb."

He waited for Chester to respond. Nothing happened. Dennis looked down at his side and found the little robot waiting as motionless as he was silent.

"Do you think I should do that?" Dennis prodded.

"It is not mine to think or not think about what you should do, Dennis," Chester said, as close to a lie as the youth had ever heard from his mouthless companion; but when Chester continued, "It may be that I can open the vault without your taking your father's keys," Dennis knew that he'd been answered after all.

"Right," said Dennis buoyantly, hopping into his suite without touching the waist-high transom. "First the fishing line and the food, then the sword—and then the jungle."

And escape forever from the sea hag, relief whispered in his mind; but he wasn't proud enough of the thought to speak it aloud.

CHAPTER 11

The burlap shopping bag brushed Dennis' pants leg
awkwardly as he walked. The bag's side-panels were
embroidered with the Seal of Emath in blue yarn—a
leaping fish with a woman's face, too crude to have
features even in better light than that of the village
streets at night.

The Seal of Emath was the sea hag—in the false,
conventional style that fishermen joked about the creature. Now Dennis understood why.

Dennis hadn't really thought about how he was going
to carry the food until he got to the kitchen. The
rope-handled shopping bag seemed the best alternative
there.

He'd collected bread and three different kinds of
sausage—summer sausage, liverwurst, and a hard, spicy
pepperoni—because he wasn't sure which was proper.
Anyway, it was difficult to make little choices now that
his mind was filled with the large one, the decision to
leave home forever.

Dennis had also collected the wide-eyed concern of

all the kitchen staff, but they'd helped him anyway. An undercook had even curtsied and offered him an apple brought from the far north . . . which Dennis took to avoid embarrassing her.

He began to crunch it quickly as soon as he left the palace. An apple just didn't seem the thing to carry along on a dangerous trek into the jungle.

Dennis was pretty sure that none of the staff would slip off to tell the king what his son was doing. The way Hale was acting now, the servants were afraid to see him even when they were required to do so.

Dennis tossed the apple core into the gutter.

"The man who uses his provisions wisely, Dennis," said Chester in a tone of cool disapproval, "will never want."

"I didn't *ask* her for an apple," Dennis snapped back.

Then he said, "I feel foolish walking about with a shopping bag, Chester. I'm sorry."

A group of children were playing around a pool of lantern light in the street, watched by an old woman in a mob cap. "Good evening, your highness!" the woman called, trembling back and forth on her rocking chair as she waved a hand in greeting. "A *fine* evening to you!"

"Good evening, lady," Dennis responded in a cheerful voice, waving his own free hand as he and Chester passed. The children stared, whispering among themselves in voices that occasionally rose with high-pitched awe.

"I don't know who she is, Chester," Dennis muttered to his companion as darkness covered them again. "I didn't think anybody could recognize me in the dark anyway."

He looked down at the clothing he'd chosen: a cloak, a plain cotton tunic, and drab blue trousers.

Of course, the bag did have the royal seal on it. And—

"It may be that I can be recognized though you are

not, Dennis," said Chester, putting words to the thought that had just struck the youth.

Well, it wouldn't matter in the jungle.

They'd had to tramp almost all the way around the harbor, since the Tomb of the Founder was on the landspit opposite the palace. Even now, Dennis wasn't willing to disobey his father by crossing the harbor the easy way—on one of the many water taxis available at the piers.

Wasn't willing, or wasn't able because of the sea hag's magic.

Most of the bars and entertainment areas for seamen were concentrated near the end of the harbor, but one brightly-lit establishment was doing a cheerful business next to the wall separating the village from the graves and solemnities of the cemetery.

A woman sat on the rail of the third-floor roof with her back to the street, singing to an invisible audience and accompanying herself on a one-string lute. As Dennis passed the tavern, the singer paused, stretched, and looked down at him. Her eyes gleamed as her jeweled combs in the light of the sconces at the tavern's entrance; her breasts were deeper shadows within the pink froth of the chemise she wore.

The singer smiled down. Dennis blushed and walked away quickly.

"He who knows how to hold his heart," murmured Chester, "knows the most important thing of all."

"Just *leave* that, all right?" Dennis said.

For a wonder, Chester said nothing more on the subject.

The cemetery was closed from the remainder of the landspit by a fence and gate. Five years before, Hale had replaced the wooden palings of Dennis' youth with wrought iron. Sections of the fence were already skewed at slight angles from one another, but the gilt spikes on top glittered bravely in the starlight.

The gate was open. Emath was crowded, but there

was no need to lock squatters out of the graveyard. King Hale's law forbade anyone sleeping within the fenced area; and King Hale's protector, hidden in the deep sea, supported the law with her own powers.

A high swell rumbled against the land, silhouetting the tombs against a phosphorescent mist. The Founder's Tomb stood out in rough-hewn majesty from the lesser monuments. It had been easy to imagine that this pile of red rock was the creation of the earliest men on Earth, far removed from the crystal refinement of Emath Palace.

I built it, Ramos had said, *and your father beside me.*

One of the dragons coughed a challenge to the jungle; the sea slapped a wave against the headland again in response.

"Let's go in, Chester," Dennis said quietly. "And leave."

Serdic's black marble mausoleum lay beside the path to the old rock tomb. Dennis kept a tight hold on his emotions as he strode past the entrance, but the tomb didn't give him the thrill of fear that he'd expected— that he'd felt in the wizard's suite of the palace.

None of what was frightening about the Wizard Serdic lay here.

The door of the Founder's Tomb was wooden. Salt air had shrunk the wood and bleached it gray, so that it shone like a patch of the skyglow as Dennis approached. The straps, hinges and latchplate were rusted the same color as the rock, and the black keyhole was the size of the last joint of Dennis' thumb.

The tip of one of Chester's tentacles slipped into the blackness like a beam of starlight. The wards quivered and clicked under the robot's hair-fine manipulation.

The door swung outward against the protest of its hinges. Chester disengaged his tentacle.

When Dennis tried to open the door a few inches further, he found he had to put his shoulders into the effort of overcoming the friction of rust in the hinge pivots. The robot's delicacy and small size could give a false impression of the strength available in his silvery limbs.

The only light within was what came through the open door, and there was so little of it that Dennis couldn't see his own shadow.

"I should have brought a lamp," he muttered.

He remembered that the interior was almost filled by a limestone sarcophagus and that the sword lay across the chest of the reclining figure of the Founder on the stone lid; but he would have to feel his way—

The darkness rustled. Dennis' heart jumped as his face froze. The Founder's Sword slid toward him, held point-up in its scabbard by one of Chester's tentacles.

Dennis took the great weapon in his hands for the first time. King Hale always carried the sword himself through the crowds on a velvet cushion in the Founder's Day procession—from the tomb, around the arc of Emath's perimeter, and to the gate of the palace before returning.

The youth stepped backward into the starlight and slid the blade from its sheath.

It gleamed like a cold gray star itself.

Dennis had been trained in swordsmanship from his earliest childhood. It was part of the education of a prince, and his father had skimped on nothing that would further that ideal. The blade of the Founder's Sword was just under a yard long and heavy for its considerable length.

Dennis wasn't used to a sword of quite this size—but he could handle it. His muscles were trained, and his frame was filling out daily with the growth spurt of his late adolescence.

The sword was perfectly balanced. Despite that, the weapon had a crudeness that surprised Dennis until he thought about it.

The Founder's Sword had been forged out of star metal, material ripped from the hulls of the ships that brought men here to Earth. Of *course* the blade wouldn't have the polished correctness of swords hammered out by modern weaponsmiths using mere steel.

This was the weapon of a hero of a bygone age. This was the weapon that Dennis would take into the jungle heart of the continent.

He shot the weapon home in its scabbard with a flourish. At last he was thrilled with his decision instead of just plodding onward, afraid to look at what he was doing.

Seeing his father face the sea hag had made Dennis a man. Buckling the Founder's Sword onto his belt made him a hero—at least in his own mind.

The guard beasts snarled again: at the night, at nothing, or at one another. Dennis' vision of himself at the head of a conquering host, waving his star-metal sword, shivered back down to present reality.

"All right, Chester," he said as though the robot's dallying were slowing him down. "Let's go."

"When worry arises," Chester murmured, "the heart thinks death itself is a release."

Dennis grimaced as he picked up the bag of provisions.

"But troubles end," the robot continued, "and death does not end, Dennis."

They didn't bother to close the tomb door as they set off, side by side, toward the perimeter and the dragons guarding it.

CHAPTER 12

The newest, largest and most solidly built structures in Emath village were those pressing up against the perimeter.

The Wizard Serdic had expanded the perimeter twice in Dennis' memory—having created it the day Emath's prince and heir was born. When houses filled the space available to them, Serdic moved the spell which enclosed the dragons farther into the jungle.

As Emath grew, so did the two beasts which paced the perimeter on ceaseless guard.

"Where are they now, Chester?" Dennis asked in a whisper.

"One of them is coming toward us, Dennis," the robot replied—quietly also, but with a clarity which the youth found disturbing. Chester's precise words seemed more likely to arouse the guard beasts' interest than a slurred whisper would.

The perimeter was a location, not a thing. Dennis and his companion stood at the back of a three-story apartment block. The walls were half-timbered; their whitewashed plaster triangles gleamed softly in the star-light. Just in front of Dennis was a line of coarse grass stretching to either side in a gentle curve parallel with the buildings.

The hundred meters between that grass and the jungle was clear. The earth there had been trampled into dust—churned to mud in the rain—by the claws of dragons.

As Chester had warned, one of the dragons was snuf-fling into sight. Dennis froze. He took his hand off the hilt of his new sword because he was afraid he might rattle the blade in its scabbard.

The dragon walked on two legs, but there was nothing about it even remotely like a man. The creature's body and tail formed the cross-bar of a T supported by the legs. Its head was held close to the ground, so that its hips—eight feet in the air—were the highest point on the body when the dragon was walking normally. The legs folded upward like complex shears, then jabbed out claws-first for each strutting, birdlike step.

The head swung toward Dennis when the dragon was no more than twenty feet away. Its nostrils were set at the end of its flat muzzle. They wrinkled with the odor of the waiting youth. The eyes, gleams of black star-light, winked as they focused.

"Maybe we ought—" Dennis whispered to his companion as he edged toward the alley between this building and the next.

The dragon charged.

"Chester!" Dennis cried, flinging down his bag of provisions as he jumped between the dragon and his friend. The dragon's lower jaw dropped. Its finger-long teeth dripped ropes of digestive slime as the beast bellowed—

And collided with the invisible barrier.

Dirt sprayed. Serdic's barrier stopped nothing but the guard beasts themselves. When the dragon's head banged to an angry halt against nothing, its feet skidded in a wave of the pulverized earth of the trackway. The youth coughed and began spitting out a mouthful of the dust.

The dragon ambled away, scratching the side of its head with one of the sharp-clawed grasping arms that were normally folded alongside its chest. The creature seemed completely to have forgotten Dennis and his companion. The dragon's head and tail swung side to side, balancing the torso as the legs lifted in walking.

Chester picked up the bag of provisions. One of the sausages had spilled out. A tentacle raised it while the tip of another flicked dust precisely from the casing. "One does not learn the heart of a brave man," the robot murmured, "until his friend is attacked."

"I didn't even think of my sword," Dennis wheezed. He brushed his face with his hands but let tears and the lids clear the dust from his eyes. A sudden sneeze blew his nasal passages open and left him feeling much better, though his nose began to run.

Far on the other end of the perimeter, the second dragon bellowed in raucous triumph as it pounced on something—probably an unfortunate lizard which chose the wrong time to scuttle across the cleared strip.

The guard beasts were intended to keep the dangers of the jungle out of Emath—the tribes of scaly lizardfolk; rumored bands of human renegades, stalking the jungle trails in search of loot and always willing to pounce on an unprotected settlement; and bogeys still more frightful because no one in Emath had fully imagined them.

But the dragons were restrained rather than being controlled. They would attack anything they could get hold of, just as a pit trap would catch even the man who dug it. When the folk of Emath wanted to let traders from the jungle into their village, the wizard had to throw a separate barrier across the perimeter to prevent the guard beasts from rending the lizardfolk.

And no one from Emath could safely leave the village by land either; though that didn't matter, because nobody wanted to do that—

Until tonight.

Dennis slipped his sword a few inches up and down in its sheath, making sure that he could draw it easily. If he remembered to draw it in the next crisis, anyway.

"Are they . . ." Dennis said.

When Dennis paused to lick his lips, he found that they were still coated with the dirt the dragon had kicked over him. He spat with difficulty because of his dry mouth. "Will we be able to get across safely now, Chester?"

"Some men trust the moment, Dennis, and it goes well with them forever," the robot replied.

Chester still held the bag of provisions. If he was willing to do that, it would help his master run the next hundred yards.

"All right," Dennis whispered. "Let's go."

He leaped the line of grass that had survived the feet of both humans and monsters and began sprinting across the churned-up soil.

It was as difficult as running in shallow water. The soft dirt clung to his boots and spilled over their low tops. He was off-balance for running anyway, twisting his body to the left to hold his new sword and scabbard with both hands. Otherwise it would flop and trip him.

He hadn't thought of that when he took the sword.

Dennis was twenty yards out into the trackway when both the dragons sensed him. They hooted with thunderous delight. Though they were out of sight for the moment, hidden behind the curve of the buildings, Dennis could feel the ground shake as the beasts lurched from a shamble to a gallop.

Chester was hopping along beside him, suiting his pace to that of the floundering youth.

Normally Chester's tentacles glided just over the ground, curving as he stepped instead of lifting the way the jointed legs of animals would. On this surface, the robot hopped like a toad in thick dust. The strength of his silvery limbs was obviously sufficient to carry him safely clear of the dragons' rush.

When Dennis was halfway across the perimeter, he wished that he'd never started. When he was two strides further, he was sure that he was going to die.

The dragons moved in clouds of the dust their legs kicked up before them. Only their outthrust heads were visible as they strutted toward their human victim from either side.

Dennis' chest burned with the effort that would leave him ten yards short of the jungle when the beasts fell on him simultaneously like scissors with teeth. He'd have thrown the heavy sword away if he could have, but he didn't dare pause in order to draw the blade without cutting his leg off.

His panicked mind also considered fighting the beasts. The idea was so crazy that he would have laughed—if he'd had breath or laughter available. Each of the dragons weighed a half ton, and there were two of them. . . .

"Not only a great lord may protect another!" Chester said.

"*Help* me, Chester!" Dennis cried.

Chester flung sausages high in the air to either side.

The dragons pivoted like dancers, the heads questing upward while their arms—clutched tight to that moment —snatched the linked sausages from the air with triple claws.

One of the beasts bugled in triumph. Its breath filled the air with the smell of fish and fish offal, the food the dragons got from their keeper to sustain them as they prowled their magical cage.

Dennis dived to safety. He lay in a thicket of flowers

and brambles, sobbing with reaction and remembered fear.

Behind him, the dragons snarled at one another. They were too focused on the thrill of spiced meat to notice that their prey had escaped them.

"There is no more sausage, Dennis," said Chester. "There is bread only, now."

"That's all right," said Dennis, responding to the words as though they were a real apology rather than a delicate way of getting him alert and mobile again. "I—thank you, friend."

"You are welcome, Dennis."

If Chester hadn't prodded him, he wouldn't have thought to ask for help; and without Chester distracting the guard beasts—

It was important to be able to do things himself. But it was real important to know when to ask for help.

The dragons were moving off in opposite directions, darting quick glances over their shoulders and growling at one another. Dennis started to get up. The thorns that gripped his clothes tore at the edge of his hand as he tried to push himself upright.

He couldn't see the vegetation that held him, though a large blossom brushed his cheek and breathed a rich purple scent into the air. He tried to pick away the vines clutching his right cuff. His left arm was entwined in a knot of brambles that anchored it as thoroughly as if he'd been tied.

"Chester—" Dennis began.

He tried to speak calmly. His mind churned with ghastly tales of trees that walked in the jungle, just out of sight of Emath, and of flowers that drank blood.

Something lanced through his cheek like hot iron.

Dennis screamed and jumped to his feet. The bramble jabs were nothing to the pain that spread from his cheek, encompassing him, devouring him—

The insect that had stung the youth buzzed away

in the darkness, led by the perfume of another night-flower.

Dennis stumbled a few paces away from the bramble patch. The ground between two of the larger trees was reasonably clear. He had his left palm raised to his cheek. He wasn't quite touching the skin, but he could feel the heat from the injured part.

"Chester," he said, slurring the words because the side of his face was beginning to swell. "I'm all right, aren't I?"

"You are all right, Dennis," said the robot. "You will be better in a day.

"Perhaps," Chester added after a pause, "you should hold a wet compress to your cheek."

"I didn't bring any water," Dennis said in sudden concern. "You said there'd be water in the jungle, Chester."

"It is beginning to rain, Dennis."

As Dennis opened his mouth to argue, the first rush of big raindrops started to hammer down, making the leaves clatter.

Dennis looked up. A drop slapped the corner of his eye hard enough to hurt; but the rain was cooling things down, and that felt good after he'd sprinted away from the dragons in the humid atmosphere. Dust pocked up from the trackway in miniature explosions. In a few minutes, the perimeter would be a sea of mud—greasy and a deathtrap for anyone who tried to bolt across it.

Dennis shuddered. "Let's get out of here," he muttered, more to himself than to his companion.

Chester moved, a faint glimmer and a crackling of brush nearby. "There is a path here, Dennis," he said. "If you choose to follow it."

"Shouldn't I? Where does it go?"

"The path goes anywhere, Dennis," the robot said. "It goes away from Emath."

Dennis pursed his lips. The side of his face felt stiff already. "Sure," he said. "Let's go."

His cloak felt clammy as the rain plastered it to his shoulders. Maybe it'd be drier on the trail, protected by the canopy of leaves.

Dennis pushed through the undergrowth, guided by the glint of his companion's pointing limbs. He was a hero, after all, going off to seek adventure. That thought should keep him warm.

CHAPTER 13

The rain continued. The canopy didn't stop it; instead, the drops collected on the tips of leaves, then overbalanced and dropped to the trail in individual cupfuls.

Dennis felt cold and wet and nothing at all of a hero.

"Even in a blameless life," said the robot, "there are good days and bad days."

"Chester, how far have we come?"

Dennis held the scabbard with his left hand. If he let the sword swing as he walked, his belt chafed the skin over his right hip. He was pretty sure he'd rubbed himself raw before he realized what was happening.

"We have come four miles, three hundred and twenty-one yards, Dennis."

"Are there—" Dennis began. He grimaced to himself, then asked instead, "Do the lizard people have villages?"

"The lizardfolk have villages, Dennis," the little robot agreed. "But there are no villages nearby."

"Oh."

A vine with spikes like a warclub caught at his head, right at the hairline. Dennis squealed with frustration— stopped—and freed himself by ducking carefully while his hand disengaged the thorns from his scalp.

The fresh pain was too minor to affect Dennis' general feeling of discomfort. His head was throbbing. He thought the pulses of heat and pressure were centered on his swollen cheek, but he couldn't be sure even of that. Maybe some of the thorns that tore him had been poisonous.

Maybe he'd feel better if he ate something.

Dennis stepped close to a tree whose vine-knotted trunk at least pretended to offer shelter. "Give me the food," he ordered curtly.

The sword shifted. The scabbard-tip rapped his left ankle hard enough to hurt.

Chester obediently offered the shopping bag. He'd been carrying it beneath his carapace, but the robot's body was too small to provide much protection.

Wincing in anticipation, Dennis reached in for a loaf of bread. It squished.

He thrust his hand down fiercely, hoping that at least some of the bread would still be dry.

It was all soaked through, a mass of soggy paste.

"*All* the sausages are gone!" he shouted. "Did you have to throw *all* the sausages?"

"I did not have to throw any of the sausages, Dennis," the robot said mildly.

Dennis hurled the embroidered bag into the jungle. It caught in the vegetation less than a yard from where it left his hand.

For a moment Dennis breathed hard. Chester remained silent, and the rain spattered them both. Then a bucketful of water from the tree's disturbed heights cascaded down on the companions.

"Patience is the gods' greatest gift," Chester said.

"We may as well keep going," said Dennis, lifting the

sheathed sword again with his left hand. The rain would clean the bread mush off his right hand soon enough.

The sword would probably be rusting. And—

"Chester, will you rust?"

"In this rain alone, I do not think that I will rust, Dennis," the robot replied, leading the way as they walked because the trail was too narrow for them to go side by side.

"That's good," Dennis said.

"And I'm sorry," he added, but he couldn't be sure that he spoke those words aloud. He was plodding forward, step after step, and the monotony of even the pain was a defense against the misery he felt.

Things had to get better soon. Things had to get better soon. Things had to get . . .

CHAPTER 14

Dennis wasn't sure how long they'd been walking when he saw the light. It was a soft gleam, yellowish orange, not far off the trail.

"There, what's that light?" he said excitedly.

When Chester replied, his voice held as much puzzlement as the robot was capable of feeling: "There is no light that I see, Dennis."

"Right over here," the youth insisted.

He plunged into the undergrowth, waddling as he forced his way through the brush that grew most thickly at the fringes of the trail. The light flickered, but it was too saturated to be merely a will-o'-the-wisp—rotting wood or gas glowing as it drifted from fallen vegetation. It looked like firelight; and when it was raining like this, a fire meant there was shelter as well.

He'd half feared that the light would somehow slip away; but as Dennis fought his way onward, the orange warmth grew clear enough to have shape through the angles of tree-boles and writhing vine stems.

There was a cabin hidden here in the jungle, and a wedge of light from its fireplace glowed through its half-open door.

"Oh, thank goodness!" Dennis cried as he freed his swordhilt from the loop of vine that caught it. "I *knew* something would turn up!"

The cabin appeared perfectly normal, built of logs like those of the trees all around; but there was no path to the door, just tangled jungle like that through which Dennis had thrust his way. Dennis paused. "Is this. . . ?" he began. "Ah, Chester? Who lives here?"

"I do not see that anyone lives here, Dennis," the robot replied coolly from behind him.

Dennis stepped to the door. The threshold was an axe-smoothed log. "Hello?" he called. "Hello? Is anyone here?"

The rain continued to dribble down.

Inside the cabin was a table holding a jug of cider, a pot of aromatic stew, and a single place-setting. The fire was burning brightly in a stone fireplace with a stack of additional logs ready to be added at need. In one corner stood a tall cabinet, and a bed heaped with feathered pelts waited along the wall opposite the fire.

No one answered.

"Hello?" Dennis repeated. His scabbard clacked against the door jamb as he stepped inside. He snatched at the hilt to keep the weapon from swinging—and realized just too late that anyone who saw him would take the movement as a threat.

But there was no one in the cabin to see.

The fire's warmth was as close to bliss as anything this side of Paradise could be. Dennis fluffed his shirt out, shaking droplets of water onto the half-logs of the puncheon floor. He looked around.

Chester still stood outside.

"Come on in," the youth directed.

Chester neither moved nor replied.

Dennis shook his head angrily. "All right," he said. "Suit yourself. Maybe you *will* rust!"

He banged the door closed—after checking that the leather latch-string was out so that his companion could get inside at will.

The stew smelled wonderful.

"Hello?" Dennis called again, half-heartedly; and, when the silence answered him, dipped the horn-handled spoon into the pot and tasted the stew. Carrots and onions; potatoes; and a flavorful meat that seemed to be lamb, all in a rich gravy and just at the right temperature to eat.

He'd apologize to the owner when he came home. Anyway, he'd leave half the potful for the owner.

And the owner couldn't possibly need the food more than Dennis did.

The youth unbelted his sword, leaned it against the stone fireplace, and helped himself to the stew without further ado. He remembered that he was going to leave half; but when the pot was half empty, Dennis felt as hungry as he had when he started . . . and after all, the food would just get cold if he left it. . . .

The room warmed up nicely with the door closed; but as Dennis' belly filled, he began to feel the discomfort of his wet clothing. The cloth was stiffening where it faced the fire and still clammy over most of his body.

He looked at the bed. The coverlet was a single feathery skin, large enough to have clothed an ox. Dennis couldn't imagine that it came from a bird . . . but he couldn't imagine anything but a bird having feathers, either.

Dennis got up and stripped off his own uncomfortable clothes. He hung them over the chair which he slid nearer the fire. Then he wrapped himself in the coverlet, tossed another log on the fire, and lay down in front of it.

The feathers were soft and warm and wonderful. Enfolded in them, Dennis forgot the rain and the misery of the hours since he left Emath. Soon it would be dawn. . . .

And soon he slept.

CHAPTER 15

Someone called him. He swam up from the sea depths, stroking through nightmare toward the sunlit surface. . . .

Dennis flung off the coverlet. The fire was a sunken glow. A jet of gas hissed briefly from the dull orange coals, providing a blue flicker and the only movement within the silent cabin.

The rain continued as a dull patter on the roof shakes.

"Who's there?" Dennis called. He groped for the chair where his clothing dried. "Hello?"

Nothing answered him. The chair was where he remembered it, but his clothes weren't hanging there as they should have been. Maybe in the dim, red light he had the wrong chair.

His sword wasn't leaning against the fireplace, either.

"What will you give me for your lodging?" boomed a voice.

Dennis whirled around with a scream of startlement,

the sort of yelp that a nearby thunderbolt would have jolted out of him. The feather coverlet tangled his feet.

No one was with him in the cabin.

Dennis ran to the door and threw it open. "Hello?" he called. "Here I am. Where are you?"

Rain spattered him. His naked body was already shivering, although the air in the cabin had been comfortably warm. The night was dark, and nothing visible stood in it.

"Chester?" Dennis shouted. "Chester! *Chester*!"

A stream of cold water shifted down the threshold log, over Dennis' feet. The voice behind him repeated, "What will you give me for your lodging?"

He slammed the door and stood with his back to it, surveying the room by fireglow. He could make out the table and chair; even the bed across the cabin. His clothes and sword were nowhere to be seen, and there was no one else in the—

The cabinet to Dennis' left creaked open. A tall figure stepped out, moving as stiffly as the warped door that had concealed him. "What will you give me for your lodging, boy?" demanded the figure, glaring into Dennis' eyes.

It was the Wizard Serdic.

The corpse of the Wizard Serdic.

Serdic's cheeks had sunk in and were blotched with mold. His hair had been black the day he died. It had continued to grow in coarse tangles, but they were as red-orange as the dim light from the fire.

Serdic's fingernails were claws as long as the digits themselves.

Dennis jumped backward and banged into the cabin door. It knocked him toward Serdic with a crash of wood. He spun and jerked the door open.

"What will you—" the corpse repeated, tottering forward on stiff, shrunken legs.

Dennis bolted into the night.

There wasn't a trail, and Dennis couldn't see the trees until he slammed into them. His eyes were wide open, but he was so blinded by fear that, for the first few minutes, he wouldn't have been able to dodge obstructions even in broad daylight.

"Chester!" Dennis cried as he ran. "Dad! *Chester!*" Every time a vine tripped him or a tree knocked him sprawling, he got up and ran again—a little slower and with a little more of a drunken stagger.

The thorns tore bright lines across Dennis' consciousness. When rough bark scraped away his skin, he throbbed with dull purple pain.

Dennis' clothes wouldn't have protected him from the punishment he was taking, but they'd have made him feel more like a man. Stumbling naked through the wet, clawing jungle he was only a hunted beast, a child screaming for his parents. . . .

His parents didn't answer. Chester had disappeared. There was no one to hear Dennis as he cried for help with tears of pain and frustration dripping down his rain-wet cheeks.

At last he ran head-on into a tree whose trunk was spongy with rot and fungus. By now Dennis was only staggering, so the impact wasn't hard enough to throw him to the ground. He clung to the tree, wheezing and crying and expecting that at any moment Serdic's long fingernails would close on him from behind.

Nothing touched him but a dribble of water; and even the rain seemed to be stopping.

Dennis straightened and turned around, though he kept one hand in contact with the tree bole. He wasn't sure he could stand unsupported. He had a stitch in his side that hurt like a hot plowshare being driven up under his ribcage.

The sky had cleared. Enough moonlight filtered down through the canopy that Dennis could glimpse—as grim, gray giants—the trees surrounding him.

He must not have slept for very long after all. Without seeing the moons he couldn't be sure, but if both of them were as high in the sky as it seemed, the time couldn't be later than midnight.

Dennis began to shiver slightly, though the air was growing warm and steamy in the aftermath of the rain. Something bellowed in the distance, a hunting call similar to that of the dragons guarding Emath.

The tree that had finally stopped Dennis' wild careen through the jungle was almost six feet thick at the base. Roots spread across the ground in wide convolutions beneath it, and the trunk was ridged by the serpent tracks of vines.

Dennis touched one of the vines. It was hairy with the filaments that allowed the main stem to cling to the bark, but it wasn't defended by thorns.

The beast called again, perhaps a little closer.

Dennis gripped the vine with both hands. It was slippery from the rain, but the stem's convolutions gave his bare feet some support also as he started to climb. His flesh winced every time he brushed against the tendrils. Their touch was unpleasant—animal-like but too cold to be alive. Still, they couldn't hurt him the way so much of the jungle had already done.

He didn't know what he was hoping to find—perhaps a branch to which he could tie himself with vines, out of reach of clawed creatures until dawn. To Dennis' pleased surprise, the bole split into a triple fork fifteen feet in the air. The pocket from which the three branches spread was a cup broad enough for him to curl up safely.

Miniature frogs croaked in startled irritation as Dennis settled himself. The cup held about an inch of water, tepid and almost comforting as it soaked Dennis' battered skin. The gold-and-crimson striped frogs which had been mating in the raised pond hopped away disgruntled.

A day before, Dennis wouldn't have believed that anyone could sleep in conditions like these. Now he settled himself, appreciating the soft, half-decayed texture of the bark beneath his head.

A frog chirruped beside his ear. Dennis thought he felt the touch of webbed feet crawling cautiously onto him, but after the events of the night thus far, not even that was going to keep him awake.

CHAPTER 16

The noise of the frogs didn't awaken Dennis, but their sudden silence did. He snapped alert and heard the grumble of voices below him.

It was still night, but his eyes were fully adapted to the moon glimmer. He peered out cautiously.

Four figures were struggling through the undergrowth, carrying a long box. Cursing with the effort, they lowered the box to the ground directly under the tree where Dennis sheltered.

"Who's got the light?" demanded one in a breathy voice. Dennis realized with a shock that the speaker was a lizardman. It shouldn't have surprised him, out here in the jungle, but . . .

All four of them were hacking at the brush with long knives, glitters slipping in vicious arcs through the moonlight. "That's enough," said one.

"It's not enough," said another, and the third speaker at least was human. "He's too cold. We'll need more."

While three of them slashed down more fuel, the fourth figure knelt and took a stick of glowing punk from the gourd roped to his waist. He blew the punk to a bright yellow-orange, then touched it to a stem of gathered brush. Despite the rain of only hours before, the brush caught. The fire spread with oily, crackling intensity.

Any urge Dennis felt to join the newcomers evaporated when he got a good look at them. If they weren't robbers, they were worse. The sole human had a patch over one eye. Dangling from his left ear was a jewel too big to have been acquired honestly by anyone of his appearance.

The lizardmen were worse. What Dennis had thought was a gourd to carry the punk was in fact a human skull. One of the lizardmen wore a collar of spikes around his neck, and the backs of all three bore the scars of brutal floggings.

Two of them set up a crude spit, using forked saplings and a long pole chopped to a sharp point on one end. The other pair tipped over the box they'd all been carrying. The top fell off.

The corpse of the Wizard Serdic spilled out.

"He's too cold," said one of the lizardmen. "It's going to take a long time."

"Shut up and help me," said the one-eyed human as he began to impale the corpse on the pole.

"Too cold . . ." the lizardman repeated, his forked tongue adding to the words a sibilance that couldn't have come from a human mouth.

Working together despite their grumbling, the four scarred outcasts lifted the pole and the cold, stiff corpse of the wizard onto forked sticks set at either end of the fire. The brush burned with a hard flame that threw shadows like teeth across the forest. It sizzled and popped angrily.

"Don't let him burn," muttered a lizardman, giving a twist to one end of the spit where a knot gave some leverage. The pole creaked against both its forked supports as it turned, rotating Serdic's body from face-down to face-up. The dead eyes stared toward the crotch and the horrified Dennis.

One of the lizardmen tossed some more brush onto the fire. "We're going to have to leave," he said morosely.

"We can't," said the human. "Who'll mind Serdic?"

"Dennis will mind me," said the corpse of the Wizard Serdic.

Dennis jerked his head back out of sight. His bare flesh shuddered in streaks, up his thighs and down his shoulders.

The corpse hadn't really spoken. The bright-colored frogs were poisonous. They'd croaked and splashed and padded across Dennis' skin as he slept—rubbing him with venomous slime and bringing on wild hallucinations.

"Dennis," called the one-eyed human in a rasping voice. "Come down and mind the fire."

"Dennis, come down," agreed the lizardmen together.

"Dennis, come down," said the Wizard Serdic. "Or I will have to fetch you down."

Dennis had heard that hard, disdainful voice almost every day of his life. He couldn't mistake it now.

But neither could he possibly be hearing it.

Dennis stretched his head over the edge of the branch, looking down and expecting to see nothing but tangled brush and darkness. The fire glittered at him, and the five upturned faces shocked the youth as bitterly as a slap in the mouth.

"Come down, Dennis," said the corpse.

The lizardman holding the knotted end of the spit gave it a turn, rotating Serdic's face downward again. The dead voice trailed off in the sputter of the flames.

Dennis climbed down from what he'd thought was his hiding place. His chest was so cold and stiff with fear that he felt his pulse only in his ears. The vines were slick with rainwater. The fire threw shadows upward, concealing rather than illuminating hand-holds.

Halfway down, Dennis slipped. He fell the remainder of the distance, banging and scraping the inside of his right knee on a gnarled hump of vines. The pain was sharp and so fierce that it turned his stomach for the moment.

Whatever this was, it wasn't something that he was dreaming.

The lizardmen hissed in muted amusement; the one-eyed human giggled.

The corpse of the Wizard Serdic wore a smile that broadened. The spit creaked another quarter turn so that he faced the naked, shivering youth again.

"Here, boy," said a lizardman wearing nothing but a belt through which were stuck at least a dozen knives—rusty, notch-bladed weapons whose wooden handles were cracking and wired clumsily onto the tangs. "Take the spit."

Dennis stepped forward. His fear pulled him, because if he ran he would have to turn his back on these . . . men.

One of the lizardfolk was tall, taller than Dennis even if the youth stood straight instead of hunching over against his fear and pain and nakedness. That one rolled a human skull in his left hand, while his right palm rested on the brass hilt of a cutlass. His tongue forked between pointed teeth as he grinned.

Dennis put his hand out to the knotted end of the spit. The bark wasn't as deeply ridged as that of the vines down which he'd just climbed. It felt as though he were stroking the scaled back of a lizard. . . .

The human chuckled. "Go on, boy," he said. "Turn it."

"Don't let me singe, boy," said the grinning corpse. "It'll be the worse for you if you let me singe."

Dennis twisted at the pole. It was hard work: the knot didn't give much leverage, and the corpse was a heavy weight to turn against the crude bearing surfaces of the forked sticks.

"That's right, boy," said one of the lizardmen. "Turn and turn until he thaws. And don't let the fire go out."

Laughing together in their varied voices, the four scarred outcasts walked back into the jungle the way they had come. The human had a limp.

Dennis watched their backs, feeling relief at their going—until Serdic repeated, "Don't let me *singe*, boy!"

Dennis began to turn the spit. The corpse's ankles were lashed to the pole nearest him; the cruel, glittering eyes stared past the mold-green feet as if they were a frame. Dennis turned his face toward the jungle and gave the spit another tug.

The warmth of the brushwood fire thawed the ice-block that was Dennis' chest. He began to shudder.

None of this could be happening . . . but the fire hissed a muted lullaby, and its dull heat dried Dennis' skin and reminded him of how tired he was. Watching the silent motion of shadows on the jungle growth, he could forget his circumstances, his fear—

Fat popped as it dripped onto the flames.

"You've *burned* me, boy!" snarled a voice as vicious and deadly as the expression on Serdic's face when Dennis jerked his eyes and attention back to his duties.

"I'm sorry!" Dennis wheezed in terror as he turned the pole furiously. "I'm sorry, I'm so sorry!"

The wizard's wrists were tied to the middle of the pole. The hands should have flopped loosely as the spit turned, but they were held in the rigidity of death. Tiny mushrooms had sprouted from the knuckles of the right hand, but they were shriveling in the fire's heat.

Dennis tried to meet the corpse's eyes as he struggled with the pole, but there was too much venom in Serdic's glare for him to manage that for long.

At first Dennis ducked his head away to gather more brush for the fire. The vine-roots and saplings burned hot, but they collapsed to black ash without usable coals. Fresh wood flashed up quickly in a nimbus of blue flame from the gas driven out to burn a fingers-breadth above the stems.

"Careful, boy . . ." the corpse whispered in a voice that mimicked the hiss of escaping gas.

A few yards into the jungle was a plant whose leaves were broad as washtubs and streaked both yellow and green. Lesser vegetation cast quivering shadows on that backdrop. Dennis began to watch a playlet in which he and Chester walked the halls of Emath Palace, greeting his parents and talking with servants and village-folk come to the palace on business. He felt warm and safe for the first time in what seemed a lifetime, and—

"Boy! You've burned me again!" blazed the corpse's thunder-crackle voice.

Dennis' mouth dropped open and his eyes flared so wide that for a moment he couldn't take in what he saw. He'd stopped turning the pole when the Wizard Serdic was face-down. The corpse's toes were black and steaming as if they were about to burst into flames. When Dennis spun the protesting pole another half turn, smoke from the shriveled digits coiled away in an awful-smelling spiral.

"Boy—"

"I won't do it again!" Dennis cried with his eyes closed. "I won't—"

"Boy," repeated Serdic in a tone of chilled steel that drove the length of the youth's spine and pithed him, leaving him no volition but the corpse's dark will. "If you burn me again, I will come off this stake; and it will be the worse for you."

"I'm sorry, I'm sorry," Dennis whispered between lips salty with the taste of frightened tears. The bark had torn the palms of his hands with the effort of turning the pole. He reveled in the pain, because he could pretend that it was the only punishment he would receive for his lapse. "It won't happen again."

". . . worse for you . . ." whispered the wizard, his awful face turned toward the fire once more as Dennis rotated the spit as swiftly as if he were winching a bucket out of the well.

The jungle was no longer the haunt of darkness and hidden violence it had been when Dennis first stumbled into its trees and clutching thorns. No one could live in a world in which there was no peace or safety . . . and for Dennis, peace was now just beyond the firelight, in the shadows that told him of home and family.

The fire muttered reassuring phrases to the back of his drowsy mind. . . .

CHAPTER 17

The cry that woke Dennis the third time was wordless and terrible.

He leaped to his feet. The Wizard Serdic lay face-up
on the pole. The fire had fallen to ash and a shimmer
everywhere but beneath the corpse's hips—where fat
had bubbled out to burn with yellow flames and a soapy
odor.

"*Now* you've done it, boy," said the corpse. It freed
its wrists by twisting them against the withie which
bound them to the pole, then hunched its knees forward and untied its ankles.

"I'm coming for you, boy," said the Wizard Serdic,
dead a month and wrapped in a miasma of decay and
smoldering flesh. He crabbed his legs sideways and
stood up, still impaled on the spit.

Dennis screamed and ran into the night.

The jungle had tricked him, enticed him from his
duties and lulled him to sleep. Now it was all clawing
thorns and saw-edged leaves again.

Dennis would have thrown himself willingly into a

hedge of spears if it were the only way to escape from the corpse. His last view of Serdic was a memory of white terror: the wizard with his arms lifted, pulling out the pole that impaled him, hand over hand.

Trees battered the youth as he clubbed himself on their trunks and fallen branches. His forearms stung from cuts and scratches, but the pounding the rest of his body took during his wild careen through the night was a red, dull ache with no end and no location.

That red pulse became the whole universe for him, replacing hope and the memory of Serdic. It was so omnipresent that when Dennis' eyes told him that there was a glow which silhouetted the dark thickets, the information merged with pain and was lost until his feet tripped on the threshold.

Then he stumbled into the cabin he had fled a lifetime before.

Dennis would have gotten up and run further, but his body failed him at last. His hands and feet scrabbled briefly on the floor of smooth hardwood puncheons, but they could raise his torso only for a moment before he flopped down again.

He wasn't crying; he had no tears left.

For minutes, Dennis lay on the floor with his breath sobbing in and out while his muscles recovered themselves enough to hurt individually.

The fireplace held a bed of glowing coals. Their light seemed brighter than it had earlier, when the cabinet opened and Dennis ran from Serdic the first time . . . but time lacked the reality it had had when this terrible night began.

The cabinet still stood in the corner, open and empty. The cabin's front door stirred vaguely in a breeze that made Dennis shiver.

The youth got up, moving like a man who'd lived with pain for decades. A cramp suddenly knotted the big muscles of his right thigh. The flesh contorted, taking away Dennis' breath with the fresh agony and almost throwing him to the floor again.

Almost. With his eyes slitted, he hopped on his good leg until he caught the edge of the door and supported half his weight on it until the fiery throbbing subsided. He slammed the heavy door; barred it; and, as an afterthought, tweaked in the latchstring that still hung out through the hole above the lintel.

The feathery pelt was gone. He'd probably lost it in the jungle when he bolted out the door.

That didn't matter. Dennis had slept with frogs in a pool of rain water. The warm puncheons were a more attractive choice now than the bed that hulked in the shadows across the room.

Dennis curled up in front of the fire, cradling his head on his crossed arms. He could feel the aches draining from him. His muscles relaxed, giving up the tautness which had doubled the pain of his injuries. He was logy with fatigue, drifting into a slumber as deep as the realm of the sea hag. . . .

"What will you give me for your lodging, boy?" demanded the Wizard Serdic from outside the cabin.

Dennis roused. He felt as though his skin were covered with needles which pricked him every time he moved. His ears buzzed so loudly that for a moment he thought he must be dreaming, because he couldn't hear any real sound over the roar of blood and exhaustion.

"What will you *give* me, boy?" the voice demanded.

Dennis stepped to the door. He didn't feel his scrapes and bruises, but pulses of heat rose until they expanded away from the top of his head as he moved.

He lifted the bar and pulled the door open. The corpse stared at him with eyes lighted orange by reflected firelight.

Dennis had been frightened too badly and for too long to have any fear remaining.

"Come in, wizard," he said, moving his arm in a

welcoming gesture. He would have bowed if he'd been sure that he wouldn't fall over if he tried.

Serdic stepped forward stiffly, not from pain but as if he were pieced together out of wood rather than flesh. The fire had tangled his long fingernails into a mass like knotted hair, giving his hands the appearance of deformed hoofs.

The hole in Serdic's right shoulder—where one end of the spit had been inserted—was puckered and bloodless.

"You *owe* me for your lodging, boy," said the corpse. "What is it that you will give me?"

Dennis stepped back and let the door swing closed behind Serdic. A greenish fungus traced patterns like tattoos on the right side of the corpse's face.

Dennis smiled. "I'll give you a story, wizard," he said. The syllables drifted through his consciousness like bubbles glimmering on dark water for the moment before they burst.

"I'll tell you about a boy—a man. . . . A man who enters a cabin open in the night and who finds a dead man there. Does this interest you, wizard? It's fair pay, isn't it, a story?"

Serdic said nothing. Either Dennis' body or his consciousness swayed. He wasn't sure he was still standing up, but his voice continued, "And the man runs, but the corpse follows him, carried by four rogues, bloody rogues. The man has to watch the corpse warming on a fire, but he doesn't mind it well and the corpse chases him down again to ask for pay."

The pattern of Serdic's cheek writhed, but Dennis couldn't tell whether it was the flesh or the fungus or his own reeling mind that caused the movement.

"And the man has nothing to pay with," he went on, almost shouting now. "He's naked and friendless and the night may never end. And so he offers a story, a wonderful story—and that's fair pay, isn't it, for it's all he has?"

The corpse didn't move.

"*Isn't* it, Serdic?" Dennis cried, leaning forward so that his face was only inches from the dead face of the dead wizard. "And if it isn't—then to Hell with you, where you belong. And to Hell with me as well, if it must be."

The corpse smiled, an expression made more horrible by the fact that decay had already begun to shrivel the gums away from the yellow teeth they held. Serdic reached out with one stiff hand, stopping just short of contact with Dennis' cheek.

"Shall we play a game, boy?" he asked in a voice like the paw of a cat dabbing at its prey.

Dennis lifted his chin in a brusque nod. He was suddenly afraid to speak.

"We will play this game, then," said the wizard. "I will leave you now. But when next my name is spoken, boy—then I will come. Understand me, boy?"

"I understand," Dennis whispered.

He could feel himself slipping away, but he wasn't sure that it was his body falling. The Wizard Serdic was dissolving, but *everything* was dissolving into the night. At the last, nothing remained but the pattern of fungus glowing green and hideous though the cheek on which it grew had disappeared.

And then even the pattern was gone, except in Dennis' nightmare.

CHAPTER 18

"Good sleep is the greatest of gifts to a man in the time of his feebleness, Dennis," said Chester as sunlight through the leaf canopy made his master's eyelids quiver.

All of Dennis' muscles flashed taut. His body thrashed as if lightning-struck by the sudden surprise. "Ch-chester!" he gasped. "Where have you—where are—"

Dennis looked around. He and the little robot lay beneath a tree whose buttress roots spread broadly out through the lesser growths of the jungle. The bark was smooth, and the contours of the roots made a comfortable cup to support the youth while he was sleeping.

Nothing in the jungle could stay dry. Dennis' hips lay in a pool of water, and the cloak that he'd pulled over himself and Chester was as sodden as the surface of a pond. He tweaked the garment back—it clung because of its weight and the surface tension of the water—and stroked the smooth, slick carapace of his friend and companion.

"Where did you find my clothes, Chester?" he asked.

"And this?" he added, noticing that the Founder's Sword was with them beneath the cloak also, belt wrapped around the hilt and scabbard.

Dennis stood up, lifting the sword with one hand. He ached all over, and both his clothes and skin were ripped by thorns—but there was no sign of the battering he'd taken when he ran through the jungle naked, pursued by the corpse of his father's wizard.

"Chester?" he repeated in concern, because the robot still hadn't responded.

"Dennis, your clothes and your sword have been with you through the night and dawn," Chester said. Concern honed the precision of his words.

"But the cabin," Dennis said. The chain closure of his cloak cut into his neck with the weight of water in the garment. He reached up to release it with his free hand, but wonder stayed the motion. "Chester, you remember the cabin, don't you?"

The little robot stretched his own limbs, raising his body on four of them while the other four reached higher yet. Droplets cascaded down the silvery tentacles, leaving no more sign than if Chester also were made of fluid.

"Dennis," he said, "there is no cabin that I remember."

The tentacles groping through the sun's dapplings lowered to the ground; the other four rose and shook themselves free of water in silky iridescence.

"Then what. . . ?" said Dennis. His hand completed its motion, loosing the clasp and swinging the cloak away from his body. He leaned the sword against the tree bole and began to wring out his garment thoroughly.

He didn't finish his sentence, because he had no idea what the rest of the question ought to be.

The air was muggy, saturated with vapor transpiring from the leaves as sunlight touched him. It was hard to remember how miserable and chilly it had been a few hours before.

"Didn't you see the—" Dennis began; and before his

tongue formed the rest of the words, he recalled the fungus-knotted smile of the Wizard Serdic saying *shall we play a game, boy?* in a nightmare voice.

"I was dreaming," Dennis muttered to himself aloud. "I dreamed it all, Chester. And it was awful."

Chester coiled a tentacle around the youth's waist. "Happiness comes out of the hardship men undergo, Dennis," he said.

Dennis belted on the sword again. The skin over his hipbone was still chafed from wearing the weapon the night before, but maybe he'd get calluses or something. It wasn't a problem he remembered hearing about in tales of past heroes.

"Well . . ." he said, looking around them.

His heart leaped. They were off the trail—that much of what he remembered from the night before was true.

But there was no cabin, and no room in the heavy vegetation for a cabin ever to have been there.

"Chester," he said, "can you find the trail from here?" He was amazed at his own calm. The night he had spent in his dreams with a dead man had burned all the fear out of him.

"I can find the trail, Dennis," Chester replied. "And I can find a road, if you would travel a road instead."

Dennis looked at his companion, wondering what the robot's expression would be now if he had a face. "Then let us take the road, Chester," he said. "And—" the grinning fungus in his memory momentarily wiped the smile from his own expression "—if it leads away from here, it leads us well."

He followed the robot through the glittering leaves which showered them again with the night's raindrops.

CHAPTER 19

Dennis didn't have a clear idea of what his companion might mean by "road." A wider track beaten into the jungle by scaly feet, perhaps; or, just possibly, a herringbone surface of stone pavers like those King Hale had ordered a few years before to clothe the streets of Emath.

The road to which Chester led him, only twenty yards from where the pair of them had weathered the night, was amazingly more durable than either of those.

The road was soft pink and a little more than ten feet wide. The surface was pebble-grained for the sake of traction, but it was so dense that the last night's rain beaded on it with no hint of sinking in.

And it was old. The root of a great tree knobbed on one side of the roadway and sprang to the surface again on the other, bracing the trunk and sucking nutriment from the thin jungle soil. The enormous hydraulic pressure swelling the root had been unable to crack the pink surface—and the tree it fed was at least a century old.

Chester's limbs clicked on the roadway, just as they had in the halls of Emath Palace. Dennis followed him gingerly. The road was slick despite the grain of its finish . . . but the youth's concern was for other things than merely his footing.

"Did the first heroes build this road when men came here to Earth, Chester?" he asked.

"The road is older than men on this planet, Dennis," the robot replied. In the same neutral tone, he added, "The road is older than Man."

"Then—" Dennis began; but if the road was that old, he wasn't sure he *wanted* to know who had built it. He didn't finish his question.

The trees to either side of the pavement closed overhead in a canopy gorgeous with flowers, fruits, and the lizards which darted to snatch up metal-glistening insects. The air was a steam-bath, even though the light that reached the ground was filtered yellow-green by the leaves through which it poured.

Dennis' boots squelched at every step. Finally he stopped and took them and the socks off, wringing the latter dry and giving all the paraphernalia to Chester to carry in the embroidered shopping bag.

"I thought I threw that away," the youth said suspiciously. Had the dream started—

"You threw the bag away, Dennis," the little robot agreed. "And I retrieved it before I followed you."

The warmth of the pink pavement felt good to Dennis' bare feet, but he needed to walk with some care. He had a habit of banging his heels down as he strode along. The road had no resilience at all. He'd bruise himself badly if he tramped that way here without wool and leather to cushion the shock.

He was getting very hungry. That was probably a sign he'd recovered from the events of the night—both real and imagined.

Dennis looked at an overhanging branch, heavy with fruit of an enticing scarlet—

A color similar to that of the poisonous frogs of the night before. Or was that only dream, too?

"Chester," he asked, pausing, "can we eat any of these?"

"Eat freely, so long as food is available," Chester quoted. One of his limbs snaked up to remove a globular fruit and offer it to his companion.

Dennis bit down. The pulp beneath the bright rind was mauve and succulent; juice dribbled off his chin as he resumed walking.

It tasted delicious, but he didn't remember ever eating the type in Emath. Forty yards further on, as he was finishing the fruit, he realized why the lizardmen didn't bring this variety in to trade. Even in that short time after picking, the pulp had softened further and begun to sour. It was a delicacy for jungle-dwellers alone.

Jungle-dwellers like Dennis, Prince of Emath.

Chester continued to pluck fruits and berries for Dennis as they strode along. The youth noticed a cluster of thumb-sized translucent fruits and said, "These, Chester?"

"Not these, Dennis," said the little robot, guiding Dennis' hand away with one of his tentacles. "For you would die, and your bones would rot before your flesh."

Dennis lost all concern over the wholesomeness of what his companion offered him.

The fruits were tasty and interesting in their variety, but they didn't satiate Dennis' appetite even after he'd eaten all his stomach could hold. "Ah, Chester?" he asked, embarrassed that he might sound ungrateful. "Is there a place we could get meat? Ah, or fish?"

"There is a pond ahead of us, Dennis," the robot said. "It may be that there are fish in it that you can catch."

That I can try to catch, Dennis thought; but he was looking forward to the chance.

CHAPTER 20

The road swept through the interior of the continent in a series of curves. The pattern had nothing obvious to do with the terrain. When one gently-radiused arc intersected a rare outcrop of hard stone in the jungle's general flatness, the roadway sheared through and left what remained of the outcrop as a gray wall to either side of the manufactured pinkness.

The pond was curved also, a crescent moon of water so large that its horns vanished to either side in the fringing jungle. The road crossed three feet above the water, unsupported and without guard rails. As the companions approached, Dennis saw touches of pink beneath the mud and reeds of the water's edge. Whoever built the road had constructed the pond as well.

There was bright, unobstructed sunlight at the center of the shallow arch that bridged the water: the pond was so wide that even the giant trees to either side could not close the sky with their branches. Dennis had spent his life in sunlight; but after less than a day in the jungle, the sharp purity of an open sky was as great a wonder as tangled greenery had been when he viewed it from a crystal tower.

Dennis looked down into the water—black as shadows except where it reflected the orange ball of the sun. Insects skimmed the surface, tracing their figures with mechanical repetition.

One circle broke suddenly in a splash and a silver glitter too unexpected to be visualized after the event.

"There are fish indeed, Dennis," said Chester approvingly.

"How did you know this pond was here, Chester?" the youth asked.

"I know what I know," said the robot. "And the pond was here."

Dennis attached his hook and cork float to the line. They'd been in the shopping bag when he flung it away, furious at the wet bread and missing sausages. If Chester hadn't retrieved the bag . . .

"The wise man is praised because he remains calm, Dennis," said the robot—as if he were reading his master's thoughts.

Dennis would have to hold the line by the small stick on which it was spooled unless he cut himself a pole, and to do that—

"I should have brought a little knife, Chester," Dennis said doubtfully. "Or maybe a hatchet. I could use the sword, but it'd be pretty clumsy. . . ?"

He let his voice trail into a question. Chester ignored it.

Well, that was what Dennis deserved. He was unsure of himself and hoping to be told that everything would work out fine. What he needed to do—what he *knew* he needed to do—was to act.

He unbelted the sword and laid it beside him. He'd use the butt to club his catch when he'd landed it. Then he started to drop the line into the water—and froze.

The large fish that rose and slapped the water only a few yards out did so in mockery.

"Chester," Dennis said, "I forgot bait. We don't have any bait."

"There is the ring on your finger, Dennis," replied his companion. "It may be that the ring will lure fish."

The ring was a diamond in a thin band, placed on Dennis' thumb for luck in his infancy and now worn on the little finger of his left hand. Its facets sent the sunlight across the surface of the pond in fiery sparkles even as Dennis turned his hand to look at it.

"Sure, that's a *good* idea," he said as he worried the ring over his knuckle. "*Thank* you, Chester."

"Many are the small things that are worthy of respect," quoted the robot smugly.

The line, with the ring attached to the tag end of the leader, plopped into the water at last. The pond was so rich in dyes leached from the surrounding jungle that the hook disappeared though it was only a hand's length beneath the bobber. The diamond remained a wink of brightness twisting in the dark.

The strike was immediate. Dennis almost lost his grip—and the pull was so strong that he nearly pitched into the water when reflex clamped his hands against the spool.

He staggered backward on the bridge crying, "We've got one, Chester!" as the line spun out.

In the back of his mind Dennis was bitterly calling himself a fool for not cutting a pole after all, even if it would have been a hard job with the sword his only tool. A pole's springiness would have given the fish something to fight besides the tension fingers put on the spool . . . but Dennis' hands were strong and calloused from swordsmanship drills, and the thrill of the struggle quickly replaced desire for a meal as the force driving his actions.

It was a big fish, big even had it come from the

hold of one of the Emath trawlers whose catches had all the salt ocean in which to grow.

At first Dennis saw nothing but the cavorting line and the insects drawn by the bubbles in the line's swift wake. A spiny fin flicked the air, long and six feet back from where the line cut the water.

The fish broke surface in a leap, tossing its head in a vain attempt to clear the hook fast in its jaw. It was huge, its head and back iridescent and its belly the white of fresh cream.

Its eyes were black. They sparkled like the diamond flopping at the side of its mouth.

Dennis let his catch run against the drag of his thumb until the line had wound almost to the end of the spool. Then he fought the fish back, loop by loop—wishing he had better equipment and proud beyond words that he was succeeding with what he had.

Dennis was doing this himself, with neither king nor courtier to ease the task.

For a time, the fish struggled in the pond-edge reeds, but there were no trees growing beyond the pink margin to break the line on their roots. If the fish came toward him, though, and crossed beneath, the road's lower edge—an immaculate 90 degrees despite the untold ages the pink material had been exposed to the elements—would cut the line as surely as a pair of scissors.

"Chester!" he shouted, already poising to jump into the pond if the water were knee-deep and its opaque surface had convinced him that it must be. "How deep is this?"

"It is twice your height, Dennis," Chester replied calmly. "Or maybe more."

The fish started its rush at the bridge, just as Dennis had feared.

Instead of reeling the line, he gathered it in great loops by the handful. He could never play it out again

smoothly, but—first things first. It didn't matter whether
or not the line were neatly coiled at the spindle end, if
the hook and the catch that was invaluable for Dennis's
self-respect were trailing their way unimpeded on the
other side of the bridge, lost forever to him. . . .

"He who thrusts his chest at the spear will surely be
slain!" Chester warned—

But the robot didn't interfere, it wasn't his *place* to
interfere, and Dennis with his blood up was in no mood
to be warned about the sin of pride

Almost the fish beat him. Almost.

Dennis bent with the spindle in his left hand as the
fish tried to shoot beneath him, its fin cutting a flat
S-curve of foam in the black surface. When he jerked
upright again, the last yard of line was in his right palm,
sword palm, and the great, glittering fish flashed up
also—will it or no.

They teetered there together, the fish's tail lashing
the water to froth as Dennis tried to twist his torso back
to balance and safety. The eyes winked at him and the
ring winked; and Dennis dropped the tangled spindle
to thrust the vee of his index and middle fingers into
the flaring gill slits.

For a moment it was an open question as to which of
them was caught, the fish or Dennis. Then the youth
curvetted, lifting with all the strength of both arms—
nearly overbalancing but not quite, while the fish flopped
and slapped and flopped back on the bridge.

Dennis panted and groped for the sword with his
right hand. The line had cut his palm, so he left chev-
rons of blood on the pink surface as he patted toward
the hilt.

"Be my lover, dear one," said the fish in a human
voice, a woman's voice.

Dennis squawked and jumped back, snatching away
his left hand that had pinioned his catch while his right
prepared to finish it. The sharp gill-rakers had cut his
fingers.

"I am the Cariad, dear one," said the fish, turning so that both its eyes watched the youth in a most unfishlike way. "Be my lover, will you not?"

"By earth and heaven!" Dennis shouted in a mixture of wonder and horror. "You're a fish and no more than my dinner!"

He snatched up the sword, and as he turned with it the fish—glimmered. He didn't see the change, but instead of its tailfins slapping him, bare human legs tangled with his legs and they both went back over the side of the bridge—the youth and what had been a fish and was now a girl who clasped him.

Dennis hit the water with his mouth open to shout surprise. The pond was as cold as it was black, and no better to breathe than water of any other temperature or color. They sank in a gout of spray, Dennis and the girl. All he could think of as he went down was *"It is twice as deep as you are tall, Dennis; or maybe more."*

When his body's buoyancy and air trapped in his clothing bobbed Dennis to the surface, the girl—Cariad—spouted a playful jet of water from her mouth and said, "Now, dear one—won't you give me the power of a wish over you?"

"Let me *go!*" Dennis shouted.

He knew an instant later that he should have saved his breath instead, because Cariad grinned and ducked him again with arms that were slim and white and very strong.

She had a pixie face with high cheekbones and a wide mouth. Her eyes were round and the color of sun-struck amber, while the nipples of her breasts were the same bright coral as her lips.

Dennis' lungs were burning before Cariad let him rise the second time. When his head broke surface, he began to cough and his eyes were blind with fear of suffocation.

"Give me the power of a wish, beloved," the girl

murmured in a voice as soft as her naked body pressing against him. "So that we may go up upon the firm ground again, you and I. . . ."

"Never will I—" Dennis sputtered, uncertain whether or not he was speaking aloud until the Cariad's hands gripped his chin and forced him down again backwards, as if she had her will to slay him or spare him—

As indeed she did, slip of a girl though she looked. . . . But Dennis' strength was nothing to hers in the water. White torture seethed in his lungs, and his eyes pulsed red with fire and death.

When the pressure released for a moment, before Cariad could speak—or he could see the sun for what might be his last glimpse—Dennis gasped, "I give you your wish! Only let me up!"

"But of course I will let you up, dear one, little heart," the girl crooned as she thrust them over to the bridge with two stokes of her slim, strong legs. "Of course I will do no harm to my lover."

Dennis reached for the lip of the bridge—low above the water when he stood atop it, but a lifetime away now. When his arm rose out of the pond, his face sank under the surface.

Help, Chester! his mind wailed. Frustrated exhaustion goaded him, but he'd learned at least not to open his mouth at such times.

Cariad gripped the youth under one armpit and splayed her free hand onto the bridge. Against the pink stoniness, Dennis could see the translucent hint of webbing at the base of her fingers. She lifted him effortlessly into the tentacles of Chester, who caught the youth when Dennis' own arms would have let him flop down for want of strength.

Girl-shaped and eel-fluid, the Cariad slipped onto the roadway beside them. Smiling, she curled her legs beneath her, knees together, and sat in a shimmer of pond water. When she tossed her head, droplets flew from the tight rings of her hair. Her tresses were of variable, brilliant colors, like the rainbow dazzle of a fish's scales or light breaking through one of the prisms of Emath Palace.

Cariad's yellow eyes were ageless, but for the rest she seemed no more than a girl as young as Dennis. Her nudity was innocent and utterly unselfconscious.

Dennis' hook was caught in her upper lip. The line trailed from it, back into the pond. As Dennis watched, she raised her hands to the injury and winced as she tried to worry the barbs free.

"Ah . . ." said the youth. "Can I . . . ?"

"Oh, would you help me, my Dennis, my lover?" Cariad replied, giving him a sunbright smile that the barbed steel hook only quirked slightly.

Dennis shifted on the pavement without standing up. His garments felt gluey and uncomfortable. He started to shrug out of his tunic but looked at Chester first. The robot was as impassive as motionless silver could be.

Dennis blushed and left the garment on as he leaned toward the Cariad.

The hook was set firmly. Dennis tried to keep his eyes focused on the steel, instead of letting them drift down as they wanted to the girlish breasts. The water that beaded on Cariad's flesh gleamed prismatically clear, with no hint of the black depths of the pond from which it came.

He tugged tentatively. Cariad gasped and tears started from the corners of her eyes. Dennis flinched away.

"No, beloved," she said, hugging the youth back against her. "No, you must hurt me to save me, is it not so? Go ahead, then, my lover."

"I'm *not* your lover," Dennis muttered to her shim-mering hair. The sharpness of his tone was meant as a reminder to his own body.

"Even a wise man can be harmed by desire for a woman," quoted Chester. His voice was slightly too distant to be called tart.

The Cariad lifted her face with another broad smile. "Come, my Dennis, you will love me forever, as I wish it," she said. "But first the hook."

Dennis felt the heat of his blush again. "There's no help for it but to push the hook through," he said firmly. "I'll cut the line and do that, though it will hurt for the time."

One of her delicate hands played with the back of Dennis' neck as he turned to find his sword, the only cutting tool he had. He kept his eyes down so that he didn't have to look at Chester—though the robot's metal carapace could have no expression.

The Cariad giggled.

The Founder's Sword was an awkward device at best for cutting fishline, and Dennis' muscles still quivered from being starved for oxygen as the girlish arms held his head under water. Dennis pinched the leader between his left thumb and forefinger, while the other three fingers momentarily steadied the cross-guard of the weapon he held point-up in his right. Then he cut the stout line.

The Cariad smiled and her hand shot out to snatch the ring Dennis had used as a lure. "Beloved . . ." she murmured as she slipped the little diamond onto her own fourth finger, the digit whose vein leads straight back to the heart with no branchings.

The swordblade was filmed with rust, especially where the sheath rubbed the chines that gave it a diamond cross-section for strength. Dennis slid the weapon back into the scabbard, embarrassed at its condition.

Embarrassed also at remembering that he'd drawn the sword to knock in the head of this luscious girl.

"I'm ready, little heart," said the Cariad, lifting her face as he gingerly reached for the hook with both hands. When she arched her chest, her nipples brushed his forearms.

With his face set in stony determination, Dennis' left

index finger probed the inside of Cariad's lip. He could feel the point, but it hadn't penetrated the skin.

Well, he'd have to push it the rest of the way.

"This will hurt," he said forcefully as he spread the lip with one hand and twisted on the shank with the other. Her flesh resisted the barbed steel.

"Push, beloved," she murmured in a voice blurred by his hands. "I don't—"

The barbs poked clear. Dennis griped them and pulled the shank the rest of the way out of the Cariad's lip.

"—mind."

Sweat was dripping from his face, making him look as though he'd been ducked again in the pond.

Dennis tried to give the hook to Chester, who had already gathered in the line and spindle before it could twirl away in the pond's slow current. His hand was shaking badly, but Chester wrapped the hook with the tip of one tentacle and wiped it clean on the side of the bag before starting to re-attach it to the leader.

Drops of blood from the cut brightened the Cariad's lips so that she smiled even more richly than before. "Now I've saved you from the water, beloved," she said, "and you've saved me from the hook. . . . Come and kiss me, my dearest—"

"No!" Dennis said, shouting to quench his own desire. Standing, the Cariad's body curved, her hips to one side and her bosom to the other. He couldn't imagine how he'd ever thought that she was innocent.

He wanted to hold her so badly; but her ancient yellow eyes seemed to laugh as they looked into his soul.

"Only the once, little heart," whispered the Cariad's ripe, red lips. "And then you will go and I will stay, if you would have it so."

Dennis looked sidelong at his companion. "That can be no harm, can it, Chester?" he asked as if the question were an idle one and his heart and soul weren't fixed on hearing the proper response to it.

"If you taste her blood, Dennis," said the robot coolly, "then you will love one another forever—for that is her wish, and the blood will seal it."

For a moment, Dennis saw his life sinking into the amber eyes and the slim arms that reached to embrace him. Then his throat made a sound somewhere between a groan and a scream; he began to run the rest of the way across the bridge, his bare feet slapping the pavement and the long sword clipping his ankle for all that he tried to control the swinging with a hand on the pommel.

"Dennis, my heart," called the girl-thing behind him, the sun an iridescent dazzle in her hair. Her form quivered at the corner of his eye and she was a fish, curving back into the water with scarcely a splash, so clean was the dive.

Chester was at the youth's side, loping easily on the warm surface. His bent limbs struck tick-whisk! tick-whisk! with a regularity that reassured Dennis.

The fish rolled to the pond surface beside Dennis and his companion. The ring shot spikes of light from one ray of a pectoral fin. "Be my lover, my Dennis, little heart," the fish called. "Do not leave me when I need you so greatly, my beloved."

"Run," Dennis gasped to himself. "Run, run . . ."

Dennis knew he was safe when the reeds of the pond margin brushed the roadway beside him, but he continued running for another thirty yards—until the tops of the great trees were a solid canopy above him, and the undergrowth was a wall to either side.

Gasping for breath, Dennis leaned against a tree-trunk streaked green by the vines using it as a support to coil skyward. He looked back the way they had come.

A slim girl sat on the roadway at the pond's edge. The sun jeweled her hair and the water droplets on her breasts.

She waved the hand which wore the diamond ring.

"We'd best be going," Dennis said to his companion.

But it was several moments more before he was willing to turn his eyes from the Cariad and resume walking along the road through the jungle.

"And I think, Chester," the youth said when they were well out of sight of the pond, "that I will be satisfied with the fruit and nuts which you tell me are safe to eat. I do not need to try fish again, for the time."

CHAPTER 21

In the evening, the sky darkened again before sunset. The needlepoint patches of blue became pools of
roiling cloud.

"He who runs abroad from evil, finds evil where he
flees," Chester said.

Dennis laughed and patted the robot's carapace. The
cut across his palm still stung, and there seemed to be a
little swelling in the hand itself. Despite that, he felt
surprisingly good. "But can the wanderer find shelter
from the rain, my friend?" he asked.

Chester rose cautiously onto the tips of his eight
tentacles. Even so, the robot's egg-shaped body was
no higher than Dennis' shoulders. Chester rotated slowly,
moving his limbs in sets of four, a few inches clockwise
at a time.

At last he said, "Here is a tree that became hollow
before it fell, Dennis. It will give us shelter from the
rain."

Dennis couldn't imagine how his companion could
see a fallen tree or anything else through the leaves and

gathering darkness, but he followed Chester willingly
into the undergrowth. A few yards away—though each
step was a battle—was the bole of a forest giant, just as
the robot had said.

Upright, the tree had been twenty feet across at the
base. Now, on its side, more than half that diameter
was a cave whose lip was orange and yellow with the
shelf fungus eating its way into the wood which remained.

Chester paused. The first drops of rain rapped against
leaves, but the downpour hadn't yet penetrated the
triple canopy.

Dennis climbed in. The interior of the trunk was
damp and had a hint of reptilian sharpness. It made
him wish that he'd drawn the sword before entering.
Chester followed, a barely-visible glimmer in silhouette
as the storm thundered down and washed away the last
of the daylight.

The hollow was slimy, and Dennis could hear water
running through a knothole somewhere farther back in
the trunk; but in comparison at least to the night before, he was dry and comfortable. The tree was real,
not a dream, not like the dead wizard's cabin, and
Chester lay beside him with his limbs coiled.

Dennis laughed. "How is it that heroes spend the
nights between one adventure and the next, Chester?"
he asked.

"You are a hero, Dennis," the robot said softly. "And
it is in a fallen tree that you are spending the night."

"I'm no hero," the youth murmured. "I know that
now."

But he slept easily, wrapped in the fuzzy warmth of
his friend's compliment.

CHAPTER 22

For seventeen days they followed the road, while Dennis learned to live from the jungle—if not precisely in it.

Each midday they rested. Dennis trained himself to lie so still that the lizards skittered past and across him as if he were a fallen log. Once he amused himself by flicking lumps of nutmeat from the tip of his thumb toward the lizard that lay like a purple-black shadow on the underside of a branch ten feet above him. At last he got a bead into the proper position—a hand's breadth from the lizard's blunt nose—and the lizard's pink tongue snatched in the nutmeat.

"It is not nuts but insects that the lizard eats, Dennis," said Chester.

"The nuts do not harm me, Chester," the youth replied. "Will the nuts harm the lizard?"

"The nuts will not harm the lizard, that is so."

"Then no harm has been done," Dennis said, smiling up at the little creature. "For which I am glad."

The lizard's throat worked as it swallowed down the pellet instead of spitting it out again as expected.

"Perhaps that's my mission, hey?" Dennis chuckled to his companion. "To convert first myself, then the lizards of the jungle, to a diet of nutmeats?"

"Lowly work and lowly food are better than luxury far from home," the robot grumbled.

But when Dennis thought of Emath, he wasn't sure that a palace or village in the power of the sea hag made a proper home for anything human.

CHAPTER 23

Chester's carapace shone with a brushed finish applied by thorns and horny bark.

Dennis' clothing was reduced to rags, but the cuts in his skin didn't fester as he'd expected on his first miserable hours beyond the village perimeter. At Chester's suggestion, he washed them in the citric astringence of a fruit whose orange pulp was too bitter for him to eat. The half-ripe interiors of large, warty-hulled nuts provided a salve that seemed to do more than merely keep insects from swarming to feed on Dennis' exposed flesh.

He topped nuts and hacked down fruit-clusters with the Founder's Sword. He was learning to use its weight with precision—and to respect the quality of the edge it would hold.

The blade was burnished, now. Chester had shown his companion a gourd which split into a mass of white rags. Dried for a day on Dennis' back as he tramped in the sun, the rags became a coarse cloth with enough embedded silica to sweep away all hints of rust.

Dennis cleaned and sharpened the sword every night,

as the rain fell from the darkness on their shelter—a log
or a cave or a thatching of tub-great leaves over a frame
of vines and saplings. A careful polish with the gourd
he'd prepared during the day, then short, firm strokes
with his whetstone to grind any hint of nicks or wear
out of the star-metal blade.

Ramos had taught him how to sharpen with a stone;
taught him also that even a king's son must keep his
tools—a blade is no more than a tool—ready for use at
all times.

But for all the tales of the jungle and its terrors,
Dennis found nothing on which to try the sword save
fruits, and nuts and—very occasionally—sharp-spikes
tangles that had managed to grow across the paved
surface.

CHAPTER 24

On the eighteenth day, the road ended.

The jungle grew to the edge of a glassy bowl a mile across, roofed with more sky than Dennis had seen since leaving Emath. Nothing grew in the bowl's interior, though the surface was crazed with a myriad of tiny cracks, and rainwater pooled in many of the smooth irregularities of the surface.

Weeks of familiarity had taught Dennis that the road was indestructible; but here the pavement ended in gobbets burned from pink through all the colors of the spectrum—indistinguishable from the soil fused to glass beyond.

The air was hot. The unhindered sun blazed down and in reflection from the sides of the bowl. Dennis felt as cold as he had when thinking of the Wizard Serdic.

"What happened here, Chester?" he asked. His voice sounded in his own ears like that of a little boy.

"This planet is not so old as the universe, Dennis," the robot said quietly. "And the thing that happened here to the road and the city beyond the road, that was not so old as the planet.

"But they are all three very old, the universe and the planet and the thing. We must not be troubled by them now, you and I."

Dennis squinted across the bowl, his eyes struggling with the haze and heat waves. He could see no hint of the pink road continuing; and even if it did, he was no longer sure he wished to walk it.

"All right," he said decisively. "We haven't seen any of the lizardmen's trails crossing the road in . . . Two days? No, three. We'll go back to where we last saw a trail and take that to where it leads us."

His hand reached instinctively for the pommel of his sword and lifted the blade an inch or two, making sure that it ran free in its scabbard. They hadn't met any lizardfolk on the way, save the three in his dream of the corpse. Dennis didn't know—no one in Emath had known—how the scaly denizens of the jungle would react when humans entered their villages instead of the other way around.

"The wise man takes counsel patiently before he acts," Chester said. Though Dennis knew the robot could move or see in any direction, the normal "front" of his carapace now looked off into the jungle as if he were ignoring his companion.

"Well, all right," Dennis said in the exasperation he always felt at his companion's unwillingness—or perhaps inability—to volunteer anything but quoted wisdom. "What would *you* do?"

"I will do whatever my master wishes me to do, Dennis," Chester said primly. "But—there is **a** city not so far away from here, though it be through the jungle with no trail save the trail that we make for ourselves."

The youth shaded his eyes with his hand as he looked back at the road they had followed so far. "A village of the lizard people, Chester?" he asked.

"It is a village of men, Dennis," Chester replied.

"Though it was not made by men or by lizardfolk either. It is called Rakastava."

Dennis thought for a moment. "It doesn't mean crossing—that, does it?" he asked. His thumb gestured over his shoulder without looking at the bowl which death itself had excavated.

"It does not," the robot said, and a light-silvered tentacle pointed the way to their right. A clump of sword-edged leaves with black, spear-shaped tips rimmed the road there for several yards. "But there is no trail."

Dennis drew the Founder's Sword and slashed a broad gap through the immediate vegetation. "We can handle the jungle," he said.

CHAPTER 25

A day and half later, he knew enough to be less positive if the question came up again. The difficulties weren't particularly from the undergrowth—away from the tunnel of light which the road let fall to the ground, lesser vegetation was stunted and easy to avoid.

The footing was worse than terrible. Streams; bogs that might be ankle-deep or over his head; fallen timber that Dennis might have to circle for a hundred yards because it was too soft with rot to climb; and the rare outcrop of quartz or other faceted stone that would slash through even the calluses his bare feet had formed tramping the hard, smooth roadway.

Dennis didn't see Rakastava until he hacked through an unexpected tangle of briars. Beyond them, he noticed that his feet were on grass and his face in sunlight.

"This is Rakastava, Dennis," Chester said needlessly.

Dennis let his breath out slowly.

No one could have doubted that the crystal spires of Emath Palace were artificial, built by the men of old with tools more wondrous than those they had be-

queathed to their progeny. No one could have doubted—
save Hale and later his son, the only men who had seen
the palace rise by itself, an organic part of the headland
on which it stood.

Rakastava seemed instead to be a great vaulting hill,
brown and barren; wholly a thing of the Earth and not
hands . . . but Dennis wondered.

The city or city-huge palace had no gates or windows,
only slopes too steep to climb. They rose hundreds of
feet in complex curves. The exterior of Rakastava was
brown; reddish-brown in its own shadow, closer to golden
in the portions which the sun flooded—but the same
color throughout, a uniformity as false to nature as the
oily smoothness of the walls when Dennis tested them
with one hand.

His other hand held the great sword which he had
thought not to sheathe.

"Chester, how do we—" Dennis began. The shrill,
broken note of a trumpet interrupted him and drew his
eyes upward.

Three men were leaning over a high battlement to
stare down at Dennis and his companion. Their tunics
were splashes of orange, yellow and chartreuse, and
their peaked caps were all bright blue. As Dennis
watched, the man in chartreuse straightened and raised
the trumpet to his lips again.

He wasn't a very skillful trumpeter. It took him three
tries to get the effect he wanted; and that (though clear
and loud) was by no means musical.

A section of solid wall near Dennis drew back to
either side in accordian pleats. The movement was
noiseless, but a medley of human sounds came from the
opening in advance of more people appearing.

"Do not tie yourself to a fiend, though he be powerful," Chester quoted morosely.

"I don't understand," Dennis said, glancing from the
gateway to his companion—and back to the gate, as his
sword shifted across his body.

"You will understand, Dennis," Chester said. The robot composed his limbs at precise intervals around his body, as if they were no more mobile than table legs.

Half a dozen children scampered out the gate, carrying banners on short poles. They made an effort to look serious, but one's peaked cap was sideways over her curls. When she tried to straighten it surreptitiously, her banner dipped across the back of the boy next to her—who jabbed with his elbow in response.

Before a general melee could break out, a middle-aged woman with a flute paced out in time with the stately music she played. Unlike the trumpeter, she was expert indeed. Her flushed face suggested that she as well as the children had rushed to get into position to greet the newcomers.

Behind the flautist came—"marched" would imply too much organization—six men wearing swords, breastplates, and neck-flared helmets. The sheathed swords looked sturdy enough to be real weapons, though their hilts were gorgeously ornamented. None of the swords had the length or heft of Dennis' star-metal blade.

The armor was too light to be intended for more than decoration. The tallest of the six, a man of at least half again Dennis' age, strode forward from his companions. His trousers and tunic were black, and his armor was plated with black chrome. The sunlight danced on its smooth curves as it had over the surface of the Cariad's pond.

The flautist paused.

"In the name of King Conall and the people of Rakastava," boomed the man in black, "I welcome you, stranger, to our community. I am Gannon, the King's Champion."

"I, ah," Dennis said.

He drew himself up straight—he was a little taller than Gannon, he noted—and said, "I am Dennis, Prince

of Emath. My companion and I are adventuring through
the jungle."

His words sounded impressive—and they were true,
though the greatest adventure he'd had outside of dreams
was to run from a fish-girl. . . . But he was barefoot and
his clothing hung in tatters. The splendidly-attired folk
of Rakastava must think him a fool and a braggart to
speak that way!

Gannon's eyes moved from the great sword to something beyond Dennis. His face paled, and there was no
mockery in it.

Dennis glanced behind him to see what it was that
affected the King's Champion. Had Chester done something, or had they been followed by a monster? But the
robot was motionless, and there was nothing else—

Except the wall of the jungle itself.

He'd become used to it in the weeks since he'd left
Emath. It was neither friend nor foe, just fringing undergrowth and the majesty of the vine-draped mon-
archs toward whose peaks Dennis stared while he lay
resting on his back.

The jungle might have denizens more fearful than
the birds and lizards which had brightened its vegetation and his life as Dennis journeyed among them,
but—

The Founder's Sword quivered as Dennis' grip tightened on it. The terrors of the jungle might find a terror
of their own to face if they met him now.

The folk of Rakastava felt the same way about the
newcomer. It was on the faces of all of them, children
and woman and armed men, as they gazed at Dennis in
his rags.

"Prince Dennis," said Gannon in a voice that lost its
tremulousness after the first syllable. "Please come with
me to our king, who even now prepares to receive
you."

Gannon gestured. The children moved in a flutter of
banners and loose clothing. They glanced back over

their shoulders in quick nervousness toward the new-comers—then squealed and scattered forward when they saw that Chester moved also. The flautist took up her measured cadence and followed them.

Dennis waited for further direction. The King's Champion gestured again, this time with a touch of irritation in his eyes.

Dennis sheathed his sword. It rustled against the scabbard sides, then chimed as it shot home to the cross-guards.

"As you will," he said, striding on after the woman with the flute while Gannon and his fellows arranged themselves behind.

"Pride and arrogance are the ruin of their owner," Chester murmured.

Dennis, with the look of the King's Champion fresh in his memory, had no doubt at all for whom the robot meant *that* bit of wisdom.

CHAPTER 26

Dennis expected a cave. Instead, the interior of Rakastava was brighter than Emath Palace at midday. The air, while somehow lifeless, was fresh and moved in gentle currents even after the gate closed behind them.

The walls glowed. Light couldn't come through them, the way it did in Emath Palace, so it must be generated by the material itself. Maybe the air did the same. . . .

The corridor down which the children led Dennis was high-ceilinged and lined with people. More spectators appeared at every moment from side halls or doorways that vanished again when they closed, just as the gate had done.

The citizens blinked at Dennis and gaped at the robot beside him, but their whispered excitement stilled when the newcomers passed close to them. Gannon was the only inhabitant of Rakastava who'd actually spoken to Dennis.

The youth matched his pace to that of the flautist. He'd have preferred to let his legs take the full stride

141

he'd found so natural on the road through the jungle. For a while he tried to meet the eyes of the people looking at him, but they ducked away. That made him uncomfortable—he wasn't a freak, for goodness' sake! —and he let his sight rove along the walls instead.

The corridor's lines were softened by bands of color, primaries as well as pastels; but there was no visual art to give the passageway a human touch.

Nothing in Rakastava was human except the inhabitants.

The corridor opened into a chamber incomparably greater than anything Dennis had expected to find within a building. Even the mountainous bulk of Rakastava as he had first seen it, a slick, brown mass rising sheer from the jungle, seemed inadequate to hold this— audience chamber, he supposed, because there were thrones and a carpeted path to them across the expanse of stony floor.

Trumpets sang, high and clear and echoing. Their well-blown notes sounded thin in the huge room.

Gannon strode past Dennis and Chester, marching toward the thrones with his head back and his armored chest thrust out. The woman with the flute had stepped to the side and vanished among the spectators.

There weren't as many people as Dennis had at first assumed. There were at least a score of corridors like the one he and Chester had followed, and all of them were spilling gaily-dressed people into the audience chamber now. But the room could hold twenty Emath Villages; and the crowd now assembling totaled less than Dennis had seen at the Founder's Day parades on any of the past five years.

In Emath, the crowds were alive—coarse, pushy; smelling of fish and spices and the sea—but alive and sure of their growing success. These folk of Rakastava were good-looking, almost without exception. They were dressed in clothes of a quality that in Emath only Hale and his family could afford—and they wore their garments with a stylishness that Dennis hadn't imagined existed before he saw it here.

But the flies glittering in circles about a corpse were brilliant to watch also; and if there was liveliness in the eyes of the folk Dennis saw around him, it was only that. Rakastava was great, but it was dead; and the people who inhabited the city spun in their courses over carrion.

The King's Champion quick-stepped toward the thrones. Dennis followed, lengthening his own stride instead of trying to match Gannon step for step. They reached the end of the carpet. Spectators were drifting along beside the newcomers, watching them avidly. There didn't seem to be much formality in the arrangements, despite the way the newcomers had been greeted.

Buzzing flies, Dennis thought again. Aloud though in a low voice he said to Chester, "I don't like this place at all. What's wrong with them?"

"Do not be in haste to quarrel with a powerful ruler," the robot quoted sharply. But a tentacle reached behind the youth and curled affectionately in his palm— his left palm, the hand he wouldn't need if he had to draw the sword abruptly.

The red carpet was thick enough to feel comfortable under Dennis' bare feet.

The pair of thrones provided Dennis with something other than vastness on which to focus. As he approached them, the visual scale of the room reduced to human norms. The face of the man seated to the right had wrinkles only about the eyes, but he was at least as old as Dennis' own father.

Certainly he was older than the woman to his left. She was the most beautiful girl Dennis had ever seen.

"Most noble King Conall," Gannon shouted, twenty feet from the thrones but still unable to sound impressive in a room so large. "Most gracious Princess Aria—"

There were ten or so additional men in decorative armor to either side of the thrones. An honor guard, Dennis supposed, like the one Ramos commanded at Emath.

And equally needless, it seemed. The men beside the thrones were older and paunchier than the ones who accompanied Gannon. Dennis suspected that the six who'd greeted him outside the gate were those who could throw on their accoutrements and race down the corridor in time to do so.

"I bring you Dennis of Emath," Gannon was continuing. "A wayfarer who begs your hospitality."

Dennis squeezed Chester's limb and stepped past Gannon. His body had gone cold when he realized what he was about to do, but it wasn't fear like that with which the dream wizard had struck him.

This was Dennis' choice; his decision not to be belittled before strangers . . . one of whom was named Aria, and whose blond hair spilled from golden combs to the middle of her back.

"Sir," he said, wondering if his own voice seemed as thin as that of Conall's champion, "I'm indeed Dennis, and I've come from Emath where my father is king. But while I wish your friendship, I need beg from no man. The jungle fed and kept me on the way here. It'll keep me again before I'll become a burden anywhere I'm unwanted."

Conall laughed and stood up.

"Pardon our insensitivity," he said as he stepped forward, extending his hands toward Dennis. "Visitors are a rare pleasure to those of us who live in Rakastava. And as for a burden—"

He gestured with one hand while the other clasped Dennis' in friendship. "There *are* no burdens here," he said forcefully. "Rakastava is Paradise on Earth."

Aria had stepped down beside her father. Her smile had as much of amusement as greeting in it. "At the very least, Prince Dennis," she said in a clear voice pitched like a viola, "won't you allow us to provide you with clothing? If only until you return to the jungle to have it provide for your needs."

Dennis glanced down and blushed. He'd forgotten

how ragged he looked. "Look," he said, grimacing. "We're traders in Emath. Traders and fishermen. Just Dennis is fine, please."

Aria herself wore a dress of gauzy blue pastel, cinched with a waistbelt. The belt's gold matched her combs and sandals, while her ring and earrings were clear, faceted jewels.

Around Aria's neck was a silver chain. Three carven crystal balls, nested one inside the other and the largest no bigger than a walnut, hung between her breasts. The pendant moved when the girl did, but Dennis realized with a shock that there was no physical connection between the chain and the crystal.

As for his clothing . . .

"Ah, I'd very much appreciate—something to replace these," Dennis said. "I—the thorns, you know."

"Clothing of course," said Conall heartily. "And a meal, at least. You surely won't deprive us of a chance to talk with you during a banquet, will you?"

"Well, I . . ." Dennis said, losing his train of thought as he stared at Aria's crystal pendant. The three balls were rotating within one another, each on a separate axis. Their carved surfaces made patterns which changed the way the shadow pictures moved when a breeze stirred the leaves of Dennis' dream.

"And maybe Prince Dennis wouldn't mind taking a bath," Gannon said harshly from beside Aria where he now stood.

"I'll take him to a room where he can change, father," Aria said coolly, turning her head as if the King's Champion hadn't spoken.

"Certainly, daughter," Conall agreed, but his eyes were on Chester. "Ah, Dennis?" the king went on. "That is a —an artifact from the Age of Settlement, is it not?"

"Yes, Chester," Dennis agreed, reaching back and feeling his palm warmed by the tentacle it had snatched itself away from a few moments before. "We came from Emath together. We're friends."

Gannon smiled.

Flushing again, Dennis said, "This may interest you, Champion."

He slid the Founder's Sword a hand's breadth from its scabbard; not quite a threat but enough to show the blade's rugged lines. "It's from the Age of Settlement too. It's made of star metal."

Conall smiled also. "How interesting," he said, bending forward to peer more closely. "May I?"

Dennis thought the king was going to take the sword. Instead, Conall flicked his hand so that the nail of his index finger rang against the flat of the blade.

He straightened. "How interesting," he repeated without emotion. "We have many artifacts of the Settlement here as well. I see you noticed my daughter's pendant."

"Is that what he was staring at?" Aria said with a twinkle of amusement.

Dennis flushed. Conall blinked. Gannon looked as though he'd been slapped.

"Yes, well," said the king. "Do please take our guest to a room. The banquet will begin as soon as he's refreshed himself."

"In our apartment, I think," said Aria.

Dennis watched the by-play between the princess and her father, but none of it made sense to him.

"I don't think—" Conall began doubtfully.

"It's closer," Aria said. "And it needn't be for long."

Gannon gave a snort.

"Yes, well, of course," Conall said at last. "Whatever you think best, child."

Aria gestured Dennis to come with her. The wall opened into a doorway just as Dennis was sure that she was about to walk into something solid.

But as he followed, watching the dress sway against her softly-curved body, he was sure of one thing: Aria wasn't a child.

CHAPTER 27

They were striding down a hallway, narrower and not as high as the corridor through which Dennis had been led to the assembly chamber. It was bland—but bright and cheerful, filled with the same diffused light as the larger volumes.

"Here, this will do," Aria said. Another door opened—would they do that for him? "Just ask for what you need, bath, clothing—whatever. Everyone's waiting in the assembly hall, but you needn't rush."

Her face lost its look of superiority though not the bitter humor that had always underlain it. "We have plenty of time here in Rakastava."

"Ah . . ." Dennis said. Chester could help him figure things out. Aria certainly wasn't coming into the room with him. He'd never thought that she would, never. . . . "Thank you."

He stepped into the room. Its walls were sand-colored, the hue of the shaded side of dunes in late afternoon.

"You aren't like most of the wanderers we see here," Aria said. "Vagabonds, really."

"Pardon?"

She turned away. Her skirt flowed silently as she swept back up the hallway. "It doesn't matter," she tossed over her shoulder.

"How do I close the door, Chester?" Dennis whispered to his companion.

"Tell the door to close, Dennis," the robot replied.

"Ah, close, door."

"If you meet a beautiful woman," Chester went on as the wall spread itself back over the door opening, "prove that your control over your body is greater than hers."

"Hush, Chester."

The room had a bed of modest size and what seemed to be an empty sideboard. There was no bath.

"Ah, bath, pour yourself," Dennis ordered. One of the beige walls quivered. Water gurgled beyond it.

Dennis whisked aside what turned out to be drapery rather than a solid surface like the other three sides. A tub shaped in the gentle curves of a half clamshell was filling, apparently by osmosis through its glistening body.

The tub was full by the time the youth had stripped off his clothes to get in. Not much in the way of clothing had survived the weeks since he left home, he admitted ruefully. He supposed he could wear leaves or bark . . . something, at any rate . . . if he were to spend the rest of his life in the jungle.

The water was hot but not quite uncomfortable. It had a slight scent and astringence which suggested that it already contained some sort of cleansing agent. He wished he had a proper bath sponge, but the multiple scabs and scrapes he could reach with his bare hands softened pleasantly as he rubbed them.

"Chester," he said. "Should I stay here? Or should I go back to Emath now?"

"The one who asks foolish questions wearies those around him," said the robot, his outline blurred by the steam rising from Dennis' bath. "Who but yourself knows where your heart is?"

"I can't see—spending all my life in the jungle," the youth went on. "This place is—very wonderful, in some ways. . . . But there's something about it I don't like. And back home, well, I was right to leave and I don't think I want to go back just yet.

"I think—" Dennis closed his eyes and rested his head and arms on the edge of the tub for a moment, luxuriating in the warm cleanliness, "—that we'll stay in Rakastava for a while and learn a little more about it. And then we can go on if we want to."

"If you ask for clothing, it will appear in the cabinet, Dennis," Chester said.

Dennis rose in the tub and stepped out. The level of the water began to drop immediately. "Clothes, appear," he said tentatively.

A set of bright yellow garments rose from—through—the bottom of what he had thought was an empty sideboard.

"Wow!" he breathed aloud. "Ah, and a towel?"

When the towel—dark beige like the room's walls—appeared, he realized that he should have asked for a sponge before he got into the bath.

The garments were slippers, a tunic and loose trousers—all of a soft, slick fabric that was similar to silk; but not silk, and not any textile with which Dennis was familiar.

"Do you suppose all the rooms in Rakastava are like this, Chester?" he asked as he slid the tunic over his head.

"All the rooms are like this, Dennis," the robot replied. "Except that they may be finer."

The slippers fit perfectly. "That's *amazing*," Dennis said. "And none of it costs anything."

He looked at the blank wall and said, "Door, open!"

Behind Dennis as they strolled toward the assembly hall, Chester said quietly, "It would indeed be amazing if there were no costs, Dennis."

CHAPTER 28

Dennis hadn't known what to expect in the assembly hall. When the hall door opened for him, he found that tables were arranged in a circle large enough to seat the entire population of the community—well over a thousand faces staring at the newcomers.

The table closest to the door was bright with the polished metalwork of Conall's honor guard. Between the king himself and his daughter, both of them turning to greet Dennis, was an empty chair.

So far as Dennis could see, it was the only vacant seat in the assembly. The thrones and carpet had disappeared. It made him somewhat uneasy to realize that the tables had probably risen from—and the thrones had vanished into—the floor, much as the clothes he wore had coalesced through a solid surface.

"Well, come sit down, silly," Aria directed with a wave of her hand toward the empty chair.

Gannon glared at Dennis from the other side of the king. That was a human sort of dislike and therefore less disconcerting than many other things about Rakastava.

He sat down and felt Chester creep past to lie curled and comforting at his feet.

There were no—human—servants in Rakastava. King Conall himself raised the lid of a serving dish and offered Dennis a slice of savory meatloaf. It was the first meat Dennis had eaten since leaving home. It smelled delicious, and the taste was wonderful and intriguing—

But he wasn't quite sure that it was meat after all.

No matter. It was good, and so were the vegetables on the platter beside it. . . . Though these vegetables weren't anything he'd eaten before, either, and they had a curious uniformity instead of the layering of garden truck Dennis had eaten at home.

"I wonder, Prince Dennis," said Conall with a casualness that could only be deliberate. "There's no question of you being a burden on us here, of course. But if it would make you more comfortable during your stay at Rakastava—"

Aria made a muffled sound and looked down at her plate, though she didn't lift the forkful of loaf to her lips.

"Yes, go ahead," Dennis asked, feeling his body tense.

He'd belted the sword on over his fine new clothing, less because of expected need than because he was afraid it might vanish into the floor the way his tattered garments had if he left it. Now he was glad of its awkward weight.

"I was thinking," Conall continued. "A bold lad like you with a fine sword, well—"

Gannon was chuckling behind the king's leonine head.

"You see, we keep a herd of cows here in Rakastava. Not for our own use, but for trade with the, ah, local people."

"The lizardmen?" asked Dennis. "I hadn't expected that. There aren't any trails leading to Rakastava—quite unusual, you know."

He grimaced internally, knowing that he was emphasizing his status as the only expert on the jungle in the room—in order to keep from open embarrassment at his lack of sophistication in the ways of this wonderful place.

"That is," he amended for his conscience' sake, "no trails by the way I came."

"Well, we do some trading," Conall continued, looking more worried than Dennis' mild comment seemed to call for. "Well. In any case, we have a herd that we like to pasture outside the walls. But, ah, none of us here are really comfortable in the—"

Conall's face grew pale as he remembered something beyond what was before him in the room. "None of us feel comfortable outside Rakastava, that is. If you think you'd be able to do this, Prince Dennis, lead the herd to its pastures. . . ?"

"Of course," the youth said. "For that matter, I can milk them, if you'd like me to. We had some goats in Emath, though cows only rarely for the problem of fodder."

There was a catch, but no one in Rakastava was going to tell him what it was. He'd learn for himself.

Between Aria's warmth close to his right elbow, and Gannon smirking from beyond the king, there was no way Dennis was going to permit himself to sound frightened.

"Fine, then, that's settled," said Conall. The older man seemed relaxed for the first time since Dennis had seen him. "First thing in the morning, then. Perhaps my daughter will point you on the way?" He leaned forward to look at Aria.

"I will not," said the princess toward her plate of food.

"I'll be the boy's guide, then," said Gannon. "First thing in the morning, princeling."

"I'll be ready," said Dennis.

For anything, his mind added and his eyes promised.

CHAPTER 29

The wall opened into a door. Dawnlight beyond looked like a curtain in contrast to the pure radiance from the walls of the cow byre. The cows began to lurch forward in the one-at-a time, dominoes-falling, manner of their kind.

"Well, there's your trail," Gannon said. His voice sounded thick, because he was holding a handkerchief over his nose and mouth. "Just follow it. I'm getting out of this stinking place."

The large, low room in which the cows were stabled was as clean as every other part of Rakastava, though the odor of the animals permeated the air. Dennis blinked at the King's Champion, trying to decide whether the man was serious or just flaunting his "greater culture."

Gannon certainly didn't look well; but the dinner of the night before was turning into a morose drinking party when Dennis left it to sleep away the weariness of the jungle. Perhaps the smell of living things turned Gannon's stomach, but the cloyingly sweet wine the champion slurped down might have more bearing on the way he felt now.

"Drink brings all manner of illness to the body," Chester said primly.

Gannon snatched the kerchief away from his lips. "What did you say?" he blazed at Dennis.

"Is there good water to drink out there?" the youth said calmly as the cows shouldered their way by the men. There didn't seem to be any point in explaining that Chester was more than a mobile decoration; and anyway, the knowledge wouldn't make Gannon less angry about the comment.

"How would I know?" Gannon muttered, slightly mollified. "The cows eat and drink, I suppose."

He looked again at Dennis, realizing suddenly that the youth carried only his sword. "That is . . ." Gannon said. "That is—someone will bring your lunch out to you. Yes."

Dennis was cold with the certainty that something was wrong. His elbows pressed his new garment tightly to his ribs. "That won't be necessary," he said. "I'm used to the jungle, you know."

His eyesight blurred despite the clarity of the artificial light. It would feel good to be out in the fresh air and daylight.

"None of you really do anything, do you?" Dennis said, voicing the insight that had suddenly surprised him.

"Don't be a fool, boy!" Gannon snapped. "We all have our duties. I'm here with you, aren't I?"

"Yes," the youth said. "But you're courtiers—not traders or fishermen or anything. And it's not even for a real king, for Conall. You're courtiers for Rakastava itself."

Gannon's face grew still. His right hand dropped to his swordhilt and lifted the weapon enough that polished steel glinted above the lip of the scabbard. The

handkerchief, caught between hand and pommel, fluttered absurdly.

Dennis balanced himself on the balls of his feet. His
hand didn't move to his own great sword, but he could
dive away to the right if Gannon attacked and then—

Gannon shot his weapon back home in its sheath. He
lifted his hand, noticed the kerchief—and flung it aside
in displaced fury. "Don't talk about what's not your
business, boy!" he said. "I *warn* you."

"Fine," Dennis said, turning and putting his hand on
the warm, shaggy flank of the last of the herd. It bleated
in bovine surprise, but there was nowhere to go except
forward at the speed of the animal ahead. "I'll be back
at nightfall, then."

Chester followed Dennis. If the King's Champion
tried to say anything further, his words were lost as the
door flowed shut behind them.

Dennis *did* feel better outside. It was as though the
huge mass of Rakastava had been pressing on his chest
all the time he was in the city. Beneath all the magic
and luxury lay a tension that was concealed until he got
beyond the range of its power.

But the folk of Rakastava never stepped more than a
few yards from their palace-city.

"If you trust your enemy," Chester said, "you will
curse the result in the end."

"I *don't* trust him," Dennis said. He shivered in the
warm air. "Chester, I don't trust any of them. Except
maybe . . . The girl seems to be different. Nicer, in a
way. . . ?"

Chester said nothing.

"Don't you think?" Dennis insisted.

"It is through woman that both good and evil came to
mankind," the robot quoted.

"All right, all right," Dennis said. "It's not something
that you can do for me."

He rubbed Chester's carapace with his knuckles; the
curve of a tentacle caressed the back of his hand.

There were forty cows and a dozen calves in the herd, all of them short-horned and white with black markings. The way to the pasture was unmistakeable: the beasts had trampled a path through the jungle.

The trail was muddy, green with droppings, and only a foot wide on the ground. Higher up, the cows' wide hips and rib cages had worn the vegetation away to a comfortable distance.

Among the familiar plants was a vine that Dennis didn't remember having seen before. It had a thin, purplish stem; small leaves; and broad, black-pointed thorns. He kept a careful eye out for strands that had crept near enough to snag him—but though the vine was common just off the trail, it didn't come threateningly close.

Dennis laughed. "I suppose if I tear up these clothes, the cabinet will give me another set," he said.

"It is not for your clothes you should be cautious, Dennis," Chester said, "but rather for yourself."

"Oh, I'll heal too," the youth remarked gaily. It felt *good* to be out of—out of sight of, even—the brown pile of Rakastava.

Dennis began to whistle a tune, the tune the tavern girl had been singing when he passed on the way to get the Founder's Sword.

The pasture, a broad stretch of sunlit grassland, was as obvious as the path leading to it.

Dennis had never seen anything like it. There were grassed plots in Emath Village, jealously guarded by their owners—and generally of approximately the same dimensions as a doorway. Beyond those small holdings, greenery meant the jungle rather than grass.

Here was grass on the scale of the jungle: a strip a quarter-mile wide that undulated on out of sight between walls of trees and clogging brambles. The cows had already cropped away a broad swath close to the trail from Rakastava, but the portion a few hundred yards beyond was knee-high and a lush green that looked delicious even to Dennis.

Scattering now, the herd ambled to its food—each cow choosing the tuft that its great brown eyes thought most tasty. They let Dennis and Chester come within a few feet of them—if the companions walked slowly. A closer approach sent the cows bolting some yards further, to stare back doubtfully at the unfamiliar figures.

Dennis paused, breathing fresh air and feeling the direct sun. It was going to be scorching here at midday, when the dew burned off and the light plunged straight down with no shadows.

He frowned at the black and white backs straggling away from him and each other.

"Chester?" he asked. "How are we going to get them back to the stables in the evening? They won't let us get close to them."

"They will return of themselves, Dennis," the robot said quietly, "to be milked by the machines of Rakastava so that the weight of their udders will not pain them."

Dennis looked at his companion in puzzlement. "But they didn't need me to drive them here, either," he said. "They knew the way. . . ."

He shrugged. "Well, maybe they just wanted somebody here to guard the cows. They're afraid of the jungle, after all."

"They are afraid of many things, Dennis," Chester said. "And who is to say they are wrong?"

"Let's go get ourselves some breakfast," the youth said. He sauntered on a slanting course toward the jungle—rather than try to follow the forebodings that Chester seemed determined to rouse.

"Crocodiles eat their portion of the fools who roam, Dennis," the robot said.

"What's a crocodile, Chester?" Dennis asked with a little more interest than he had intended to display.

"There are no crocodiles on this Earth, Dennis,"
Chester replied.

The youth grimaced.

He wondered idly how the pasture was kept in grass.
Grass survived hard use better than broader-leafed greenery, so heavy cropping by animals would keep the
jungle from reclaiming the open area . . . but a few
score cows weren't by themselves enough to achieve
that here. Perhaps the folk of Rakastava mowed it
occasionally.

Perhaps Rakastava itself extended a brown, slick-
textured pseudopod that sheared away the vegetation.

"Fah!" Dennis said loudly. "I'm away from the place
for now."

As he got nearer, he saw that the jungle was making
small inroads already. Plants with coarse, colorful leaves
spiked up several yards into the grass—springing from
deep-buried roots. Vines trailed surreptitiously across
the pasture edge, ready to snag Dennis' foot if he
placed it carelessly.

There was a boulder, gray and as big as a house,
lying not far ahead at the jungle margin. The grass in
front of it had been trampled down.

Dennis glanced over his shoulder. None of the cows
had wandered in this direction. The boulder didn't
seem to be a salt lick or—

He was walking forward and his head was moving,
turning toward the boulder, but the boulder moved
also. Half of its front—it was bigger than he'd thought—
slid aside in a rippling motion.

It was a hut of lichen-gray leaves woven onto a wicker
framework. Something shifted across the opening from
within.

*This has to be a boulder, humped and gray and
rolling out through the doorway toward me. . . .*

The humped thing straightened onto two of its six
legs. Its eyes were faceted red glints. The remainder

of the body was gray and yellowish and fish-belly white.

The creature was alive and half again as tall as Dennis. Its jointed legs had spikes and knife-sharp edges of chitin. They glittered as the creature flexed them with scissoring clicks.

"It's time and past time," the creature said, "that Conall remembered that he owes more than beef to feed Malbawn."

CHAPTER 30

Dennis drew his sword. His whole body was trembling.

Malbawn's voice was deep and breathy; the plates of its beak flexed sideways as it spoke.

"Run, Chester," the youth whispered.

All Dennis could remember was the corpse of the Wizard Serdic lurching toward him as it drew the sharpened pole from its body. Dennis had run then, and he wanted to run now—

But there was no escape from nightmare.

He would face Malbawn with his star-metal sword; face the creature striding through the grass on saw-edged limbs, nine feet tall and armored in chitin. The inexorable certainty of the corpse had taught Dennis never to run from fear.

It was only intellectually that he could grasp the fact that Malbawn would kill him. He *knew* that, but he'd never been killed before and the concept had no emotional reality.

The creature paused when its human quarry didn't flee as expected. Malbawn's head was a flat triangle with the beak on its forward point and the fiery eyes behind to either side. The four raised limbs moved slowly, like the claws of crabs fencing in the water.

They had triple-bladed pincers: a pair of long claws folding in opposition to a single spike.

"My sword's star metal!" Dennis shouted in sudden bravado. He moved the blade slightly in its on-guard position so that the sunlight ran across the well-honed edge. "I'll hack you to bits!"

Malbawn gave a cackling laugh. It dropped its middle pair of legs to the ground and rushed Dennis.

Dennis cut at the creature's head without any attempt at subtlety. A yellow-gray forearm blocked the sword with a ringing crash.

Dennis shifted back. His right palm quivered with the shock of impact. There was a notch in the blade of the Founder's Sword. Malbawn's forearm feinted toward him, uninjured.

Dennis circled slowly, keeping his sword at mid-chest. The creature lifted onto its hind legs, waving the other limbs slowly. They spanned three yards or more from tip to clawed tip. It was like fencing practice for Dennis, but instead of one of his father's retainers he was facing a creature that—

Malbawn dropped into a four-legged charge again.

Icy and prepared, Dennis thrust with the precision of light glancing from the facets of a crystal. He was using his speed and skill instead of just his strength. Despite Malbawn's attempt to parry, the point of the Founder's Sword clanged into the center of the creature's chest.

The steel slid away without marking the chitinous plastron. Malbawn's wide-spread arms closed like the spring-loaded jaws of a trap.

Dennis ducked, but he was off balance and the saw-toothed limbs slammed toward him from either side. One of them raked the back of his head and left shoulder.

An acrid odor hung over Malbawn, making Dennis gag as he grappled with the huge creature. The beak dipped toward him as the two middle legs lifted off the ground. Their pincers flared.

Dennis flung himself backwards, pushing with his left hand against the limb that had struck him. He expected the spiked arm to resist like a tree trunk or a cliffside, too massively powerful to notice Dennis' merely human efforts. But the youth's arm was stronger than that of the monster he fought, for all the other's size and horrid looks. . . .

Malbawn gave a gurgle of frustration. It lurched forward again without first rising onto its hind legs.

Dennis breathed through his open mouth. The left side of his head felt cold as his blood evaporated in the open air. He supposed his ear had been torn off. He couldn't feel it. He couldn't feel anything but cold and the searingly hot air he drew into his lungs.

There was another bright nick in his swordblade where a set of Malbawn's pincers had closed on it.

Malbawn lumbered only a few steps toward Dennis as the youth back-pedaled. The creature didn't seem able to move quickly. It paused and waved its right foreleg. The sharp chitin was streaked with Dennis' blood.

Dennis thrust, handling the Founder's Sword as if it were a fencing foil. His body made a smooth, straight line from his left foot to the point crushing into the joint of Malbawn's bloody foreleg.

Dennis knew the blade had gone home even before the creature screamed. He could feel his metal grate into the soft tissue between plates of armor. Malbawn rushed forward, but its own movement completed the work of destruction. The pincers thrashed convulsively; then the whole forelimb flopped, held to the body only by a scrap of the gristly connective tissue that permitted Malbawn's joints to bend.

Malbawn's remaining foreleg swiped at Dennis. Instead of dodging back as he had done before, the youth ducked and let the muscles of his back absorb the blow as he thrust at the lowest joint—ankle joint—of the creature's right hind leg.

The spiked arm struck Dennis like a falling tree, driving out his breath in a grunt of pain. He'd underestimated how much it would hurt.

The middle legs reached for his torso as the forelimb squeezed him against the yellow-gray plastron. He chopped his sword pommel at the joint of the limb holding him—felt it crunch and felt Malbawn release him as the hind leg his point had severed gave way.

Greenish fluid oozed from Malbawn's damaged joints. The grass was spattered with it; so were Dennis' hands and clothing. The creature staggered onto its three good legs. Its beak opened and closed, but the only sounds it made were clicks and a soft hissing.

"I'll hack you to bits!" Dennis heard himself repeat in a hoarse, horrible voice.

Malbawn tried to sidle away. It lowered its left fore-leg to the ground so that the middle limb on that side could take a step backwards. The damaged joint collapsed under the weight. Dennis moved in, thrusting between the chitinous ridges of the creature's neck and torso.

Malbawn threw all its mass forward, lurching at Dennis like the rolling boulder he had at first thought it. The left forelimb swung at him, its last segment hanging loose like the end of a flail. It struck him across the side of the head, turning his whole universe into heat and bright, roaring pulses. . . .

CHAPTER 31

The blaze of white warmth cooled to sunlight and pain. Dennis had fallen forward, his knees on the ground and his torso sprawled against Malbawn.

One of Malbawn's middle legs was prodding at Dennis with the disconnected sluggishness of a windmill with broken vanes. Sharp nodules on the back of the pincers left a line of bloody welts over the youth's ribs every time they struck him.

Malbawn was dead. Half the length of Dennis' sword had slid through the neck joint and was buried within the creature's body. Green ichor oozed from the beak, and the only light in the faceted eyes was the sun's reflection.

One of Chester's tentacles wrapped the twitching leg and prevented its autonomic motions from injuring Dennis further.

"Is it your wish that I continue to run, master?" the robot asked.

Dennis couldn't remember his metal friend ever coming so close to disobeying an ill-conceived order.

"Thank you," the youth whispered.

The creature's acid stench had left the inside of Dennis' mouth raw. He tried to raise himself, but the movement caused spasms in the muscles of his ribs and lower back. He couldn't even scream.

Three of Chester's tentacles lifted Dennis gently, taking his weight and permitting his muscles to quiver out of their tension.

"Thank you," Dennis repeated. "Thank you . . ."

"He who loves his friends, Dennis, finds his friends around him at a time of need," the robot said. He stepped back, carrying Dennis without apparent difficulty.

Malbawn's limb twitched once when Chester released it, then stiffened into rigidity. Sparkling insects gathered in clusters around the creature's dripping wounds.

Dennis tried again to stand up. He managed it this time with his palm braced on Chester's carapace and one of the robot's tentacles curled about his waist for further support.

"Wait," the youth said in a voice so soft that only Chester could have heard the word.

He tugged at the hilt of the Founder's Sword with his right hand. The deep-thrust blade resisted. Curling the fingers of his left hand around the cross-guard to spread the effort, Dennis leaned back and let the weight of his upper body work for him.

The blade slid free. Slimy fluid made a sucking gurgle as it gushed from Malbawn's beak.

"Is it into the shade that you would like me to help you, Dennis?" the robot prompted.

Dennis took a deep breath. He laid the flat of the blade across the fingers of his left hand, the only way he could carry the heavy sword without letting its point drag on the ground. He knew he wouldn't be able to use the weapon for—he didn't dare think how long. His whole body felt as if it were encased in bands of hot iron like a barrel while the hoops were being shrunk onto it.

"They sent me out to die," Dennis whispered.

"That is so, Dennis," the robot agreed calmly. "But you did not die."

Dennis cautiously lowered his left hand and let his right take all the weight of the Founder's Sword. Light shivered across the metal and the slime that covered half of it, but he could hold it after all.

"There's shade in Malbawn's hut," he said. "Let's see what else is waiting there."

Together, a tentacle curled in Dennis' palm for support and for friendship, the companions strode into the creature's dwelling.

Dennis had expected a cramped dome. Instead, the interior stretched back into the jungle, carried on arched saplings. Light crept through chinks in the leaf-mat covers, but the same openings let in the daily rains. The atmosphere within was dank and thickened by the mold growing on the walls and the dirt floor.

Dennis slipped as something turned beneath his foot. Chester steadied him. He looked down, his pupils dilated in the dim light.

He gagged. If there'd been anything in his stomach, he would have lost it.

"Do not let life be spoiled for you because another has died," Chester quoted.

"I should have expected the bones," Dennis said.

Most of them were cattle bones, broad ribs and femurs massive enough each to carry its share of a half ton of cow.

The human skull that had almost thrown Dennis now quivered on the packed ground before him, smiling for the rest of eternity.

"How many. . .?" Dennis started to ask, but he let his voice trail off because he didn't really know what he meant by the question. How many deaths? How many men?

How many years had this gone on, Rakastava sending visitors out to have their bones sucked clean by Malbawn?

Just inside the door was a pile of weapons, their metal parts rusty and the wood on many rotted away. There were a few swords, but for the most part it was a rustic arsenal: spears, only a few of which had steel points; crude, single-edged knives; flails; and a club inlaid with sharpened flints. . . .

I can see you're a bold lad. You won't mind leading our cattle out in the morning. We keep a herd for trade with the locals.

But not trade with the lizardfolk. For a thing that lived in the jungle and called itself Malbawn. And so long as Rakastava fed Malbawn, Malbawn wouldn't disturb Rakastava.

Dennis' vision blurred with tears of anger and frustration.

The only thing within the hut that wasn't the detritus of a carnivore was the mirror to the left of the doorway. It was a large glass mounted between two piers, as high as Dennis was tall. He stared at the ghost of himself on the surface, vague because of the lighting but not distorted.

"Chester," the youth asked. "What's this doing here?"

"If you wish to see a thing, Dennis, or a place," the robot replied, "you may ask the mirror and it will show you."

"Huh?" Dennis said. He blinked. His reflection blinked back.

The sword was getting heavy. He lowered the point carefully, setting it on a cow's pelvis rather than the slimy floor. He didn't want to sheathe the blade until he'd wiped it clean and smoothed the nicks from its edge with his whetstone. Gray light trembled on the sword and on the glass before it.

"Show me—" and he meant to say "Emath" but his tongue formed instead "—the Princess Aria."

The mirror clouded into dull uniformity, then brightened. It reflected the interior of a room in Rakastava. The walls were mother-of-pearl, sunless but glowing sun-bright with their internal radiance. The bedspread was the color of red coral.

The princess was sprawling on her face across the bed. She wore a shift as gauzy and translucent as the fan of her blond hair.

She was sobbing into her hands, making the bed and the curves of her body on it tremble.

Dennis turned his head. "I don't want to watch this any more," he mumbled; but his eyes glanced sideways for a last look at Aria as the glass blanked and then became only a mirror again.

"The fortunate house is praised because of the character of its mistress," Chester said approvingly.

Dennis felt dizzy. For a moment he wasn't sure he could grip his sword, much less hold it up. Even after the spell passed, he knew he was light-headed with weakness.

"Let's get outside," he said to his companion. "I need to eat and drink something."

He paused. "I need to get outside."

The cattle watched uncaring as Chester helped his master into a bower of broad-leafed fruiting vines at the jungle's edge. Dennis dozed or stared with empty eyes as the robot's tentacles squeezed juice into the corner of his mouth and sponged him with leaves still dew-damp from the shade.

Nearby, the insects buzzed and sparkled in their dance above Malbawn's corpse. Their music eased Dennis into a sleep of pure exhaustion.

CHAPTER 32

"It is time . . ." someone whispered to Dennis as he floated in a lake of fire.

Dennis flailed out with his arms and legs. The healing nightmare broke into white shards, opening the youth's eyes to the reality of the evening-shadowed pasture. The cows, driven only by habit and the weight of their udders, were drifting back along the trail to Rakastava.

"It is time that we return to Rakastava," Chester was saying. "If you wish that we should return to Rakastava."

"All right," Dennis said, pretending that not he but the robot had made the decision. Then he added, "Wait."

Chester had slipped off the remnants of the yellow tunic in order to clean the wounds on the youth's torso. Dennis wadded the tail of the garment, relatively unstained by blood and the foul ooze from Malbawn's wounds. With the cloth he carefully wiped the blade of the Founder's Sword.

The nicks which the chitin edges left in the metal

were too deep to worry about now. With a few strokes, he cleaned away the flashing that would make the sword stick in its scabbard; but it would be the work of hours to smooth the sword-edges back into the smooth lines they had before he fought Malbawn.

"Help me . . ." and Chester's gleaming limbs were lifting the youth to his feet even before his lips formed ". . . up, Chester."

The last half dozen of the cows, chewing their cud in sideways motions as they waited to enter the narrow trail, shied back as the companions approached.

Dennis planted one foot in front of the other, taking full strides and knowing that every time his heel hit the ground, the shock would make the top of his head ring like copper cymbals. No matter how careful he was, he'd have to bear the pain anyway. He strode forward as if he didn't feel it.

After a time, he *didn't* feel the pain. His eyes weren't focusing properly, but there were no longer hammer-blows to his skull. He could walk on, guided by the black-and-white blur of the cow ahead of him and the delicate pressure of Chester's grip in his left palm.

Dennis tripped.

He didn't fall, though for a moment he wasn't sure that he hadn't because everything turned gray and pulsed at the tempo of his heartbeat. Then his vision cleared and he saw the thorny purple vine over which he had stumbled.

Even as he watched, the vine's feather-leafed tip retracted toward the side of the trail on which it was rooted.

There was sluggish motion throughout the under-growth fringing the trail. More of the spoke-armed vines quivered where there was no wind, pulling back to where they wouldn't be trampled by the returning herd.

After Dennis passed in the morning, they'd woven their thorny tendrils across the path in a net that doomed anyone trying to flee Malbawn's lumbering advance.

If Dennis had run—as so many before him had certainly run—he would have been held screaming on the thorns while Malbawn's pincers closed on him from behind.

Dennis drew his sword. The rush of adrenalin cooled his body and made supple again his wound-stiffened muscles.

He slashed at the vegetation. It fluttered and fell before the keen edge of the Founder's Sword.

Dennis stepped into the arc his blade had cleared and brought the sword back in another wide sweep. Vines squirmed like headless snakes. The trunk of a wrist-thick sapling thumped down beside its severed stump, unable to fall sideways because its branches were interwoven with those of the trees nearby.

"Going to trap me, weren't you!" Dennis screamed as he cut a third time at the silent vegetation. "Going to hold me like a goat being slaughtered!"

"Dennis," said the robot behind him in an urgent voice. "You know that the vines had no choice but to obey Malbawn. It is for Conall and his folk that your anger is meant."

The youth was gasping for breath. "Don't tell me what I mean," he said, but he'd already paused. The cows who'd begun to follow down the trail at a safe distance stared at Dennis with brown, nervous eyes.

Chester silently offered Dennis the scrap of tunic which he'd dropped. The youth polished the blade again, cleaning away the sap that gummed and might corrode the metal.

Sheathing the weapon, Dennis and his companion followed the trail marked by the herd's steaming droppings. He lengthened his stride, warned by the gathering darkness.

"Chester," he said as the great pile of Rakastava loomed before them. "I don't think the people here had a choice, any more than the vines did."

Then, as they entered the stable with the last of the herd behind them, Dennis added, "It's hard to be afraid. And they haven't learned that you have to face fear. . . ."

CHAPTER 33

"My, there's no one to greet us," Dennis muttered in renewed bitterness as the stable door closed behind them. The cows were making their own docile way to stalls where mechanical fingers milked away the pain of their udders. "You'd think they didn't expect us to be back."

"Indeed, they did not expect us to be back, Dennis," the robot said. "Is it to your room that you wish to go?"

"They'll be at dinner now, won't they?" Dennis said.

"It may be that they will," Chester said in qualified agreement. Then he added in a different tone, "A fool who forgets balance is not far from trouble."

"I've seen trouble, Chester," the youth said quietly. "And now I will see Conall and his people."

"We will go to the hall, then, Dennis," the robot agreed. "And if they are not there, we will find where they are."

The corridors had a bright sameness of illumination.

It wasn't harsh, but it grated on Dennis' eyes because it didn't vary the way light did in a natural setting. He was beginning to get dizzy again; or perhaps that was just the hormonal surge of fury wearing off.

He was very tired.

"This is the door to the assembly hall, Dennis," the robot said.

Dennis came to full alertness. His skin flashed hot and crawled as though there were tiny bugs crawling *under* its surface.

He looked at the blank wall and said, "Door, open."

He strode forward even as the fabric of the wall stretched itself aside.

The effect of his entrance spread throughout the big room like a drop of oil on a pond's surface. A face turned toward him; then the faces nearest; and then, in expanding circles, all the population of Rakastava—staring, rising to their feet, climbing onto the tables to gape and murmur.

The first eyes to look at Dennis were those of the Princess Aria. They were clear and blue and fearless.

Dennis walked toward the king's table. There was no place set for him between Conall and Aria this night. Gannon was sitting to the princess' other side, his arm raised to not-quite-touch her shoulder in a proprietary gesture. When he looked at the returning youth, the arm dropped and his staring face went white.

"Here, here," Conall babbled, sliding sideways on his bench. The armored courtier beside him got up hastily to make room and scuttled off, staring over his shoulder.

Dennis smiled at Gannon and drew the Founder's Sword. He flicked a finger at the King's Champion.

No one breathed for a moment; then Gannon realized that Dennis was demanding his space, not his life. He crawled over the bench also and backed away.

Dennis put his foot on the seat and stood the sword point-down beside it. He looked over Aria's blond head at her father. Steadying the pommel with his left hand, he began to stroke his whetstone across the nicks in the metal.

"I watched your cows," he said, "just as you told me to do. And they're all safe, King Conall. Every one of them. And I am safe as well."

Sring! went the stone against the swordblade. *Sring*! *Sring*!

"Sit," Conall murmured, patting the bench beside him as he raised his fine, noble face to the youth with the naked sword. "Please sit, P-prince Dennis, and we'll . . ."

The king met Dennis' eyes instead of fluttering his gaze across the younger man's bruised forehead; the bloody gouges streaking down from his hair and across the bunched muscles of his shoulders; the scabs and purple swellings on his ribs where Malbawn's corpse had continued to strike Dennis' unconscious body. . . .

"We didn't mean—" Conall said in a firm voice; but he broke off the sentence because he couldn't speak the lie after he thought about it.

Aria slipped from the bench and stood before Dennis. The fall of her hair blocked his view of the seated king. She reached out, touching Dennis on the forearm. Her cool fingers traced along his biceps, just beneath a scabbed gouge left by Malbawn's first blow.

"Come," she said softly. "These must be bathed."

She nodded solemnly to Chester, an equal to an equal, and began to lead Dennis back to the door by her touch on his arm.

"*What*?" Gannon blurted.

"Aria!" Conall cried.

She looked at the men: coldly at the champion; a softer but still inflexible glance toward her father. "Come," she repeated to Dennis.

A great babble of sound broke out behind them as the doorway closed. Dennis started to glance back, but Aria strode on—and he followed, down the hall and into the room that had been assigned to him.

"Fill, bath," she directed with the same assurance with which she had led the youth. "And I'll have unguents—as well as some food for later."

Dennis looked at Chester for support. The robot stood to the side, as still and silent as a piece of furniture.

"Well, get into the tub," the princess said. She was wearing a dress of the same bright chicory-flower blue as her eyes. It had long puffed sleeves which she was rolling up while the nested crystal spheres spun in her cleavage.

The door opened.

Gannon stood in the frame of the doorway. He stood with his thumbs tucked into his sword-belt, arms akimbo, with a hectoring expression on his face and his mouth open to speak.

Dennis' face went blank. Light trembled on the blade of the weapon he still carried bare in his hand.

Aria turned and pointed her index finger at Gannon. "*Go*," she said in a tone like that of the sword crunching into Malbawn's throat.

Gannon backed as though steel and not a delicate hand were thrust toward his face. "Princess," he blurted, "you—"

The wall closed with a rushing certainty that cut off any words he meant to add.

Aria turned to Dennis, too controlled to be calm. "Get your trousers off," she ordered. "No one can open the door again until I say so."

"I—" Dennis said.

The steam rolling from the warm water was scented. He was feeling dizzy again and very tired. Without arguing further, he sheathed his great sword; unbelted the scabbard; and slipped out of his torn and stained trousers.

The water in the shell-shaped tub was a caress that melted the agony from his strained muscles even as it dissolved the scabbed blood on his skin.

"Oh . . ." Dennis breathed, slipping down so that his scalp and whole body were under the surface. His eyes were closed and he was on the quivering edge of un-consciousness. "Oh . . ."

A lemon-pungency of ointment filled the air. He felt Aria's fingers reaching through the water to work un-guent into the scrapes and tears and punctures that he had accumulated during his weeks of travel and a battle for his life. Her touch was cool despite the tub and the healing sharpness of the ointment.

"Turn now," her voice whispered through the fog of exhaustion and steaming water. "Turn . . ."

There were flaps of loose skin on his shoulders where he had deliberately accepted punishment from the crea-ture's armored limbs. Aria kneaded the ointment into the wounds, then forced the skin back over Dennis' bare flesh while he rested his chin on the sloped rim of the tub. The sudden pain made him suck in his breath . . . but after the first rush, he could feel the injured surfaces starting to knit together.

"I'm beginning to think I survived after all," Dennis whispered. He wasn't sure whether he was speaking aloud or only in a pink-misted, lemony dream.

"I am glad that you survived, Prince Dennis," mur-mured the woman's voice from the mist. "Now it is time for you to get out of the water and to sleep."

The tub was draining into itself. Hands and tentacles as gentle as hands were helping Dennis, drying his body with towels and clothing it again in loose, light garments before lifting him to the bed.

Dennis could see the crystal spheres spinning, so close that if he blinked his eyelashes might brush them.

"I am glad that you survived," the voice said. "And I am very glad that you have returned as well. Now, sleep. . . ."

His mind obeyed that instruction, as Dennis had obeyed every instruction Princess Aria had given him this night.

CHAPTER 34

Dennis saw faces in the nightmare world of the following hours. Aria came to him—and Conall; Selda sponged his forehead while King Hale talked earnestly about kingship and necessity . . .

Serdic's fungoid sneer gibbered behind them.

Then the fever broke and Dennis awakened to reality. Chester was half supporting his torso so that another tentacle could hold a cup of soup to Dennis' mouth.

"Oh!" the youth said. His eyes were prepared for the brightness, but his conscious brain had been existing in a dim netherworld for . . .

He swallowed soup, then asked, "How long have I slept? Is it morning?"

"It is morning, Dennis," the robot said. "And it is two nights and a day that you have slept."

"Oh!" Dennis repeated.

"The wise and goodly man may come close to death and yet survive," Chester quoted, "because of his goodness."

"I can't claim that," the youth muttered. He rotated his legs over the edge of the bed and stood up. The fever which purged his body had left deep aches in all his muscles.

He balanced for a moment, weak and light-headed from the pain. But it was an overpowering thrill to be able to move after hours that were lifetimes in his dreams. . . .

In dreams he had no control, neither over himself nor over the other inhabitants of nightmare. Reality had real pain, but he could move; and—

The Founder's Sword leaned against the wall beside the bed.

Dennis slipped it out of its sheath. The weight and balance of the weapon brought memories of Malbawn. The stress, instead of doubling Dennis over with cramped muscles, returned him to strength and suppleness as the hormones of battle leaked back into his system.

In the waking world, Dennis could affect those around him—no matter how terrifying their form.

He was wearing a nightgown of slick fabric, but there were other clothes ready in the cabinet. He'd finished dressing—slacks and a tunic of blue, slashed diagonally with orange—and the sword belted around his waist, when the wall opened into a door.

"Oh!" said King Conall. "You're, ah, recovered."

His daughter stood behind him, looking cool in a dress of the same yellow-white as her hair. There was no emotion in her eyes as they looked at Dennis.

He'd been delirious with fever. The fever had brought fanciful imaginings. . . .

"I am recovered enough to go out with your cattle, your highness," Dennis croaked. His vocal cords were as stiff as all his other muscles.

Conall blinked. Aria looked as though Dennis had slapped her.

"Ah, that isn't really necessary. . . ." the king muttered.

"But it is necessary to *me*, King Conall," Dennis said

in a tone that even to him seemed to be rising toward madness. "For I undertook as my duty that I should be your cattle-guard and on my *honor*, King Conall, I will do that thing. You would have none in Rakastava but honorable men, surely?"

"Yes, yes, of course," Conall muttered, turning his face down and away. "Well, in that case—"

"Since you are recovered and able to make your own decisions, Prince Dennis," said Aria sharply, "then you are welcome to the hospitality of Rakastava—and we are pleased to have your company."

Dennis bowed stiffly.

"There is no further agreement between us, Prince Dennis," the princess continued. She was on the verge of tears. The hard set of her face was the crust above a pool of flaming lava. "None! If you choose to go to the forest, then only your own will sends you there!"

Dennis bowed again. "If your highness—" he said to Conall, who was gaping at his daughter, "—and you, milady, will forgive me, I'm already behind the herd by some hours. Come along, Chester."

"The fool who is in the right, Dennis," Chester murmured as he followed his master, "is more annoying than the one who has wronged him."

CHAPTER 35

The hot, humid air of the jungle's margin drew away Dennis' strength and left him sleepy again. The cows had watched him approach with greater aplomb than they had shown the day before.

Two days before. He'd lost a day.

Insects still buzzed around the corpse of Malbawn. Two of the creature's limbs rose at twisted angles. The breeze whistled across their hollow interiors.

Dennis flexed his aching muscles. More had been at risk than a day of fever dreams.

He looked at the cows, nestled for the most part into bowers their bodies had flattened out of the jungle's edge. Their jaws moved in quiet contentment, chewing cuds of the grass they'd cropped in the cooler hours of morning.

"You know, Chester. . . ?" the youth said. "If I'd brought a pail, I bet I could get some fresh milk. I don't like depending on the—you know, food in Rakastava."

"I have brought a pail, Dennis," the robot said. He reached into the battered shopping bag from Emath and came out with a large bowl of the same smooth, brown material as Rakastava's surface.

Dennis smiled at his friend. "We will gather some fruit, Chester," he said. "And some nuts, may be. And then we will try whether to milk a cow is the same as a goat, and whether I remember to do even that."

He paused. "But first," he said, looking at the gloomy, cave-like entrance of Malbawn's hut, "we will look in the mirror and I will see my father."

When Dennis entered the hut immediately after his battle, he'd been keyed up by the fighting and nervously ready to react to any new horror.

The second time he saw the interior, it was dingy and depressing; nothing more. He couldn't imagine anything willingly living in such squalor, not even a creature as foul as Malbawn.

But he couldn't imagine people willingly living in Rakastava, either; and he was willing to live there himself for a time, with its food that had no flavor and its air that had no life.

Dennis thought of Aria and said, "Mirror, show me my father."

The surface blurred and cleared into the remembered brilliance of Emath Palace.

Hale was on his throne in the audience hall. He'd aged more than the few weeks since Dennis saw him last.

A deputation of villagers, leading citizens in their robes and heavy golden chains, stood before the throne. They were angry and, though no sound came through the mirror's glint, it was obvious that several were shouting at once while they shook their fists at the king.

Nothing like that had ever happened in Emath.

"What. . . ?" Dennis said, more to himself than to Chester.

The robot responded anyway. "When a fool refuses the service he owes," Chester quoted, "he will lose his goods to another."

Parol stood at the foot of the throne, facing the delegation with a set smile. A merchant whose cheeks were as ruddy as his thick velvet robe turned from Hale and pointed toward the apprentice wizard.

Of course. The villagers were demanding that the perimeter be expanded—and that meant replacing Parol with a competent wizard.

Parol's face didn't change. He gestured, and a phantom formed in the air. It had smokey bones and the head of a pig, also in shadowed outline. It stepped toward the delegation.

Villagers backed, stumbling on their unfamiliar formal garments. Then they turned and ran. Parol's expression was the unchanged. Behind him, Hale covered his face with his hands.

"I don't want to see this!" Dennis shouted. His words were still ringing in the air when Emath Palace became the gray reflection of a hut and a young man staring back from the glass with an anguished look on his face.

"I don't understand why that's happening," Dennis whispered.

"Your father was a king because the sea hag made him a king, Dennis," his companion said. "Now he must be a king on his own—or no king at all. . . ."

Chester's tentacle squeezed Dennis' hand.

Dennis hadn't looked at himself since he awakened. The ointment had done a wonderful job of healing his wounds. Pink welts marked the tan of his skin, but he'd expected deep scars at the least. . . .

Dennis' left hand rose and tugged at his ear as he watched the mirror. He'd been sure that Malbawn had torn it off with his first blow, but the ear was fine, just twinges of pain in it as in almost every muscle of his body.

"Show me the Princess Aria," he said softly, and the mirror shimmered in response. . . .

She had set the bracelets and jeweled combs from her hair on the table inside her bed, but she still wore the crystal pendant. As Dennis watched, she took off the dress she'd been wearing when she and Conall visited his room.

When Dennis had insulted them both; and they'd deserved it, Dennis *knew* they'd deserved it . . . but they'd been coming to check his condition, and their faces from his delirium were surely memories of earlier visits.

She tossed the dress toward the cabinet into which it vanished like fog melting before the sun.

Aria wore nothing beneath the dress. The fine hairs on her body gleamed like liquid gold as she stepped into the tub. Steam rose as her slim legs stirred the surface.

She settled. The crystals between her breasts spun dancing light over the room and the water as it bobbed, now beneath the fluid and now above it. . . .

"I don't—" Dennis said. He couldn't finish the command until he turned his face toward the doorway. He was gasping for breath.

"Don't show me this either," he said in a husky voice. "Let me—"

He bent at the waist and the rush of blood to his head restored his balance. "Chester," he said, "let's go—"

A cow blatted from across the field.

Dennis straightened, looking at his companion.

"Do not undertake a duty unless you have the power to enforce it," Chester said.

"I've got the power," Dennis grunted, lifting the sword a finger's breadth in its scabbard to prove that it would slide freely. He stepped out into the sunlight.

Malbawn was dead. The odor of his decay permeated the air around him.

Therefore it wasn't Malbawn who stalked toward Dennis from the other side of the pasture.

CHAPTER 36

The cows were in restless motion. Their sidling movement away from the creature, always with their black-
and-white heads twisted back to watch for surprises—was
punctuated as a half dozen of the beasts suddenly decided to bolt a hundred yards in a snorting gallop.

Their eyes rolled when they saw Dennis. They bolted
from him as well.

Dennis drew his sword. The grass the cows had
cropped short brushed his ankles as he strode toward
the yellow-gray creature. He saw Chester in the corner
of his left eye, following on liquid-rippling tentacles a
pace behind and a pace to the side.

The creature was advancing on all six legs. Fifty
yards from Dennis it lifted itself and waved the saw-
edged front and middle pairs.

"You have come to Malduanan, fool!" it croaked
through its cruel beak. "Malduanan will drink your
blood!"

Dennis ran the index finger of his left hand across the
flat of his blade as he advanced, reminding himself of

186

the sword's hard reality and the battle it had fought for him.

"Your brother's a stinking corpse!" he shouted. "I'll kill you too!"

His body fluttered with anticipation and fear of failure, but all the aches and reminders of his previous fight were gone.

This was what he needed. This was what would make him forget his anger at the folk of Rakastava who had sent him to die.

This is what would make him forget the touch of Aria on his body and the way he felt as he watched her take off her clothing in the mirror.

"I'll *kill* you!" Dennis shouted as he lunged.

Then he nearly died.

Malduanan was bigger than Malbawn. Standing on its hind legs, it was easily twice as tall as the youth. As Dennis thrust, the creature toppled forward, letting gravity move its mass faster than Dennis expected muscle power to do.

Dennis shifted back expertly, a swordsman again and not a boy randy with the thought of a naked woman more lovely than he had ever dreamed flesh could look. He blocked Malduanan's right foreleg with his sword near the guard where the metal was thickest—and still the blade notched like a furrow before the plowshare.

Malduanan's left foreleg struck from the other side. Its pincers closed over the youth's ribs hard enough to slice flesh to the bone as they gripped.

Dennis screamed and cut over his own back. Luck aided skill. The sword cracked the horny integument at the joint which permitted the pincers to move in their plates of armor.

Malduanan wheezed foul air over Dennis and jerked away, lifting the injured limb high. The single blade of the pincers sagged at an angle.

The youth staggered several paces backward. He was breathing in quick, shallow puffs because it hurt to expand his chest fully. He thought a rib must be cracked. He was bleeding all over that side of his tunic, though the tough fabric itself hadn't been cut.

Malduanan balanced his weight on the middle pair of legs, a maneuver that Malbawn had never attempted. Dennis panted, wondering whether or not he dared dart in again. He wouldn't know how much the pain handicapped him until a sudden stitch cost him his balance and he fell—

Malduanan's hind pair of legs flung a loop of silk at Dennis.

The youth started to parry it the way he would a swordstroke—but he saw the sun gleaming on beads of adhesive just in time and slashed his sword away.

The creature moved toward him on its four forward legs. Their jointed scissoring seemed leisurely, but the legs were so long that they covered the ground as fast as Dennis could back-pedal.

His heel turned. Another loop arched toward him on a glistening trailer from Malduanan's spinnerets.

"Help me, Chester!" Dennis shouted as he hunched, turning his misstep into a diving thrust. His whole body was in line with the three-foot blade of the Founder's Sword when its point sliced into the knee joint of Malduanan's right middle leg. One of Chester's curving tentacles caught the forelimb whose slashing blow would have gutted Dennis like a trout had it landed as the creature intended.

Malduanan tried to flatten itself, but the joint with the sword sticking into it was jammed partway open. The creature's body stuck at an angle to the ground, wedged by a limb that could neither fold nor help support the creature.

Dennis rolled sideways and jerked his point free. Malduanan's damaged leg flopped loose below the wound, but the upper limb pivoted in its ball-and-socket joint with the body, as though it still carried weight. The youth curled against a pincered kick or a stab from Malduanan's beak.

Nothing hit him. As he spun to his feet he heard the clang of the creature's forelimb batting Chester through the air like a shuttlecock, swaddled in ribbons of silk.

There was a gouge thumb-knuckle deep in the metal where Dennis had parried the creature's blow with his sword. The same limb had just struck Chester squarely.

Dennis' face was white as dead bone. He stabbed. If Chester had been killed or reduced to crippled impotence for the rest of eternity because his master was a boastful fool. . . .

He hadn't thrust for a limb joint this time. Dennis didn't know how cold a murderous rage could be—not until he saw the creature smash down at Chester for a mistake that was Dennis' own, all his own. The point glided butter-smooth over the armored collar and into Malduanan's neck.

The creature snatched itself aside.

Dennis thought he'd missed, cut only air because his sharp blade hadn't even quivered with contact—

But there was slime on a hand's breadth of the swordpoint and there was a spurt of gray-green ichor hanging in the air behind Malduanan's head as the creature lunged forward again—and stumbled.

Chester clung to both undamaged limbs on the right side, and the legs didn't scissor apart as Malduanan expected them to.

"*Got him!*" Dennis cried in triumph at his friend's life; but it was a warrior's cry too, and a swordsman's. He thrust, ignoring the pain in his torn side as he'd ignored it ever since he realized that he *had* to function normally—even if his body didn't think it could.

Malduanan's eyes were pools of glittering blood. Its beak opened as the legs on its right side forced themselves apart against Chester's metallic grip.

The sword slid through Malduanan's beak. The point

jarred to a halt on the inner surface of the creature's armored braincase.

The creature's six limbs flailed in a convulsive motion swifter than anything they'd managed under conscious control. Dennis jumped back, dropping the swordhilt of necessity. He stumbled, from weakness and not because his foot had caught on a tangle of dry grass.

The left side of his garments, trousers as well as tunic, was sticky with the blood that oozed from cuts over his ribs.

The ground shook as Malduanan fell. The creature's legs beat a drum-roll that scattered dirt and grass high enough to throw a long shadow.

Dennis sat up. He had to lean on his arms to stay upright. His vision was clear, but he saw double images of everything around him.

Malduanan's armored back arched; then the creature's belly slammed the ground again and its tail lifted, spinnerets spewing out gobs of silk that fell over it and the landscape promiscuously.

The creature's whole huge body shuddered and grew still.

The doubled images in Dennis' eyes drew back together. The scene shrank down to a pool of white light.

He barely felt the ground's impact as he collapsed.

CHAPTER 37

There was something damp and cool over Dennis' eyes. All the rest of his skin prickled as though burning needles were being driven into the surface of his body.

"Is the sword all right, Chester?" he whispered.

His lips were cold and stiff until he moved them. Veins of fire razored through them like lava rising in the crevices of a glacier.

"The sword is with us, Dennis," the little robot said. "It was used hard in the struggle, as you were used hard; but both of you will be well, that is so."

A sponge mopped Dennis' breastbone, then moved cautiously across the torn left side of his chest. He shuddered. He was cold to the core.

He knew he was dying.

"Chester," he said, "you're all right, aren't you?"

"Indeed I am well, Dennis," the robot replied. "And you have slain Malduanan."

"*We* killed him, my friend," Dennis said.

When he smiled, he felt a little better. The empty cold of his body mixed with his burning skin. He wondered where he was lying. He didn't feel the grass heads tickling him as he expected.

His smile faded. "You'll tell my parents, won't you, Chester?"

"When next we see your parents, I will tell them that you are a hero and have slain Malduanan, Dennis."

"And—and Aria?"

"What is it that your friend can tell me that I don't see for myself, Dennis?"

Dennis lurched upright. The cloth fell from his eyes, but for a moment dizziness blinded him to all but the light.

"Oh!" he gasped. Arms enfolded him to keep him from falling—the resilient metal of Chester's tentacles and Aria's soft, warm flesh. She'd dropped the sponge she was using to clean and cool his torso—

Pain—genuine, all-embracing pain—shot through Dennis like a thunderbolt striking him in the side of the ribs. He gasped and fainted and revived so suddenly that the hot buzzing and disorientation were like those from a blow on the head.

But he was alive again, not cold and consigned by his own mind to death.

"Oh," Dennis repeated.

His brain was staggering back to the fight with Malduanan because he wasn't able to understand his present surroundings just yet. He looked down at his bare knees, because if he looked up he'd see Aria; and he said, "I made a mistake, Chester, rushing in like that. I could've . . . I thought I'd been . . ."

"The youth who learns from punishment," Chester quoted proudly, "need not be punished again."

Aria held a cup to Dennis' lips. "It's milk," she said. "From the cows."

They were in Rakastava. Dennis lay in a brown room, on a slab that was perhaps not so bare as it seemed because there were hair-fine pricklings when his skin pulled away from the surface. He looked down at it

doubtfully, but the two of them, Chester and Aria, wouldn't have brought him here if it weren't for his benefit.

Dennis drank the warm, sweet milk with care.

The cut in his side was a bad one, and even the slightest shift sent shards of pain quivering away from his ribs. Chester's touch steadied him, though Aria had moved back a trifle. He thought he could still feel the warmth of her.

He met Aria's eyes and smiled. "The herd's all right, too, then?" he asked.

He thought he was blushing. They'd draped a blue cloth over his midsection after they stripped him, but the sight of his own bare legs reminded Dennis of watching the girl undress in the mirror.

Watching the *woman* undress. Her pendant, a relic from the age before men landed on Earth, spun to draw his eyes and memories.

She looked away; embarrassment hardened her tone unexpectedly. "You didn't have to do that. None of us knew about the—other one. Nobody had . . ."

She met his eyes and pursed her lips in a grimace, but still she couldn't finish the thought aloud: *none of the visitors we sent out had ever lived that long before.*

"I didn't mean that," Dennis protested. "I just—"

He couldn't finish his sentence either, because the thought was so clearly *I just wanted to talk about something harmless, so that I didn't tell you how beautiful your breasts are when the pendant plays its soft light over their inner curves. . . .*

"I told you that whatever you did out there was your own choice," she said hotly. "I *didn't* send you out to, to be hurt!"

And she hadn't, but the look in her eyes showed that she thought she had. *Dennis* knew he'd tramped out to the pasture the second time from only his own stiff-necked pride.

He finished the milk, letting the cup hide his face

and give him time to think of what to say. "Can I get up, now?" he asked quietly, studying the faintly iridescent film which the fluid left in the bottom of the cup.

"Clothing!" Aria directed the wall brusquely. In obedience, a suit of silver-patterned red fell to the slab beside the youth.

Aria turned her back courteously, though Dennis knew she wasn't modest in the mincing, fearful sense. She was as firm and willing to do whatever was necessary as the women of Emath Village, fishermen's wives and tradesfolk who took jostling and occasional disaster as mere incidents of life.

The only problem was that here in Rakastava, life proceeded without incident.

Or it had, until Dennis arrived.

"Aria," he said as he pulled on the fresh garments. The movement still brought flashes of giddiness, but he was in much better shape than he'd expected from the amount of blood he'd lost. "Princess, I went outside the, the city here because it—I wouldn't like to be here all the time. But . . ."

She turned to him, sidelong, when his voice trailed off.

Dennis was fitting his feet into the new slippers and wondering how to say what he meant without . . . "But I'm glad to be here where you are, too. And the milk was very good."

Aria smiled like the sun on a calm sea. "Chester taught me to milk a cow," she said with coy pride. "He thought you might like that instead of—"

Her face lost its joy. "It isn't the food that makes us—what we are in Rakastava," she said harshly. "It's us. I knew that before you came."

"I—" Dennis said. "I think I could use a proper meal, Aria. There's nothing wrong with the food here, I know."

"You can eat alone in your room, if you like," she said. The tone of self-loathing in her voice hurt Dennis as much as if the dissatisfaction had been directed toward him.

"I'd rather eat with all of you," he said humbly. "If that would be all right?"

She smiled again and took his arm. "Of course it's all right, silly," she said. "It's a *pleasure*."

CHAPTER 38

When they reached the hall where the whole population was assembled as usual for the evening meal, Dennis found that Rakastava had left two places on the bench beside King Conall. The foresight no longer surprised him.

CHAPTER 39

Dennis went out with the herd the next morning.

He felt a little tired and all his muscles ached, but he was in amazingly good condition for someone who'd been near death from his wounds less than a day before. The room with its slab that pricked his skin had done much more than speed the healing of his surface injuries.

"Rakastava takes good care of its citizens, Chester," he commented.

"Rakastava takes good care of its herd, Dennis," the robot replied crisply. "But it was the purpose of the cows to feed Malbawn and Malduanan."

Dennis reached out to stroke the flank of the nearest of the cows plodding to fresh grass beyond the arc they had already cropped. She twisted aside at the touch. When the cow looked back and saw Dennis, she made a grumbling sound—brushed her tail against the youth—and resumed her course.

"They're getting to like me," Dennis said with quiet satisfaction. "I think—"

He paused. "—Aria may like me too."

"If a fool has no work," Chester snapped, "his groin thinks for him."

Dennis grimaced. "I want to see Malduanan's hut," he said. "He came from this side of the field, so it's— yeah, that must be it."

Another great lump stretched from the pasture edge back into the shadows of the jungle. It was perhaps larger than Malbawn's hovel, but they were both made of leaves gray with their coating of mildew and other fungus. The door, a curtain of twigs and woven bark, hung open as Malduanan had left it to meet the youth who'd slain Malbawn.

Dennis drew his sword, though he didn't think he'd need it.

"The best remedy is to prevent trouble by foresight," Chester quoted approvingly.

Dennis stepped inside with his blade chest-high.

The dirt floor was littered with bones—scrubbed clean of flesh and ligament. Malduanan's beak had punched the larger ones with thumbnail-sized holes through which the creature sucked marrow. Some bones were fresh, and some had rotted away into splinters; but all the bones were cattle bones.

Dennis realized he'd been holding his breath. He let it out in relief.

"I thought—" he said aloud. "I was . . ." He looked around the dim interior.

"Malduanan didn't kill people," Dennis said, finally managing to organize his thoughts clearly enough that he could wrap words around them. "I was afraid there'd be—"

Skulls to trip over, his mind said.

"—bodies here too," his mouth completed.

"But," he added as his irrational relief turned to gloom that didn't really make any sense either—what was done, was done: "There aren't any men here, because Malbawn killed them all before they could meet Malduanan."

"There was a man who met Malduanan, Dennis," Chester said softly. "It was so long ago that his bones are dust and the dust of dust; but *this*—" metal pinged softly as Chester's tentacle touched something in the shadows "—is not yet dust."

The sound was from behind him, beside the door. Dennis turned in curiosity. His blade shifted, point forward, as his heart jumped in surprise. A figure stood there, as tall as Dennis and as silent as Death.

Metal rang on metal again. "It is not a man but a man's armor, Dennis," Chester said. "Nothing in this place is alive, except the mold on the walls."

Dennis scuffled his way through the beef bones to see the armor. It was black and so highly polished that it gleamed even in this vague light.

Dennis ran his left index finger across the metal. It felt cool and water-smooth. There was no dust on his fingertip when he looked at it closely. The black surface was more than glassy: not even dust would cling to it, over these—

"How many years, Chester?" he murmured. "How long has this been here?"

"For fewer years than men have been settled on this planet, Dennis," the robot said. "But by only a generation of years fewer."

Dennis tapped the breastplate with a fingernail. It rang like a wind-chime, a high-pitched sound that resonated in the armor for a dozen heartbeats.

The youth could see, from where plates overlapped to let the wearer move his arms, that the metal was paper-thin. He shifted his sword to his left hand and squeezed the hollow wrist with the full strength of a grip that could crush the hand of anyone he'd ever met.

The metal didn't quiver. It was as if Dennis were squeezing a solid steel bar.

He let out his breath again, slowly.

The suit of armor stood on its own legs without external support. The slotted visor was raised. A glance within assured Dennis that there was no framework inside either.

Nor were there bones. If the suit's owner had been wearing the armor when he died, that had been long enough ago to permit even a human skull to vanish utterly.

Dennis shifted an arm of the suit up and down, as though he were shaking hands with the dead owner. The hinged plates of the wrist and elbow whispered across one another, almost frictionless in their movement.

"Chester, this is *beautiful*," Dennis said. "Should I—"

He thought as he sheathed his sword, freeing both hands. "Ah, Chester? Is this something that I need?"

"It is not now that you need it, Dennis," the robot replied in a flat, uncompromising tone.

"Oh," the youth said. Well, he didn't need it. Would he wear it, tramping through the pasture under a sun that would heat black metal like an oven? "Well. I guess it can stay here."

He poked his foot morosely into a pile of debris; but that's all it was, debris. Garbage, really, picked too clean to smell. "Let's go out and see what else there is in this . . . place."

The sunlight felt good, though Dennis found himself twitching together his fingers to recapture the ghostly smoothness of the armor. It had been so *beautiful*. . . .

Chester offered him a cluster of magenta berries. The kernel within each berry was large, but the layer of flesh around it was sweet and tart in trembling alteration.

The berries were delicious—and everything the food of Rakastava was not. But Rakastava had surely saved Dennis' life the day before. . . .

The cattle were avoiding the area in the center of the pasture, where Malduanan lay in the grass like a gray hillock. The air above the corpse glittered as gorged insects spun in the sunlight.

Dennis touched his sword hilt. Sucking on the last of the berries, he began to walk across the field toward

Malbawn's hut. He would look in the mirror again. He wanted to see what was happening in Emath.

And he wanted to see Aria.

Malbawn's legs had fallen in tattered segments to the grass. The great plates of the creature's torso were beginning to separate as well. Dennis wondered if the chitinous armor would resist the elements as effectively as it had the edge of his sword. The pieces might lie there forever, empty reminders of a monster the folk of Rakastava had thought must be bribed because it could not be slain.

He shivered. They'd nearly been right.

Chester touched his companion's shoulder and said, "He who perseveres in a crisis makes his own fate, Dennis."

"If he's lucky," the youth grunted. "And if he has friends."

But he was swaggering as he stepped up to the mirror and demanded, "Show me Emath. Show me my father."

As obedient and certain as the law of gravity, the gleaming surface grayed, then brightened on the turrets of Emath Palace for a moment before it swooped dizzyingly down through the crystal walls.

King Hale sat in the drawing room of the royal suite. Selda lay on a divan across from him, her face pressed against the bolster. She seemed to be crying. No servants were present.

"That's funny," Dennis muttered. He peered out the hut's door to make sure that his time sense hadn't been distorted by his injuries and whatever process the city had used to heal them.

The sun was just short of mid-sky—the time Hale always spent in the throne room, hearing deputations and discussing the business of the village with his advisors.

"Show me the throne room," Dennis directed. His

voice was neutral, but his face glowered like a thundercloud.

The mirror's image shifted queasily, a seeming motion like that of a diver executing a fast back-flip. The throne room filled the surface when it came to rest, though at first Dennis thought the mirror had made a mistake. The bright, sparkling chamber of his recollection couldn't have been transformed into *this* nest of shadowed gloom.

But it had been. The walls and ceiling were draped with black cloth: not velvet, like those of the Wizard Serdic's apartments, but sailcloth painted black and hung to cover crystal that paint wouldn't stick to directly.

Parol—pudgy, pock-marked Parol, with his smirk and his cringing agreement with anyone willing to face him— sat on the throne.

CHAPTER 40

Takseler, one of Emath's leading citizens—a merchant whose shop covered a block of the waterfront and who owned three trading vessels himself—faced Parol with a shocked expression and very little clothing. He'd entered the audience hall wearing robes and a chain of office. Now he stood in his undergarments with his valuables in the hands of guards in orange livery.

Those were the human guards. At either side of the throne shimmered a demon, orange also but clad in flames that vanished upward in curls of filthy smoke.

Parol cackled and pointed at the merchant. The guard holding the chain of office in his soft hands laughed in agreement. He stepped closer and slapped a loop of the heavy gold across Takseler's face, then kicked the merchant as he stumbled to his knees.

The guard was Rifkin. King Hale's butler now had new livery and new duties. He seemed comfortable in both of them.

Parol laughed. The human guards joined him.

The demons raised their snaky heads. Billows of fire surged from their throats, curling so high that they threatened to blister the painted sailcloth. . . .

"No more!" Dennis shouted, to the mirror and to fate.

The mirror obeyed, showing the youth only a reflection of himself.

Fate—the doom which closed on King Hale and his subjects when he determined to cheat the sea hag of her bargain—would be harder to avoid.

Dennis' left hand was caressing Chester's carapace. The metal wasn't even scratched by the blow Malduanan had struck it the day before. It provided Dennis with the touch of something that had stayed unchanged since his earliest memories.

His parents had aged and shrunken from the wonderful, all-powerful creatures of his youth. Emath Palace was no longer the glittering wonderland of whose halls the boy Dennis had gamboled.

Chester said quietly, "Do not tie yourself to one who is so much greater that your life becomes a toy."

Dennis rubbed the robot affectionately.

He'd changed too, although—

He shrugged his shoulders, watching the play of his muscles in the mirror. A man's muscles, and a sword at his side that he'd used as a man—with the scars to prove it.

Change wasn't necessarily a bad thing.

"Mirror, show me the Princess Aria," he demanded. His chin was lifted and eyes turned resolutely away from Chester. The robot had no expression, but Dennis knew that he'd imagine a look of disapproval on the metal if he let himself see it.

He realized with a lurch of dismay that he'd hoped—dreamed, prayed—that Aria would be bathing again. But—

The mirror showed what *was* rather than what the

viewer wished. Aria sat cross-legged on a stool, with a twelve-string lute nestled into her lap. The strings flashed light as her fingers played over them and her lovely mouth shaped sounds which Dennis couldn't hear.

Gannon could hear them. The King's Champion lounged on the floor, his right arm leaned across the end of a low divan.

There were twenty or more people watching Aria's performance, young men and women—all the women beautifully gowned and none of them as beautiful as the princess.

Gannon, with his black garb and dark good looks, was in the center of the group. His eyes were on Aria, and it seemed to Dennis that she looked back at the champion more than chance would require.

Gannon smiled.

"No!" Dennis cried, turning his head.

He'd come to the mirror for reassurance. The mirror instead gave him truth; two truths, and neither of them reassuring in the least.

"No," Dennis repeated as he looked again, his voice now a whisper. His tortured expression gazed back at him, looking for help that the youth didn't know the words to ask for.

His face hardened, and he shrugged loose the sword at his side. "Show me—" he ordered. "Show me any other huts that are, are beside this pasture."

Dennis was wondering how he could rephrase his question and make it clear to the mirror—to the demon or device which controlled the mirror—that he wanted to find another creature like Malbawn or Malduanan.

"Before they find me," Dennis muttered aloud.

Chester made a metallic snorting sound.

"All *right!*" the youth snapped as he looked down at this companion. "But it's something I *can* do something about. Not like Emath."

And not like the Princess Aria, who could look at
anyone and sing to anyone she pleased. Whether Dennis, a vagabond and visitor to Rakastava, liked it
or not.

Dennis was blushing as he turned back to the mirror.
Chester knew him too well.

Chester had saved his life against Malduanan.

The mirror had understood his instructions. On it
gloomed the image of Malduanan's hut, hunching in the
woods where Dennis had left it less than an hour before. The vision had remarkable depth and detail: when
a scarlet lizard scooted up the doorframe, its tail seemed
to flick beyond the surface of the glass.

"That's good," Dennis said encouragingly, as though
he were speaking to another person instead of a thing of
glass and bronze. "But show me a different one. Is
there a—"

The picture was shifting before Dennis could finish
his question. As he blinked at the new scene, he thought
the mirror had made a mistake after all: this was a real
house, not a hovel of twigs and moldy leaves.

It was small, but no smaller than the old houses in
Emath village which had been built before space in the
bustling community became too valuable to waste on
one-story dwellings. The house sat at—in—the margin
of the jungle, the way Malbawn and Malduanan's huts
did, but it had a proper, human-sized door with a
window to either side. The walls seemed to be shingled, and the roof was probably covered with thatch.

It couldn't be hair, though that was what it looked
like no matter how carefully Dennis squinted.

"Show me the inside," he ordered.

He was getting very used to the mirror. It didn't
make him uncomfortable, the way he'd felt when using
the Wizard Serdic's device.

That had put him into an unreal scene—unreal because it was part of the past and therefore dead.

Malbawn's mirror was no more than a window through which Dennis could look. He could *understand* the mirror.

So long as he didn't think too closely about it.

The image in the mirror flipflopped as though a painting were being spun—front-side, back-side, and both images executed in meticulous detail.

Inside the house, a plump old woman in bonnet and apron was sweeping the floor with a twig broom.

"Oh!" Dennis gasped.

He'd expected some horrific monster, though why. . . ? This was a human dwelling. A man as tall as Dennis would have to duck to step through the doorway. A creature like Malbawn or Malbawn's brother—

Well, either of those monsters was nearly as big as this whole house.

The house had only one room. The woman stood her broom in the corner and checked a pot of something on the brick stove. Apparently satisfied, she opened the door and finished her sweeping with firm, quick strokes. Her face was old—lined and gray.

Dennis felt his nose wrinkle in distaste, then felt embarrassed. His nurse had been old and ugly too, with a perpetual scowl and a hair-sprouting wart on her chin. No one could have had a kinder heart—or have been dearer to him until her death when he was ten.

But what were the house and its occupant doing here?

The only thing Dennis saw that disturbed him was the sword resting above the doorway on wooden pegs. It seemed completely out of place in this homely dwelling. As out of place as the house itself was.

Dennis ran his finger along the mirror's bronze frame. It felt much cooler than the humid air.

"Enough," he said quietly, and at once he was facing his dim reflection in a sheet of glass. "Chester," he went on, still facing the mirror, "can we find that house, or is it too far away?"

"It is at the end of the field, Dennis," the robot said. "It is a mile from here, or somewhat less." Chester's voice was empty of inflection or implied advice.

When Dennis let his mind wander, it showed him Gannon smiling and Aria smiling back at the champion.

"All right, let's *go* then!" he said harshly.

He strode out of the hut, gripping his sword pommel crushingly. For a hundred yards he walked very fast, squinting against sunlight and the tears of frustration that were prickling their way out of the corners of his eyes.

Sun and exercise warmed the youth, slowed him; made him calmer. He glanced to the side and smiled to see Chester mincing along with his tentacles fully extended so that the high grass only brushed the bottom of his carapace.

Dennis reached toward the robot. Chester *humphed!* internally and ignored the gesture. He was making it clear to his master that Dennis' enthusiasm—for getting into trouble—was no more than a way to work off other frustrations.

Dennis understood. He smiled ruefully and waved his right palm to the robot. It was blotchy from its pressure on the swordhilt.

"The man who is violent like the wind will founder in the storm he raises, Dennis," the robot said grumpily, but a tentacle snaked up and curled into the offered hand.

"Still," Dennis said, "it's not a bad thing that we're doing. . . ."

Though to be honest with himself, he wasn't sure what he *was* doing. Visiting a little old lady, very possibly. But it just didn't seem *right* that a perfectly normal house should be here, where nothing else was normal.

The pasture rolled and curved through the jungle. The cows were out of sight before Dennis got his first direct glimpse of the house nestled into the jungle side.

The sun was near mid-sky, so the overhanging thatch shadowed the front of the little building. Flowers grew in little boxes beneath the shuttered windows.

Something was very wrong.

Dennis paused and took a deep breath. "Well, it won't be anything we can't handle," he said. "We beat Malbawn and Malduanan, didn't we?"

"That is so, Dennis," Chester agreed unemotionally.

"And," Dennis went on, slipping the Founder's Sword up in its sheath and letting it ring as it slid down again, "I've got a star-metal blade, have I not, Chester?"

"That you have not, Dennis," Chester said in the same cool voice as before. "The Founder's Sword is steel and smith's work, forged for your father when he became King of Emath."

The youth's vision went gray, as if for a moment the whole world were Malbawn's mirror in a state of flux between reflection and distant images. All this time he'd been sustained by the thought that he had a weapon of magical potency, while in fact—

Dennis drew the long sword, fingering the fresh nicks and notches he'd tried to grind smooth with the whetstone. He remembered Conall tapping the blade with his nail and smiling. . . .

"They knew it wasn't star metal, didn't they?" he said. "Conall and the rest? They were laughing at me."

"There is much in Rakastava from the Age of Settlement, Dennis," the robot replied. "It may be that they knew the blade was not of star metal."

Dennis winced in embarrassment over the past.

"But Dennis?" Chester continued. "They do not laugh at you now."

"By heaven, they'd *better* not!" the youth muttered. The sword trembled with the fierceness of this grip on it.

He shook himself and managed to chuckle, though the sound as well was shaky. What was done, was done.

"At any rate, Chester," he said, "it's good steel."

"It is that indeed, Dennis," the robot agreed. "And there is a good man to use it."

Dennis patted his companion in a rush of pride. "Let's go see what this house is doing here," he said.

CHAPTER 41

The grass at this end of the field was uncropped. The long stems were bent in graceful curves by the weight of their bristly seed heads. Thistles shot up like dark green pagodas, eight feet high and crowned with splendid purple flowers. Insects buzzed and quivered within their miniature landscape.

Ten yards from the front of the house, Dennis set his hand on his swordhilt and hesitated while he decided whether or not to unsheathe the weapon. The door opened.

The Founder's Sword trilled like a mating frog as Dennis swept it from its scabbard.

"Oh, heaven *save* me, noble prince!" gasped the old woman, throwing her hands to her cheeks to amplify the amazed circle of her mouth. "Oh! You mustn't be so frightening to an old body as me—begging your pardon, that is, for speaking so when it's not my place."

"Who are you?" Dennis demanded.

He lowered the point of his sword. Had it been smaller, he might have shielded it behind his body; but it was too long for that, and sheathing the blade again would have been as embarrassing a production as drawing it in the first place.

"Me, noble prince?" the old woman said, pulling out her drab skirts as she curtsied. "Oh, I'm no call for such as one as yourself to notice. Mother Grimes, they call me—"

She looked up. "Used to call me, I might better say. When there were folk here, and not all traipsing off to the fine city and leaving poor Mother Grimes to her loneliness."

"Off to Rakastava?" Dennis said, frowning as he tried to understand the situation. "But then why didn't you go too?"

Mother Grimes curtsied again. "Ah, noble prince, but there's the question. It's my sons, you see, head-strong lads that they are. They left me years ago to find their own way in the world, but it's home they'll return some day, for I'm sure of it. And what will become of them if I'm not here to greet them, tell me that?"

Dennis shook his head as if to clear cobwebs from his brain. He could understand what the old woman was saying, but . . . Rakastava had existed for—from before men settled on Earth. And what about Malbawn and—

"But noble prince," Mother Grimes was saying. "Forgive me my presumption, for I know my hut is unworthy of your highness' feet, but—will you not come inside and talk with me for only a moment? It will remind me so of my boys, fine young lads that they were when they left me to seek their fortune."

Dennis opened his mouth to refuse. The old woman held out her work-worn hands. The youth thought of his own mother, weeping for her son and for herself now in Emath.

"I have cider, noble prince," Mother Grimes wheedled. "Fresh squeezed and cool in my root cellar."

Dennis wiped his brow with the back of his left hand.

He looked down at Chester and said, "Well, she seems glad to see us. . . ?"

"She is that, Dennis."

"All right," Dennis said. "A mug of cider would be very good, mistress."

"After you, then, noble prince," Mother Grimes said, gesturing toward the door. Her beaming expression was enough to beautify even a face as ugly as hers.

Dennis shook his head as natural caution reasserted itself. "No," he said brusquely. "You go first."

"It's not for me to take precedence over such as you," said the old woman with a shake of her head. "But if the noble prince insists . . ."

Bowing to him, she stepped back through the doorway.

Dennis followed her, looking around sharply. It was just as the mirror had shown it, except that the lines of things—the stove, the cracks in the floorboards and walls—didn't seem quite as *crisp* as they ought to.

"She is very glad to see you," Chester said. "She is glad to devour you and revenge her sons, Malbawn and Malduanan."

Mother Grimes turned. Her face was full of hideous glee.

Dennis chopped through her neck with a back-handed stroke. The head bounced on the floor and began to giggle.

Mother Grimes bent over—he thought she was falling—and picked up the head. She lowered it onto her dripping neck-stump.

Mother Grimes' bodice of dumpy gray homespun split apart. Two clawed, chitinous arms thrust through the torn fabric. The pincers of the left arm held a short baton, black on one end and white on the other.

Dennis raised his sword. His face wore a set expression; he was beyond fear.

While Mother Grimes' human arms held the head in place, a pincered limb rubbed the white end of the baton across the wound. The puckering edges healed, leaving no sign of injury except the stain of blood that had already leaked out.

Something tugged at Dennis's sword.

He touched his left hand to the pommel for a hand-and-a-half grip and swung the weapon with all his strength. The sword pulled out of his grasp anyway and clanged flat against the ceiling. It began to glow red.

Mother Grimes chuckled and minced toward the youth, holding out her baton.

Dennis' scabbard twisted as the same power that drew the blade to the ceiling gripped the sheath's steel tip.

Dennis screamed in horror. His hands wrenched at his belt, but his whole weight hung from it and his fingers couldn't release the brass buckle. He watched like a cricket in a spider's web as Mother Grimes approached.

Reason overcame horror at last. "Chester! Hold her!" Dennis shouted.

The Founder's Sword and the scabbard tip exploded in white fire. Showers of sparks danced across the room. They burned holes in Mother Grimes' garments as well as blistering Dennis' skin and melting knots in his hair with an awful stench.

Chester gripped Mother Grimes in a shimmer of metal, wrapping her slight form in four of the tentacles which had proved strong enough to hold Malduanan. Her grinning face turned; her chitin-armored pincer twisted; and the black end of the baton brushed the robot's carapace.

Chester slumped away. His tentacles fell slack and threatened to separate as if their segments were the beads of a necklace which had come unstrung. The robot's carapace had retained its smooth sheen for all the youth's lifetime—and the life of every man on Earth since the Settlement. Now a greenish corrosion grew across the surface like mold on fruit, etching deep pits in the metal.

Mother Grimes laughed deep in her throat.

The scabbard tip burned away, freeing Dennis to move. He dodged as the baton thrust at him . . . but that was a playful gesture anyway, not a real attack. He was to provide entertainment—

Before he was eaten.

The walls of the room were losing definition. Individual floor boards and stove bricks were blurring into one another. Pale slime oozed through all the surfaces; some of it dripped from the ceiling and burned Dennis as badly as the blazing sparks had done a moment before.

He wouldn't have been able to tell where the doorway had been, except that the ancient sword still hung on the wall.

Dennis spun away from Mother Grimes and snatched at the sword.

He didn't expect to be able to move the weapon, but it came away easily into his hand. Only gravity held the blade onto the pegs, not the fierce magnetic flux which had stripped the Founder's Sword from Dennis and devoured it.

Mother Grimes moved closer. Her foot brushed Chester's carapace. The metal rang hollowly.

Dennis shouted and swung his new sword in a glittering arc. The blade was lighter than steel, sharper than thought. It razored through Mother Grimes' torso from shoulder to breastbone, whickering in and out as though nothing but empty air impeded the stroke. Blood misted the air.

This sword really *was* forged from star metal.

Mother Grimes giggled and sealed the gaping wound with the white end of the baton.

Dennis backed—bumped the wall. Shifted sideways as the baton twitched toward him like an adder's black tongue—bumped what had looked like a stove when he entered the room and was now a fungoid lump. The slime beading its surface burned as it began to devour Dennis' skin.

He thrust for Mother Grimes' mouth. The sharp point flicked her grin into half a smile that continued up the side of her skull and tore her bonnet away in a flutter of cloth. The black end of the baton missed Dennis' hand by so little that he thought the breeze ruffling the hairs of his wrist was the touch that had slain him.

Giggling maniacally, Mother Grimes began to heal the horrible cut before coming after Dennis again. The walls and ceiling of the room were clearly drawing in.

The realization wasn't clear in Dennis' mind before instinct guided the next quick cut. The star-metal blade sliced chitin as easily as it had the human-looking flesh of Mother Grimes' neck and torso.

One of the creature's middle limbs spun to the floor with the baton still locked in its pincers.

Mother Grimes screamed. The sound became a whistling sigh when the youth's keen blade slashed across her cheek and throat again in a blood-spray. She stumbled back, her foot slipping on the greenish ruin of one of Chester's tentacles.

"He was my *friend!*" Dennis shouted as he swung overhand. The swordtip slit a line through the ceiling as the blade cut over and down.

Mother Grimes' body fell in two halves.

On the floor, the elbow of the arm holding the baton straightened and bent; straightened and bent. Dennis stabbed at the pincer's joint. The sections flew apart, letting the baton roll clear. The sword drove six inches deep in the flooring, but a quick tug cleared it easily.

Mother Grimes' five remaining limbs were scrabbling weakly. Most of her head was still attached to the right side of the torso. Everything was covered in blood—Dennis, the walls, and the remains of Chester.

With the dress slashed to rags, Dennis could see Mother Grimes had a jointed exoskeleton like that of Malbawn and Malduanan. A thin filament attached the creature's right heel to the floor.

Dennis sliced through the filament. Mother Grimes thrashed momentarily. Then all the pieces, arm and body halves, became as still as meat in a locker.

"My *friend*!" Dennis repeated. In a rush of loathing, he began to slash at the quiescent body, grunting with the effort of blows that sent his sword deep into the floor and walls.

When he paused, he was gasping for breath. His body felt as if it were crawling. When he looked down, he found his clothing was in rags, dissolving in the juices that still dripped from the wall. Angry blotches rose wherever the slime had touched his skin.

Mother Grimes' baton lay between his feet, not far from the hollow shell that had been Chester.

Dennis gasped with the suddenness of the thought that struck him. For a moment he remained frozen in the slump to which exhaustion had reduced him. Then he straightened and cut an opening in the front wall with four long, deliberate strokes. What fell away looked like the rind of a gourd.

He paused again, still panting.

Light had seeped through the walls of the hut, but the opening brightened the interior considerably. For this, Dennis had to see what he was doing very clearly. . . .

He picked up the baton between his left thumb and forefinger. The surface was sticky with blood, but apart from that, the baton felt as though it were a piece of wood.

Dennis gingerly moved the white end toward the robot's carapace. Just before the two touched, he looked away. He couldn't let himself watch the failure of a hope that meant so much to him.

The baton went *chank*! on the hollow metal.

"I want to die," the youth whispered through his tears.

"Do not turn away from life because someone else has died, Dennis," said Chester in a cross voice.

"Chester!" the youth shouted. He started to hug the robot, then remembered the baton he held. If the black end touched him or the robot—

Grimacing with horror, Dennis flung the object through the opening he'd hacked in the wall. Then he clutched his life-long companion with his free hand and the elbow of his sword arm, holding the weapon point-up and safe during the embrace.

"I thought I'd killed you," he babbled. "I thought I'd never see you again, Chester, and I wanted to die."

There was a faint wash of verdigris on the robot's limbs and carapace, but the metal was whole again and the tentacles that encircled Dennis' shoulders were as smooth and supple as ever before.

"Whether we stay here or go back is up to you, Dennis," Chester said quietly.

The digestive juices were burning almost the whole of the youth's body by now, as though Mother Grimes had surrounded him with fire before he slew her.

"Oh," Dennis said. "Of course."

He reached his sword arm out through the opening, then cocked his body free like a contortionist avoiding further contact with the house.

Avoiding contact with the creature that looked like a house with a little old lady inside.

The new sword fit well into the scabbard made for the old one. The smith who'd hammered out the Founder's Sword for King Hale must have seen the real thing somewhere to copy the style and dimensions so accurately.

Dennis sheathed the weapon, stripped off his ragged clothes, and rubbed his body with handfuls of dry grass. The stems and leaves prickled, but they scraped away the fluids that smeared him and seemed even to reduce the redness and swelling which the slime had already caused.

The exterior of what had been Mother Grimes looked like a puffball, half-deflated and already rotting. Dennis couldn't imagine how he'd thought it was a house.

"Let's go back to Rakastava, Chester," Dennis said. Now that things were calm, his body sagged with the effort it had delivered.

He left his clothing where it lay. The garments were still crumbling, though the weight of direct sunlight seemed to be slowing the process. He carried the belt, the damaged scabbard, and the star-metal sword instead of wearing them against his bare, swollen skin.

"Is it me or yourself that you would have carry the baton, Dennis?" the robot prompted.

"There's nothing of men in that thing, Chester," the youth replied with a vehemence that surprised even him. "I'll take the sword, for it's a fine sword and I've lost the one I came with. But that other thing—"

He spat. "I want it no more than I want Malduanan tramping at my side, Chester."

"Do not slight a little thing, lest you suffer for its lack," Chester murmured.

But one of his tentacles looped around the scabbard, taking the weight from his exhausted master as they trudged back to Rakastava.

CHAPTER 42

Rakastava was so underpopulated that Dennis encountered only three of its citizens on his way to his room.

He expected to be laughed at. He was a ludicrous figure, tired, naked and blotched with swellings.

The woman and men who faced Dennis, from around corners or a doorway, fled in the opposite direction as soon as their eyes took him in. A naked wildman might frighten anybody, but there was more to it than that. One of the men bobbed a nervous bow, and the woman muttered, "Prince Dennis," before she bolted away.

They were in awe of him. Not even because he'd killed monsters.

The folk of Rakastava were in awe of Dennis' willingness to go well beyond the city's walls.

"They're all cowards," he muttered as the door of his room opened with its promise of bath and balm. He was too exhausted to put real venom into the observation.

"Not all of them are cowards, Dennis," Chester disagreed in a mild tone. Then he added, "The Princess Aria will be at meal in the assembly hall when you have bathed."

Dennis grinned. "Not all of them," he agreed.

But the cheerful expression faded when he remembered the way Gannon's image looked at the princess— and the way the princess looked back.

CHAPTER 43

The evening meal had started by the time Dennis joined the gathering. There was an empty space on the bench between Conall and his blond daughter.

Aria glanced around as Dennis approached. The way her face brightened to see him made memories of her mirrored image less bitter.

Conall peered at the youth. "You've been—" he said, then looked down and took another forkful of "meat."

"Always glad to have you with us, boy," he said gruffly.

Aria's finger traced a splotch on the side of Dennis' neck where a drop of slime had splashed the youth soon after Mother Grimes' door shut behind him. The swelling had gone down, but the skin was still tender.

He turned. She touched a similar blotch on his forehead.

"You've been fighting again," she said. If her touch was cool, then her voice was cold, clinical. "Did you have a good time?"

A disinterested adult talking down to a six-year-old.

"Well, I . . ." Dennis said, taken aback by this kind of hostility, from—from Aria.

She was concentrating on her plate again, though a certain stiffness in the line of her back suggested that she was no less aware of his presence than she'd been before.

Well, I . . . Dennis thought; but he couldn't find a useful way to finish the sentence even in his mind, so he didn't attempt it aloud.

They'd seen the damage Mother Grimes had done him. It wasn't their fault, hadn't anything to do with Rakastava and her people; but it reminded them of those they'd sent to die in the past. King Conall was embarrassed. And Aria—

Dennis blushed. He didn't understand Aria, but he suspected the fault was in the way he felt about the princess.

"Say, boy," said the King's Champion, leaning forward to speak past Conall. "Some more flotsam tossed up in Rakastava. See them?"

He pointed to the next down of the circular arc of tables rising from Rakastava's floor.

A couple, brightly dressed but obvious from their emaciation, sat gawping at the splendor around them. They looked ancient, though after staring at them, Dennis decided neither was more than thirty. Their faces were smeared with gravy from the food they'd shoveled in—with their bare hands, from the look of them. The time they'd spent in the jungle had left them with no more table manners than the lizards.

If they'd ever *had* table manners to lose.

"Maybe you'd like to go join them, boy," Gannon continued. "They're more your type, aren't they?"

"Gannon," Conall murmured to his plate.

"What will you do with them?" Dennis asked. There was no more emotion in his voice than there was on the edge of his sword.

"Well, they'll stay, I suppose," Conall said in surprise. "I don't imagine they'll want to leave again, now that they've found safe—"

He broke off when he realized exactly what Dennis meant. "Oh, good heavens!" the king blurted. "You mustn't think we did—the things that happened, that is, because we wanted to. Rakastava welcomes strangers. It was only necessity that caused us to . . ."

Dennis thought of the weapons piled in Malbawn's hut, clubs and knives and spears of sharpened wood. The sort of weapons simple folk, like the ones at the next table, would carry if some catastrophe sent them wandering through the jungle.

"You're right," Dennis said. "It doesn't matter now."

He began to eat, uncomfortably aware of the way Conall stared at the cup he held in both hands and Aria turned her torso at such an angle that Dennis had only her back to look at when he glanced to his right side.

The lights dimmed.

Dennis continued eating. He was hungry, even for the bland offerings of the city's table, and there was still enough light to see the food. He didn't know why the glow from all the room's surfaces had shrunk to a fraction of its usual intensity, but there wasn't very much about Rakastava that he *did* know.

He was going to have to leave this place. Despite Aria.

Because of Aria.

There was a long, hushed sound, a combination of wailing and sobbing, from the people in the assembly hall.

Dennis set down his fork and dropped his hand to the pommel of his new sword.

All around him, the citizens of Rakastava were covering their eyes or staring fixedly at the empty air in the huge room's center. The other newcomers to the city, the stragglers at the next table, were as confused as Dennis—though they reacted by clutching one another and hunching down as if they were about to slip under the table.

There was something in the hollow air after all.

It glowed with a pale green light, expanding slowly—the way a puffball swells in the hours before it bursts. It had a snake's body and three heads from which snake-like tongues slipped and forked as the creature grew.

It hung twenty feet in the air; and it wasn't real. Dennis could see ceiling moldings through the glowing shadow of the creature's body.

"Humans," said the head on the left. The voice thundered with echoes from a hollow even greater than that of the assembly hall. "It is time to pay Rakastava again."

One of the guards at Dennis' table began to sob in terror.

"Who shall it be this time, humans, that you send to Rakastava?" asked the head on the right.

There was a serpentine hiss in the way the creature pronounced sibilants. The voice was more than ample to be heard throughout the hall which Dennis had thought was too large for sound to fill.

There was a general cry of terror, muted by the very fear which wrung it from the throats of the cowering citizens.

Dennis' hand slipped from the pommel to the hilt of his sword, though he didn't draw the weapon for the moment. It was time for a sacrifice, and he knew where the folk of Rakastava looked for sacrifices. . . .

"This time, humans," boomed the center head, appearing to stare straight at Dennis, "it is with the Princess Aria that you will pay Rakastava for your lives and the comfort in which you live them."

The assembled citizens gasped. Though horror may have been a part of the sound, most of it was relief.

The citizens chose the ones who went out to keep Malbawn at bay. But *this* creature chose his own victims. . . .

"She will meet me in the morning—" said the left head.

"—with a single champion," said the right head.

"If she *has* a champion," the central head concluded with mocking emphasis.

The shadowy creature began to fade, or perhaps the increasing brightness of the room made it seem that way. But the vision was gone before the last echoes of its voice had vanished from the assembly hall.

Everyone was babbling to their neighbors with covert looks toward the king and princess. The volume of the creature's voice was underscored by the relative hush that a thousand humans talking brought to the big room.

"Daughter," Conall said in a choked voice. His face was turned toward Aria, but Dennis—between them—doubted the king could see anything through his tears.

"Well, of course I'll go," said Aria, answering a question that hadn't been asked aloud. She carefully folded the napkin in her lap, set it beside her plate, and stood up.

Gannon had gotten up already and was walking toward the door behind them with tiny steps as though he were a statue being pulled on casters.

"Well, Gannon," the king said—briskly, royally. "This time it'll have the tables turned on it, won't it? You'll have its heads off in a trice."

Gannon looked like a man who'd just heard the twang of the crossbow aimed at his chest. "Indeed, sire," he said. "I was just going off to prepare myself to meet Rakastava in the morning."

Dennis put his hand on Aria's wrist. "Please," he said, looking up at the standing woman. "I don't understand. *This* is Rakastava. What's going on?"

Aria smiled at him sadly. "This is Rakastava's city," she said. "*That*—" her index finger pointed toward the vault's empty air again "—was Rakastava; and every so often, we pay him for the use of his city."

Her smile grew coldly bitter. "At a price of his choosing, as is fair."

"But that's a *ghost!*" Dennis said. "A shadow! There's nothing really there, it's just a—"

He didn't have the words to finish, but his companion—

"Chester!" Dennis said, "tell them that Rakastava isn't a real thing."

The little robot slipped from beneath Dennis' seat at the bench. "What you have seen, Dennis and Princess," he said, "is not real but a projection—light interrupting light in the air."

"You see?" Dennis crowed. He jumped to his feet, straddling the bench, and took each of Aria's hands in one of his own.

"But beneath the city, Rakastava is very real," Chester continued inexorably, as if he were unaware of his master's false joy. "And it is to Rakastava, not his projection, that the princess is to go in the morning."

Part-eaten dishes had disappeared into the tables. Goblets of strong, sweet wine rose from the surface in place of the food—many goblets, and the citizens attacked the wine with enthusiasm and relief.

From the corner of his eye, Dennis saw the King's Champion drain one cup, then—after a moment's hesitation—replace it with the full one sitting unnoticed before Conall's bent head.

"Wait a minute!" Dennis cried. "If it's real, this Rakastava, then I'll fight him!"

The youth's loud voice carried to the immediate circle of the king's table and those standing near it. Gannon looked at him, and for a flashing instant Dennis was sure that he saw hope and agreement in the champion's eyes.

Aria took her hands from Dennis and turned away.

"You're a very brave young man, Prince Dennis," Conall said with kind formality. "But this is a task for one with more experience."

"Go back to your cows, boy," Gannon cried harshly. "Leave man's work to a man."

"A ruler is punished for giving honor to a fool!"

Chester rasped in the same hectoring tone. Gannon jumped in surprise.

But pride had more of a grip on the King's Champion than fear. He straightened and struck a heroic pose, knuckles against the points of his hips, beneath his polished armor, and his elbows splayed out to the sides.

"Gannon, there's no need to be—" the king said mildly.

"Wait!" Dennis repeated. He put a hand on Aria's shoulder with enough pressure to beg, though not force, her to turn. "Aria. Tell them you want me to fight Rakastava with you."

Aria met Dennis' pleading gaze. There was no warmth in her eyes, but she put a hand over the youth's where it rested on her shoulder. "Many champions have gone down to fight Rakastava, Dennis," she said quietly.

She turned to her father, squeezing Dennis' hand as she lifted it away. "I desire that Gannon be my champion and companion in the morning," she said in a clear, ringing voice. "When I go to meet Rakastava."

Gannon winced. Dennis didn't notice, because he was stumbling toward the door in blind humiliation.

There were cheers behind him in the assembly hall, but he doubted many of the citizens could have given a reason for their enthusiasm—

Beyond the fact that someone else would feed the monster this time.

CHAPTER 44

The cows' breath sweetened the morning air with the scent of the fodder they'd grazed the day before. One of the calves rubbed its black-and-white head against Dennis in a friendly gesture before frisking off after its mother.

The sun hadn't risen over the fringing jungle, but the sky above the pasture was already bright.

Dennis rubbed his face with his palms.

"Dennis?" said the little robot.

"Yes, Chester?"

"It is now that you have need of the armor in Malduanan's hut."

"To do what?" Dennis asked in amazement.

"To wear, Dennis," Chester replied. "To watch, and to wait."

The jungle was reclaiming Malduanan's hut. The woven leaves of the roof were tattered, creating pools of light. Plants were beginning to sprout among the bones.

The black armor stood in calm magnificence. Chester's tentacles worked the catches with a speed and ease beyond that of a human attendant, dressing his master piece by piece while another pair of limbs readied the next of the accouterments.

The armor covered Dennis completely. Each piece fit as perfectly as if it had been made for him instead of for some long-dead hero.

Where the armor touched bare flesh—his wrists and neck, and his hands which flexed and released within the gauntlets—the metal had the feel of satin. It seemed to weigh no more than the ordinary clothes he wore beneath it.

"This is star metal, isn't it, Chester?" Dennis said in awe. He worked the helmet's slotted visor with his left hand while the robot fitted the swordbelt around the sliding bands that permitted him to bend at the waist.

"It is star metal, Dennis," Chester agreed smugly. The robot backed a pace as if to view his handiwork. "And now,'" he continued, "we will go to Malbawn's hut."

Dennis swallowed. "To—watch the Princess Aria?" he said.

"Yes, Dennis. And to wait."

CHAPTER 45

The back of Malbawn's hut had collapsed from the weight of evening rains and a branch the rain had brought with it. Vines were crawling through the sagging remainder of the structure, but the mirror was still clear.

Dennis stood before the glass—if it *was* glass—with his visor raised, waiting for Chester to prompt him.

"There are those," the robot quoted acidly, "who know the path but do not take it."

Dennis blushed. "Mirror, show me the Princess Aria," he ordered.

He needed Chester's help to guide him through this. But he also needed to act on his own when he could.

The mirror shimmered, but for a moment Dennis thought it was still displaying the interior of the hut and the shadowed jungle beyond. Then his eyes focused on the new scene; he recognized Aria. She stood at the bottom of a sloping staircase. There was a lamp in her hand and a look of mastered fear to make her lips quiver.

There was illumination beyond the sphere of lamplight which hung in the humid air. The half-light was a gray ambiance, scarcely bright enough to be called a glow. It soaked the floor—and perhaps the walls as well, but they were too inconceivably distant for Dennis to see them.

The staircase down which Aria had come was made of stone, not the slick material from which most of the city was constructed. The treads had been worn hollow in the center, though Dennis couldn't imagine that anyone came by this path except at Rakastava's demand.

Aria's lips moved as she called out.

"Chester, where's Gannon?" Dennis demanded. "He's supposed to be with her."

"Gannon came with the princess to the bottom of the stairs," Chester explained calmly. "And now he is in the darkness behind her, where she does not see him . . . and he hopes Rakastava will not see him either."

"W—" Dennis said. "Will it see him?"

"Rakastava cares nothing for Gannon, Dennis," the robot said. "Rakastava's business is with the Princess Aria."

The youth's eyes stung with tears. "She should've taken me," he mumbled. "*I* wouldn't have run."

"She knew you would not run, Dennis. And she did not want you to die."

Aria stepped forward carefully. Only a few yards from the base of the stairs was a stone coping. Beyond that was water, smooth and black and limitless in expanse.

The glow from the walls fell on this underground sea as on glass. The princess was a white blur, a statue of Grief reflected in a cemetery pool.

The water rose, slopped over the coping and the princess' sandals. Her lamp bobbled as she took a startled step backwards. She covered her mouth with her free hand.

The sudden wave receded, then rushed forward again and soaked the lower treads of the staircase.

Aria dropped the lamp to sputter and die in the foam as she clapped both hands to her ears. Dennis couldn't hear the bellow but he'd heard Rakastava's voice in the assembly hall, and he could imagine the thunder that was beating on the princess now.

"Chester," he moaned, "why did you let me leave her? I should have—I should have gotten down there. . . ."

His eyes were closed and his mind was so concerned with punishing him for his failure—cowardice, he should have *found* a way—that he didn't for a moment understand the words when Chester said, "You can go there now, Dennis."

"You mean?" the youth said as his eyes flew open and flashed around him, somehow expecting to find that he was in the city instead of the hut a mile away. "*No*, it's too far to get there in time!"

Something was moving in the distance glimpsed through the mirror. It was as black as the water, but the water surged away from it; and above were its eyes, six sparks as bright as rubies from the floor of Hell.

"You can be there now, Dennis," Chester said, "if you step through the mirror."

Dennis drew his sword and stepped through the mirror. He didn't ask or question, because Chester had told him what he wanted to hear.

The youth's left elbow rang on the bronze mirror-frame, but of the glass there was no hint or hindrance. The atmosphere was humid and sticky with salt, and the air rebounded with monstrous bellowing.

Rakastava was coming.

The creature's scaly breast raised a tide on the underground sea, washing Dennis knee-high as his feet clanked down onto the stones. The star-metal armor sealed his legs against the sea's rush, but the pressure of the water made his footing chancy for a moment.

God in heaven! but the monster's roars were loud. Even when the triple throats were silent, the distant echoes competed with the slap of water against stone.

"Gannon?" called the Princess Aria. "Gannon? Who *are* you?"

She was a cloud of virginal white, but Dennis didn't dare let his mind dwell on her.

"Get back!" he shouted through the bars of his visor. "I've more to think of now than you!"

Dennis clenched and unclenched his left fist, proving to himself that his hands moved freely in their metal gauntlets. He lifted the point of his sword another inch.

Rakastava was bigger than its projection in the assembly hall, though most of the creature's dragon-length was hidden by the water. The body moved snake fashion, side-to-side loops that drove it forward and made the saw-edged comb on its back wobble.

The creature's eyes were red and burning. Behind its serpent necks streamed manes. They burned too, but with a sickly light deep into the violet end of the spectrum. The heads to right and left wove complex patterns as Rakastava approached, but the head in the center drove a line as direct as a beam of light.

The rippling slowed and the body straightened out, letting Rakastava's mass glide forward like that of a boat nearing dock. More of the back rose out of the water, slanting upward in a line which paralleled that of the shelving sea-bottom. As it moved closer, Dennis saw that Rakastava had short, clawed limbs at the base of its triple throats, where the pectoral fins of a fish would have been.

"Step aside, little man," the center head rumbled. The eyes glared ten feet above the water and ten feet away from Dennis, so that he had to look up to meet them. "I will take the Princess Aria, and I will let you live."

Dennis said, "You won't take—" and the head on Rakastava's left struck at him.

The helmet cut off some of Dennis' peripheral vision so he didn't react quickly enough to meet the attack with his point, but reflex lifted the cross-guard and the meat of his blade against the rushing jaws. Though the impact slammed him back, his star-metal edge cut a notch from Rakastava's lip.

Blood with orange fire as its heart spattered. The head drew back and jaws from the other side clamped Dennis around the waist.

Teeth squealed on star-metal armor. Neither broke or flexed, but Rakastava began to lift Dennis off the ground.

The youth swung, aiming down near the base of the neck where his arm had the leverage of a full stroke. The creature's scales were rock-hard and rock-strong, but they split under the force behind Dennis' new sword. Shattered bits splashed into the water, and more glowing blood oozed out to brighten the scene.

The head bellowed and dropped him. Rakastava lunged forward, using its weight to slam Dennis back. The claws on the right foot splayed open as they raked down his torso, sparking and pinging without being able to penetrate the armor.

All three sets of jaws opened. Their forked tongues jabbed out, armed with suckers and spiked nodules like the stinging cells of jellyfish.

Dennis was off-balance but he stabbed anyway, as much to give himself time as to do real harm to Rakastava.

His point glanced off. The star-metal blade was sharper than fear, but Rakastava's scales were very nearly the blade's equal. Only a well-aimed stroke would cut them— and even that they resisted.

A tongue curled around Dennis' right ankle. He swung for it but the center head was dipping toward him. . . .

Dennis struck upward, but the neck was already swinging away. The youth's left leg shot out from under him: Rakastava's right tongue had curled and gripped during the center head's feint.

The center head lifted. Its laughter boomed. Dennis crashed backwards onto the wet stone as the creature drew up on both his legs.

Dennis' armor transmitted the shock of impact in a numbing flash from the base of his spine. Rakastava spread the youth's legs sideways as well as lifting them, as if the creature were a sailor preparing rope for splicing. The youth's groin muscles began to blaze as Rakastava stretched them more than even fencing exercises had done in the past.

Dennis reached out with his left hand, trying to grip one of the heads. His gauntlet slid off the armored muzzle, then groped with the tongue holding his left ankle. Even Rakastava's tongues had the texture of quartz, not soft, spongy flesh.

Fiery pain filled Dennis' eyes. He swung into the center of it, judging where the head must be from where the tongue pulsed within his grip. He felt his sword strike, but in his spasm of hysterical strength, he couldn't be sure whether the blade bit, glanced off, or flew from his hand.

He didn't feel the floor when he fell back on it, but salt water spattered his cheeks through the helmet visor. Rakastava was roaring like an earthquake through its two remaining throats.

The stump of the third neck spouted like an orange-lit fountain.

Dennis rose to his knees. He hadn't lost his grip on his sword. His thighs clicked together in their armor. The feel of his overstretched muscles relaxing gave him a feeling of success greater even than seeing one of Rakastava's heads on the coping before him.

Rakastava was sliding its body backwards. Its two remaining heads were high, but the third neck trailed limp in the water and the third head was Dennis' prize.

"One is off, but two are on, human," Rakastava's main head called as the creature backed into darkness. "I will return for the princess—and for you."

The sea boiled. Dennis braced himself to receive Rakastava's rush and vengeance. The water surged instead—breast-high as the youth knelt and staggering

in its impact, but only water and the creature's real
farewell as it dived to whatever depths it called home.

Dennis waited on his knees and left hand while his
body gasped its breath back. His eyes were focused on
his sword.

The blade still smoothly reflected the cavern's light.
No nicks or scratches marred the pallid metal, despite
the battering it had taken in the fight.

Neither salt water nor Rakastava's glowing blood
beaded on the flats. The star-metal sword was as perfect
as it had remained through the millennia before it came
into Dennis' hands.

"Oh . . ." the youth whispered.

Aria's motion was a white shimmer where water pooled
in the low spots of the stone floor. Dennis turned and
tried to stand—then decided that he'd stay where he
was instead. He balanced on one foot and one knee
with his left hand near enough the ground for a third
point of contact if he became that dizzy.

"Are you all right?" she asked as she knelt beside
him. She touched his shoulder with the fingers of one
hand, but the metal's unearthly feel made her flinch
away.

"Better than he is," Dennis grunted. He prodded the
severed head with his sword-point.

The eyes were dead black now, and the mane had
lost much of its violet fire. Dennis leaned forward and
ran his fingers through the seeming hair. It rustled like
glass against his gauntlet.

"Are you really Gannon?" the princess asked. Her
hands framed Dennis' face as she started to raise the
visor of his helmet.

He stood up suddenly, pulling away from her touch.
He slammed his sword into its sheath, his motion driving Aria back a step.

The underground sea had grown as still as volcanic
glass. On its surface Dennis could see the reflection of
something that wasn't there—the mirror in Malbawn's
hut, and Chester waiting at the edge of it.

He stepped toward the coping.

"Wait!" Aria called. Her slim, smooth hand was pale on the armored elbow.

Dennis turned. He wanted to clasp her; but there was nothing in that for him except the thought, and nothing for her beyond pressure from a slick, grim casing of star metal.

"Give me your ring," he said, wondering for how long the visor and the cavernous echoes of this underworld would hide his voice from the princess.

She obeyed without hesitation, twisting the ring off her little finger to put it in Dennis' metal palm. It was a circle of carven crystal which matched her earrings and complemented the triple pendant between Aria's breasts.

"Now will you—" she said; but Dennis, hoping that he understood what he saw, stepped back toward the reflection—

And into Malbawn's hut, where Chester's quick support kept him from falling as his boots hit the floor.

"There are men who trust their moment," said the robot, "and for whom it goes well forever, Dennis."

"Just get me out of this suit, Chester," the youth said. He could hear the metal-to-metal whisper of Chester already beginning to loosen the catches of the black armor.

The mirror was only a mirror again. Dennis decided he liked it that way.

At least for now.

CHAPTER 46

Aria gasped. The water didn't tremble when the man in armor stepped into it. He and the rectangular shimmer—reflection, she would have said, but there was nothing to be reflected—disappeared as suddenly as if they'd never existed.

Rakastava's head, larger than that of a horse, lay at her feet. The neck-stump was still oozing blood.

She bent to touch the head. The scales were hard and as slick as the armor of the hero who'd left the grisly trophy behind when he vanished.

Gannon's step was so soft that his hand was on her arm before Aria heard him. She leaped upright. She was too shocked to scream.

Gannon smiled at her, his face unreadable in the dim light. "A pretty thing, isn't it?" he said, lifting the head by the mane. "A pretty thing to show the folk who didn't think Rakastava could be defeated, even by me."

"It wasn't *you* who fought . . . ." Aria whispered. Even she couldn't be certain whether she was denying his statement or begging him to confirm it. It had been dark. . . .

Gannon still held her arm. His grip tightened. "Not me, Aria? *Not* me? Princess, I fought a monster that no one else could face, much less defeat. It was a terrible fight, though I won it, and—were anyone to deny me my honor, Princess, I can't answer for what I might do to them in a fit of righteous indignation. To *anyone*, Princess."

Gannon's fingers continued to squeeze, harder and harder as he spoke. Aria's face worked in pain, expecting the big man's thumb and fingers to meet through the flesh of her arm.

He released her suddenly. "We wouldn't want that, would we, Aria?" he said as softly as a cat purring. He lifted Rakastava's head, staring at it instead of at the princess. "That wouldn't be a good thing at all."

Aria wasn't sure whether or not Gannon was the hero who had saved her.

But she was quite sure that he meant his velvet threat to murder her if she spoke her doubts to anyone else.

"No," she said in a calm voice, massaging her smarting arm with her other hand. "That won't happen, Champion Gannon."

Gannon's teeth were a gleam in the pale lighting. "Not so formal, my dearest," he said. "Now, let's go and display my triumph to the others."

CHAPTER 47

Dennis smoothed the new trousers over his thighs as he and Chester walked down the corridor to the assembly hall. He squeezed the big muscles at the back of his thighs, trying to rub some of the ache out of them.

"Even with the armor and the sword," he said softly, "I thought I was gone there, Chester. I thought it would . . ."

His tongue didn't finish the sentence. Clear in his mind was the image of a chicken's wishbone, being pulled apart between the fingers of two children.

"He who runs from evil," the robot said, "finds evil waiting for him."

"I ran from Emath's evil, Chester," Dennis replied. "Not my own."

The door opened, just as cheering filled the assembly hall as thoroughly as human throats could manage.

"Rakastava is dead!" Gannon shouted. He raised the severed head so that everyone in the room could understand him, whether or not they could hear his words.

Dennis paused. Gannon, Conall, and Aria were alone

at the table where Dennis had sat on previous nights. The remainder of Conall's glittering "guards" were divided among the tables to either side; and Gannon stood now between the seated king and princess.

Conall glanced back and saw Dennis. He gestured the youth to a seat among the guards.

"And now, King Conall," cried the champion, turning to the older man beside him. He lowered Rakastava's head so that its weight rested on the table. The stump smudged the smooth surface.

"In recognition of my saving your daughter—and in saving all of us for the future from the monster's exactions—I claim the Princess Aria in marriage."

"*No!*" gasped Dennis.

"*Hurrah!*" cried the nearest citizens.

"*Hurrah!*" the shout went on in an arc expanding around the circle of tables. Someone threw a hat; the air began to spin with bright cloth.

Gannon took Aria's hand. She resisted his pull for a moment, then rose to her feet. Her face was turned aside and toward the floor.

"I request that our wedding be held at—"

The assembly hall was growing darker.

"—once!"

Rakastava's laughter boomed through the sudden hush.

"Humans, humans," called the monster's glowing image from the center of the hall. "You are not yet free of Rakastava."

Gannon tried to release the severed head. His fingers were wrapped in strands of the mane. His hand twitched with increasing violence, like that of a man who's touched something foul and sticky.

"In the morning," continued the image, "the Princess Aria must return to me . . . and with her must return my head."

Only the head on the creature's central neck was speaking. The stump hung limp, though at least in hologram there was no sign of the blood that had spurted from it earlier.

Dennis thrust his right hand into the side pocket of his trousers as he watched Rakastava.

"And the champion who fights for the princess may come or may not come," said Rakastava in a voice as close to a caress as a roar could be. "It is all the same to me. But if he comes, he will stay."

"Ooh . . ." murmured the crowd as the lights brightened and the threatening image faded away. All eyes were on Gannon.

The King's Champion was shaking.

And in his pocket, Dennis fingered Aria's crystal ring.

CHAPTER 48

Chester's tentacles closed the two halves of the star-metal helmet over his master's head.

"Gannon sneers at me," the youth said. "He and I both know he's a coward, but *he* sneers at *me*."

"There is no remedy for the sting of a fool's tongue, Dennis," the robot quoted. A latch clicked as it locked together the helmet's hinged segments.

The mirror showed the cavern beneath Rakastava—beneath Rakastava's city. It seemed even darker than it had the morning before; but Dennis' eyes had adapted then, and they would adapt again today, he was sure.

It wasn't as though he had to see for any distance, after all.

Aria was waiting at the bottom of the stairs. The severed head lay on the stone beside her, but Gannon was nowhere to be seen.

Dennis shifted his stance, making sure that all the joints and fastenings of his armor were firm but flexible. He slid his sword, a ribbon of reflected gray dawnlight, from its battered sheath.

"Chester," he said without looking at his companion. "I wonder if you'd—you know, help me today if I need help."

"If you ask my help, Dennis, I will give it," Chester replied.

"I didn't think to do that yesterday," Dennis admitted, skirting the question of whether Chester would have come to his aid *without* being asked. "I—anyway, it won't be as bad today. He's—it's been wounded."

"Today's fight will be twice as fierce as yesterday's fight, Dennis," said Chester quietly. "If you struggled then, then you will strain indeed today."

"It's time," said the youth, gripping his sword as he stepped into the cavern washed by the waves of the monster's approach. Sound echoed crushingly about him.

Aria stepped forward when the youth in black armor splashed out of the darkness. Her lips moved as she called something, but the words were inaudible and unnecessary.

Dennis motioned her back with an imperious wave of his sword, toward the darkness that hid Gannon and would preserve Aria from the wild thrashings of the battle to come.

Rakastava's whole body glowed a deep red, like the surface of a banked fire in the early morning.

The stump had withered like a snake's cast skin. The creature slid forward with its two remaining heads raised high, a great one and a lesser one to the side. The tongues flickered, and the manes flowed with the dark sheen of cobalt glaze.

As before, the creature glided to a halt just short of the coping. "Did you bring my head, little human?" the central head asked Dennis.

"Your head is here, Rakastava," Dennis shouted through his visor.

"And I will put the others with it when I take them."

The mouth of the lesser head opened so wide that the lower jaw pointed to the water and the upper jaw to the cavern's distance-shrouded roof. Dennis braced himself.

Instead of striking directly at him, the open gullet spewed an arc of liquid against his chest.

Dennis staggered. Where the heavy fluid spattered onto the sea, water fizzed and sputtered.

Where it struck the floor and coping, stone cracked and bubbled away in white foam.

The main head opened its jaws part-way. Dennis advanced, raising his sword for a stroke, not a thrust, at the knot of scale-armored muscle where the head met the neck.

Lightning bathed him; his ears rang with the shock of thunder.

Dennis' armor protected him from the worst effects of the thunderbolt as it had from the gout of acid, but his eyes were flash-stunned and his skin was momentarily too full of needle-prickling pain to have any feeling. He stabbed out blindly, knowing he was about to be swept beneath Rakastava's rush—

And amazed, an instant later when he could see, to find the monster in the slim, serpentine tentacles of Chester, who was trying to clamp shut both fanged mouths at the same time.

Rakastava's forepaw gripped the robot's carapace and slammed Chester down in the shallow water. Dennis rocked forward, aiming his sword again for the blow the shock had forestalled.

The forked, suckered tongue from the lesser head caught Dennis' sword-wrist. The stroke chopped scales and drew blood from the main neck, but it didn't bite deeply enough to do fatal harm.

Lightning blasted Chester as the robot writhed in Rakastava's clawed grip.

A scallop of sea vaporized in the sizzling flash. Instead of a natural shore, Dennis could see a pavement of fitted stones extending outward at a steep slope.

The blast threw Chester into the air. The robot's

limbs thrashed in mindless convulsions with blue sparks popping from their tips.

Dennis didn't let his conscious mind consider what the battle might already have cost him. His eyes gauged the distance and angle. Then, with all his strength and the pull of Rakastava's own tongue to aid, he struck a backhand blow at the neck of the head which held him.

The core of the stroke was his heart's memory of Chester flailing in blue fire.

The sword bit clean and deep. The tongue gripping Dennis jerked the youth to his knees in the instant before the retracting muscles went limp and the fire died from the two blazing eyes.

The newly-severed neck spasmed. Acid sprayed out as from a hose; Dennis covered the slots in his visor with his left forearm, hearing the droplets snap and burn as they runneled off the armor.

Rakastava's remaining head reared. Dennis braced himself against the lightning he expected when the mouth opened.

"Two are off, but one is on, human," the monster thundered. "The third day is my day."

The serpent body pulsed a brighter red with each syllable; the sea around Rakastava began to steam. As the monster sank into the deeps, Dennis could follow its glowing descent for hundreds of feet through the dark water.

Chester curled a tentacle around his master's armored ankle and pulled himself up onto the coping. The robot's carapace was unscarred, but the eight limbs trembled noticeably as Chester lifted himself.

"Water extinguishes the fire," he muttered. "But the water boils as well."

Dennis hugged him.

Echoes died; the sea settled back to turgid calm. The loudest sounds in the cavern were Dennis' dragging breaths. His sword trilled as he sheathed it.

Aria was walking toward them. Her slippers whispered on the wet stone, and the jewel between her breasts spun with a light as clean and yellow as the sun.

"Go back!" Dennis called.

The cavern was very dark now. The princess was a blur without shape, dress and streaming blond hair merged in paleness.

"Are you all right?" she asked. She continued to approach.

The sea had not yet settled into a mirrored surface by which Dennis could make his escape. He lifted Rakastava's two heads and carried them toward the princess. He stepped slowly and his boots rang on the pavement, weighted by the trophies and the youth's exhaustion.

Aria's hand touched his armor, his visor.

"Go back," he repeated.

Dennis bent and began to knot together the manes. There was still a tinge of glowing color in the strands from the head he had taken off minutes before, but the other mane was as lifeless as asbestos fibers growing from a cliff face.

"Please," Aria said. "Come back with me."

He shook his head violently. The slotted visor brushed her away.

"Go on," he said. "Take these and go."

He lifted her hand in one of his and transferred the weight of the joined trophies to her. The manes' hard strands pressed deep into her bare palm.

"Wait," she said as Dennis backed from her. She reached up with her free hand, too proud to drop the heads first, and fussed within her hair.

"Here," she said. The earring she handed him chinked against the black armor of Dennis' palm.

The youth turned and strode for the reflection on the water. Chester waited for his master, much as he had the day before; but this time on the cavern-side of the mirror.

Together, hand and tentacle linked, they stepped into the water—

And stumbled out in the hut that had been Malbawn's.

Dennis raised his visor and rested, panting, while Chester clicked and tapped and spun the armor's fastenings. The earring was of crystal so brilliant that at some angles its core seemed to move the way the pendant nestled on Aria's breast did.

Chester lifted the helmet off.

"Tonight at the banquet," Dennis said, "Gannon'll brag again that he's slain the monster."

"The donkey is not praised for braying while it carries a load, Dennis," the robot said. He slipped off the left gauntlet, then paused with the right while the youth transferred the earring to his bare hand.

"He'll be praised," Dennis said grimly. "And she'll . . . Chester, when that lying coward sneers at me, I'd like to split him all the way open!"

"It is better to bless someone than to harm one who has insulted you, Dennis," said Chester as he snicked away the brassard, cubitiere, and vambrace from his master's left arm, leaving it bare from shoulder to wrist.

"Why does *she* lie for him, Chester?" Dennis said, closing his eyes because he was afraid he might begin to cry with frustration.

"Aria tells no lies, Dennis," Chester replied, stripping the youth's right arm with two tentacles while two others freed the gorget and epaulets from Dennis' neck and shoulders. "And if it is not the whole truth she tells—then the princess knows nothing for a certainty, and little enough even by conjecture."

Dennis sighed. "If I told them the truth, Chester," he said, "they'd call me a liar."

"Would the princess call you a liar, Dennis?" the robot asked softly. He unfastened the hinged plates that had covered Dennis' back and chest.

When Dennis' torso was free again to expand and twist without the armor's constriction, memory of the battle he'd fought began to blur away. It was as if he'd dreamed it, the acid and the vision of Chester flailing in the blue-white grip of a thunderbolt. . . .

"What good would that do, Chester?" Dennis whispered. "Her knowing and me knowing . . . There's nothing we could do to change the others' minds."

"Lift your foot," said the robot, "that I may take off your boots, Dennis."

"We'll go back to the city," the youth said in a reverie. His mind was melding what had happened yesterday and today with what would happen tomorrow. "We'll see. And if Rakastava returns— "

"As Rakastava will return, Dennis; depend on it."

"—then they'll *all* see."

CHAPTER 49

Dennis sat at the end of a table adjacent to the one now reserved for Gannon, Conall—and Aria.

The trophies, their manes knotted together, rested on the board before the King's Champion. The jaws of the head severed the day before were open. The tongue had lolled out and was beginning to shrivel. A faint odor of decay permeated the air near Gannon.

"Say," said the middle-aged man next to Dennis on the bench. "You're the boy who herds the cows, aren't you?"

Dennis looked at him. "I herd the cows, yes," he said softly. "What is it that *you* do?"

The man's hair swept back like the waves of a calm, gray sea. His moustache and beard were full and perfectly kept. "Why," he said, tapping his breastplate, "I'm Dalquin. I'm a member of the King's Guard."

The breastplate was silver, delicately etched with scenes of hunting. Dennis couldn't recognize many of the animals being pursued through the stylized forest, nor were the shapes of the trees familiar to him.

The silver was soft and thin enough to pierce with a dinner fork. It flexed slightly where it attempted to confine Dalquin's paunch.

"Yes," Dennis said. "But what do you *do?*"

Before the non-plussed citizen could find an answer, Gannon stood up at the royal table. Rakastava's heads wobbled as Gannon lifted them as high as his arm could reach, buoyed by the cheering room.

Dennis looked from the champion to Aria, seated at Gannon's left side as though she were already his queen. She met Dennis' eyes briefly, then stared at her folded hands instead.

Gannon let the heads drop with a thump. King Conall jumped a little. He wore a smile that became a little doubtful whenever his control slipped.

"I have defeated the monster again," Gannon cried, pausing for the enthusiastic response from citizens whose hearts turned cold at the very thought of following the steps down into the dank, deadly cavern beneath the city.

"When the monster realized that I was getting the better of him again," the champion continued with a meaningful glance at Aria, "he tried to slip past and take the princess instead of facing me. I forestalled him—but it was a near thing."

Aria's fingers were interlaced in her lap. The tips squeezed white dimples on the backs of the opposite hand. In all the great hall, only she and Gannon understood the threat—

And Dennis, watching them and toying with the pommel of his sword.

"If the monster dares return—" Gannon continued; but his voice broke and his face went sallow as the lights dimmed.

The champion sat down as suddenly as if he'd been hamstrung. Everyone watched the center of the hall.

Everyone except Aria and Dennis.

"Little men, little men," Rakastava thundered. "Do you think you've cause to cheer?"

Nothing but echoes answered the creature.

Dennis raised his eyes from Aria's perfect beauty. Both of Rakastava's injured necks had shriveled away to stubs that wobbled when the creature's body moved. The right forelimb extended slowly, shooting out its glittering claws as if for the citizens to admire them.

Rakastava's body was an orange blaze. The eyes in its remaining head were pits down to the red heart of anger.

"Mark the Princess Aria well tonight," said the glowing image. "For tomorrow morning she must come to me, and you will never see her again . . . or her champion."

The hot orange light beating from Rakastava's image was brighter than the normal lighting that returned as the creature faded back into the air.

Citizens got up from their benches and began to mill and stretch. Dalquin walked over to Gannon and clapped the champion on the shoulder, blustering words of congratulation and certainty.

At least Dalquin could be sure that *he* wouldn't be facing Rakastava alone in the morning.

Well, Gannon wouldn't be facing the monster alone either; but Gannon couldn't be sure of that or of anything except his own fear.

"Chester," the youth said to the robot curled at his feet, "I think it's time for us—"

"Prince Dennis," said Aria. "How are you finding your stay in our city?"

She was standing beside him. Dennis hadn't seen her get up from her seat. From the black look the King's Champion was giving the pair of them, Gannon hadn't noticed either—until Aria was already beyond his ability to stop her without a public scene.

"Comfortable, lady," the youth replied. He avoided a stutter by not looking up into Aria's eyes until he'd gotten the first syllables out. "Very comfortable."

"I'm glad to hear that," she said. "You're looking

worn, you see. I wouldn't want it on my conscience—in the morning, you see—that we of this city had been remiss in the way we dealt with an honored guest."

Dennis felt his face color. He wanted to get up, but Aria was standing so close that he'd bump her if he tried. He slid a few inches down the bench, into the area Dalquin had vacated.

Golden combs caught Aria's hair and swept it across her right ear and shoulder, concealing the fact that she wore only one earring. She toyed with the thick, lustrous strands as she continued, "You know, it was rather odd. I thought I saw your little friend, there, battling Rakastava this morning."

Her open-toed sandal indicated but did not quite touch Chester's carapace.

"I'm sorry, lady," Dennis said, rising as he now had room to do. "You must be mistaken. Chester was with me this morning; and I was in the pasture as always, with the herd."

"No doubt," the princess agreed with icy unconcern. She tossed her head. "I must be getting back to Gannon. After all, he's saved my life twice already. It's a small thing, isn't it, that he have my body in exchange?"

Dennis' expression shrank into a bony grimace. "As you wish, milady," he managed to say.

When Aria did not move for a moment, he added, "Princess? I wish you well in the morning."

Her face softened. "Thank you, Dennis," she said. "And I wish you and your friend well."

She turned around very quickly; but Dennis thought, as he strode for the door and his room, that Aria had begun to cry.

CHAPTER 50

The helmet locked over Dennis' head.

"Well, this is it," he muttered to himself. "I'll finish it, kill it for good and all, or—or . . ."

"The fool who wanders, Dennis," Chester quoted sharply, "loves neither peace nor the man of peace."

Dennis drew his sword. "I'm sorry, Chester," he said. "I don't—know what I want."

"Is it losing that you want, Dennis?" the robot asked.

"No. No, I'm not here to lose. Not that."

"Then you know what you want, Dennis; and the rest will follow."

The mirror's surface was almost black. The ambient light in the cavern had faded with each blow Dennis struck Rakastava. Aria was as faintly visible as a tuft of thistledown floating over a dark sea.

Something sunbright appeared in the cavern's distance.

Dennis locked his visor down. "Chester," he said softly. "Come with me, my friend, and we'll finish Rakastava this morning."

"As fate wills it," the robot said. He touched a gauntlet.

The companions stepped together into battle and a darkness already thundering with Rakastava's voice.

The serpent body glided in a cloud of steam, like a bead of sodium skittering in a bowl of water. Rakastava glowed a bright yellow-white. It was a fierce, foul color like that of gases blazing above the crevice of a volcano.

Rakastava's eyes had no texture. They were pure light and pure hatred.

Dennis felt motion beside him. Aria touched Dennis on the shoulder.

If she was trying to speak, he couldn't hear the words over the monster's wordless threatening; but Dennis wasn't sure that she spoke, just touched him.

He waved her back. Aria bent closer and kissed the bars of his visor, then stepped away to give Dennis the room he needed for slaughter.

Rakastava blazed like sour daylight as it came closer, illuminating angles of the cavern that had been dark for all previous eternity. The severed heads glinted where they lay on the coping, scales catching light and reflecting it as if they crawled with life and not decay.

Water surged ahead of Rakastava's approach. It caught and tumbled the trophies, then receded. The dead jaws gaped and the tongues lolled out—flaccid, now, and harmless.

Chester gave back the light with a sheen like gold, and Dennis could see Rakastava's glowing reflection elongated in the star-metal blade of his sword.

"I have not come to kill you, human," the creature boomed. "Let me past and I will let you live."

"You won't kill me, Rakastava," Dennis shouted. "And if you try to pass me, you will surely die!"

Rakastava's neck swayed slowly, side to side. The vertical bars of Dennis' visor turned the movements into slots of dark and light at the corners of his eyes, threatening to mesmerize the youth. He blinked.

Rakastava lunged at him.

Chester looped a tentacle around the blunt, scaly

muzzle and kept the jaws from opening. The head struck Dennis like the tide racing through a bore, slamming him down. His armor rang with the impact and on the stone he fell back against.

Dennis couldn't remember where he was. It was too bright. He was in a cavern of gray, dripping stone that he'd never seen before, struggling with a fiery serpent instead of a thing of shadow.

He rose to his feet. His skin prickled all over, but his muscles responded like the parts of a machine.

Like a machine. Rakastava's mouth was open. The suckers of his tongue clasped Chester's body while the robot's metal tentacles wrapped around the monster's neck. Chester was trying to prevent Rakastava from twisting him down so that a forefoot could crush his carapace against the stone.

Dennis, seeing that the monster was fully occupied, took one step forward and thrust with a surgeon's precision at the joint of Rakastava's head and neck.

Sullen red beams shot from the monster's eyes. They clung to Dennis like streams of bird-lime. He cried out, but his movements were as slow as a swimmer's. He tried to reach Rakastava before—

Foreclaws locked around the small metal egg of Chester's body. The robot's tentacles resisted for a moment, but the monster's relentless grip broke them loose at last.

Rakastava banged Chester down on the coping like a lizard smashing open a bird's egg. Chips of stone spalled away. Chester wrapped his tentacles around the foreleg that held him, trying to pry loose the claws.

Rakastava struck the robot again while the red eyes glared at Dennis.

Where the light touched his armor, the star metal grew hot. Dennis twisted.

The beams from Rakastava's eyes slipped from the polished black surface, allowing the youth to lunge forward unexpectedly. Dennis was off-balance and almost as surprised as the monster, so his stroke was an inexpert one—

But driven by the hysterical strength of his fear for his companion. The sword's keen edge split scales and the flesh of Rakastava's forearm. It stuck in one of the bones instead of slicing through the gristle of a joint as it would have done had skill rather than desperation aimed the blow.

But the bone cracked.

Rakastava howled like sheets of rock sliding past one another in an earthquake.

Chester rolled free, scuttling as if he were a mouse after the cat has gouged it deep. Dennis braced himself, panting and flexing his arms. His armor cooled slowly; and, in cooling, it heated the flesh it had protected.

Rakastava squirmed toward the youth. The movement might have been intended as a feint, because when Dennis stood his ground, the monster didn't press the attack home.

The eyes focused on Dennis. The youth trembled with adrenalin, waiting to squirm free of the immaterial grip before he cooked in his casing of undamaged metal.

Waiting to strike home and feel his blade grate through the vertebrae of Rakastava's remaining neck.

The beams of light pinned Chester to the ground.

Dennis lunged. Rakastava's left foreleg hung useless, oozing fiery blood, but the right leg shot out and hooked its claws around Dennis' foot as he slid forward to support his thrust.

The youth skidded. His sword cut a jagged, empty arc in the air above him.

Rakastava's eyes drew Chester, rasping and sparking on the stone, close to the massive serpent body while Dennis struggled to get up. When the robot was directly in front of Rakastava, the good foreleg clamped firmly around Chester's carapace.

Dennis swung, but the eyes' red beams jerked at his arm. He stumbled forward; the stroke went aside.

Rakastava's eyes held the sword arm up at an angle. "Now you will die, little human," the creature said as its jaws crashed shut on Dennis' neck and torso.

The black metal belled but didn't give under the pressure. Rakastava's teeth squealed vainly against the armor.

Dennis was sweating from heat and exertion. The vambrace covering his right forearm looked red when he saw it through the visor slots. He couldn't be sure whether the metal was glowing or just colored by the bloody light that bathed it.

The monster stopped chewing on the refractory metal and jerked its head back while the eyes still pulled at Dennis' wrist. The two antagonists were only inches apart, both panting. Rakastava's breath was a hot, moist cloud through the visor.

"Could I but close your eyes, Rakastava," Dennis shouted as his arm pulsed, "I'd have your head off."

"Could I but wrench your helmet off, human," Rakastava boomed, "I'd suck you from your armor like the meat from a shrimp. And so I *shall!*"

The sucker-knobbed tongue flicked out. One fork groped to either side of Dennis' neck.

He heard the click of a latch opening. The suckers began to tug apart the halves of the helmet.

Something fell over the combatants' heads like a white cloud.

Dennis thought he'd been blinded by panic—or else his vision went white when the monster's tongue broke his neck—

But his sword arm was free, and he brought the blade around with all the strength he'd put into vainly fighting the grip of Rakastava's eyes.

He expected the monster to scream as the blade bit deep, but there was silence except for the banging of

scales on stone and the crash Dennis' own body made
when Rakastava thrust him away convulsively.

Dennis lay on his back. He'd lost his helmet. He
pushed himself up into a reclining position on his left
elbow.

His right arm burned, but there was nothing he
could do for it except ignore the pain.

Rakastava was a writhing shape where the sea met
stone. The harsh, damning light had faded almost en-
tirely from the supple body.

The hologram in the assembly hall had been decep-
tive: Rakastava was much longer than Dennis had
guessed. Now he saw the tail flailing against the cavern
roof, a hundred feet in the air.

Rakastava hadn't roared at the final sword-stroke,
because its third head lay on the stone beside Dennis.
Wrapping the head was the white gauze dress of the
Princess Aria.

Dennis looked around. The only light in the cavern
was the purple glow of Rakastava's mane, and even that
was dying as the creature itself had died.

Aria was rising to her feet. Foul, faint illumination
could not make her naked body look less than beautiful.

There was blood on her face.

"You're hurt!" Dennis blurted, forgetting his own
pain for the moment. He got up, and the effort of
moving his right arm reminded him of everything.

Aria touched two fingers to her lips. They came down
dabbed with blood. "I didn't feel anything," she said.
"You said, 'Could I close your eyes . . .' And so I
covered its eyes."

Darkness hid the princess, but Dennis felt the warmth
of her body—through his armor, through his pain. His
hand reached for her; then he remembered that he
wore star-metal gauntlets, and that she wore nothing
but golden sandals.

Dennis turned and, with his left hand, lifted the
newly-severed head by its mane. He unwrapped the

dress as carefully as he could from the angles and pointed scales. The gossamer fabric was already torn, and dim light made the task still harder.

"Ah, here," he said, holding the rescued garment with his eyes averted—though Aria was only a pale shape in the shadows, and he'd stared at her nude body in clear light through the mirror.

But then she didn't know.

Dennis busied himself with knotting together the manes of all three heads. The whisk of air indicated the princess was dressing beside him.

She stepped very close. "Come up with me," she said. "Now."

"No," Dennis whispered. His voice caught in his throat, making it sound like a growl. "G-give me your earring."

Aria reached into the cascade of her hair and came down with a faint sparkle that clinked into Dennis' gauntlet. Then she put both arms around his neck and kissed him.

"Oh!" Dennis said, backing as though she wore armor and he only gauze. "Oh," and he turned, striding to the sea's edge. Rakastava was stone silent, but waves kicked and spattered like the echoes of its thrashing.

A low spot on the stone floor had collected a puddle, shallow and still. Chester crouched beside it, holding Dennis' helmet; and beyond him, silhouetting his egg-shaped body, was the faint rectangle on the mirroring water. They stepped through together without leaving even a splash in the cavern behind them.

Dennis sat on the mud and dried bones of Malbawn's hut, his head bent and his elbows resting on his knees. He knew he'd have to stand up for Chester to finish stripping off the armor, but for now . . .

He licked his lips and tasted blood.

"She risked her life, Chester," he said. "I had armor and my sword, but she had nothing at all when she closed with Rakastava."

"That is so, Dennis,'" the robot agreed as catches snicked and loosened beneath his touch. Dennis realized how warm the right vambrace still remained when it came away and cool air bathed his forearm again.

He stood up. When Chester had lifted clear the cuisses that guarded his thighs, Dennis reached into his side pocket and brought out the other bits of jewelry to join the earring in his palm. Looking at them and not his companion, the youth said, "Chester, I think I love her."

"Oh, aye," Chester agreed as he loosened the greaves. "And will love her forever, Dennis; for that was the spell of Cariad, was it not? And you tasted her blood on your lips, to seal the spell."

Dennis licked his lips again. Only the salty memory remained.

"Whatever," he said. But love remained also.

CHAPTER 51

The assembly hall was vibrant with banners and the boisterous enthusiasm of the citizens of Rakastava. Dennis had not been sure the city would survive the death of its ancient ruler, but the tables arranged themselves with food and beverages just as before.

Dalquin nudged Dennis and pointed to Gannon as the champion stood up at the royal table. "Truly a great hero," the guardsman murmured. "To tell the truth, lad—Gannon has a fine figure, but I wouldn't have thought he had *that* in him. Rose to the occasion, you might say."

"Oh, the true Gannon must be a surprise to many," Dennis said in what the citizen thought was agreement.

Dennis had expected to be nervous. Instead he felt loose and dangerous, much as he had done the morning he swaggered into the hut of Mother Grimes. Something was going to happen. He wasn't sure what; but he was sure that he'd be in the middle of it.

And that it was better than standing by, leaving events to others.

263

The cheers that greeted Gannon's rise died away. King Conall still had a doubtful expression as he looked up at the champion.

Aria's upper lip was swollen and slightly cut. The injury made an odd background to her sardonic smile.

The princess wasn't staring at her folded hands this evening. Her gaze wandered across the hall; to the serpent heads on the table; and occasionally to the King's Champion, standing beside her.

When she looked up at Gannon, her smile grew broader.

"Fellow citizens!" Gannon cried. "I have slain the monster!"

The assembly cheered, as though their cheers in the past two days had been only practice for the real victory. Dennis noted a few furtive glances toward the center of the hall. Some of the citizens wondered whether this celebration, too, might not be premature.

The doubters were wrong. This time, Rakastava was really dead.

"King Conall," Gannon continued, looking down at his titular monarch, "I claim your daughter as my bride tonight!"

Aria stood up, unsummoned. She lifted her hair away from her shoulders with both hands, displaying her lack of earrings.

"Father," she said in a clear voice, "I gave my crystal ring and earrings to the hero who slew Rakastava. Gannon, will you return the jewels to me now?"

Gannon's face went dark with blood and fury. "Later, Princess," he said. "In our bedroom."

Aria let her hair fall.

"Very well," she agreed. "But do me one thing, noble Gannon. The hero who slew Rakastava bound the manes of the three trophies. Do thou separate them here, so that all can see proof of thy prowess."

Gannon drew his sword.

Dennis was on his feet, but the champion's intent

was not the murder he had threatened if Aria denied him. He waved the shining blade high and called to the assembly, "Indeed, I will separate the heads—as I separated them in life from the living monster!"

He brought his blade down with a crash, hacking the knot against the table like a butcher jointing meat on a chopping block.

When Gannon lifted his sword again, the steel edge was notched and the glass-hard manes were as they had been before the vain stroke. The King's Champion gaped at his blade.

Dennis stepped forward, remembering his own shock when he cut at Malbawn's forearm with the Founder's Sword and succeeded only in putting a thumb-deep notch in the steel. Now the blade he held bare was truly star metal, and in his left hand—

"Princess Aria!" Dennis called. "I believe these are yours."

He held his left hand high. When he opened his fist, everyone in the hall could see the crystal jewelry tumble into her cupped palm.

There was a gasp so general that it seemed the room itself drew in a breath.

"And these—" Dennis went on.

He expected Gannon to try to stop him as he reached for the joined heads. Instead, the King's Champion only watched. Perhaps he was still stunned by events; perhaps he was arrogant enough to think his failure was everyone's certain failure.

The weight of Rakastava's lifeless heads was nothing to muscles as charged with adrenalin as Dennis' were. He lifted them high, his thumb and forefinger locked in the nostrils of the freshest trophy and the other two dangling like charms from a bracelet.

Dennis brought his sword around. The knot sang like a lute-string parting. Two heads bumped and jounced onto the table, then rolled to the floor. Dennis waved the third higher yet, then hurled it toward the center of the hall.

"*Dennis!*" Aria screamed.

He turned, and Gannon cut down at his skull.

But Gannon was a courtier, while Dennis was a swordsman whose skill and reflexes had been honed to a wire edge around and beneath this city. He raised his own long blade without having to think about it, a blocking motion and not a lethal stroke.

Dennis didn't need to kill the King's Champion. Gannon had nothing, and Dennis had everything his heart desired.

The swords met at the cross-guards, the thickest part of the metal. Gannon's blade rang in two notes, the stump in his hand vibrating at one frequency and the rest of the steel quivering an undamped song as it spun to the floor.

Dennis put his left arm around the princess. "King Conall," he said formally. "I guarded your herds. I slew Rakastava to save your daughter. Now I ask you for your daughter's hand, for I love her."

He looked at Aria, nestled against his side. "If she will have me," he added.

Aria put her arms around Dennis' neck again and kissed him in the sight of all.

Gannon flung down the hilt of his weapon and ran toward a door. The remainder of the honor guard had been seated nearby. With Dalquin in the lead, half a dozen of them grabbed their one-time champion.

"Kill him!" somebody called. A thousand throats echoed the demand.

Dennis raised his sword so that its point seemed to threaten the high ceiling. "Wait!" he cried; and as the hall quieted, "Wait!" again.

"You don't need Gannon here," he said to the faces watching him fervently. "But you don't need his blood on your hands either."

He was like all the rest of you, Dennis thought but did not say. *Only more so*.

"Put him in the jungle. He'll survive, if he wants to. And maybe it'll even make a man of him."

As it did me.

King Conall looked at Dennis, then at Gannon. He nodded toward the guards. "Yes," he said. "Do so."

The guards hustled Gannon toward an archway, the corridor by which Dennis had first been led into the assembly hall. Gannon began to kick, but they lifted him off the ground with many hands. Then he began to scream, but the sound was drunk by the vast hall and the loud joy of all those around him.

Dennis sheathed his sword so that he could put both arms around Aria. Citizens were crowding the couple on three sides—but not the fourth, where Chester perched high on his limbs.

"Are you smiling, my friend?" Dennis said to the robot's featureless carapace.

"There is no blame in using the portion of happiness fate gives you, Dennis," quoted Chester approvingly.

And the crowd cheered its enthusiastic approval of the royal wedding.

CHAPTER 52

Gannon was in shadow.

Something called out in the jungle. The sun was still high, but it was behind the massive pile of Rakastava.

Gannon looked over his shoulder. There was no help in dark vegetation and vines with spikes like spearpoints. He battered his fists at the slick surface of the city in which he had been born and raised, the city that had been his whole life.

He pounded while he had the strength in his arms, and he screamed as long as his voice lasted. The shadows lengthened. The sky grew black.

And the jungle behind Gannon began to whisper with more than the sound of wind rustling the leaves.

CHAPTER 53

The walls of the bedchamber counterfeited morning light. Dennis stretched luxuriously as Aria nuzzled his chest.

As his wife nuzzled him.

"I'd like to go see the, the pasture, this morning," he said.

Aria lifted her head and pouted, mostly as a joke. "Two days and tired of me already?" she said.

Dennis touched the white line on her upper lip, the only remaining sign of the cut she had received there. "Never, my love," he said. "Never."

She didn't understand the significance of his touching her lip, but no one could doubt the sincerity in Dennis' voice.

"Anyway," Dennis went on, "I thought you might come with me. There are some things I'd like to show you."

"Outside . . ." Aria said in a tone that Dennis couldn't read.

"It, ah . . ." Dennis said. "I suppose it could be dangerous. It *could* be dangerous."

"More dangerous than beneath the city, with Rakastava?"

"No, not—" he started to reply, but she smothered his seriousness with laughter and a kiss.

After a time, they both got dressed.

CHAPTER 54

One of the cows mooed in approval as Dennis led Aria and Chester into the clearing. The princess gasped and shaded her face with her hands.

"Are you all right?" Dennis asked quickly.

"Yes, I'm . . ." she said. "It's just that I never *saw* this before. The sun, directly."

Then she added, "Dennis? Could you be happy, living in Rakastava?"

"Do not let your tongue differ from your heart when you are asked for counsel, Dennis," Chester said.

Dennis laughed without humor.

"Love," he said, "I can be adequately happy wherever you are. But if that means Rakastava, I will be happy despite the city."

"Then perhaps we should go back to where you came from, Dennis," Aria said coolly. She put her arm around him. "Would that be better?"

"I don't know," he admitted. "Let's—look at something in Malbawn's hut. I came here to do that anyway."

Scavengers and decay had scoured Malbawn's corpse

into a heap of chitinous plates, yellowish and translucent. Aria paused by the hut's opening and stared at them.

"That was. . . ?" she said.

"Yes."

She took a deep breath. "I'm sorry," she said without emotion.

"Love, that was the first. There were two more that were no one's choice but my own." Dennis kissed her and held her soft body in his arms.

"I left Emath thinking that only a great hero would dare the jungle—and I was wrong. But don't be sorry because—your community gave me the chance to be what I left home saying I wanted."

Aria gasped when she saw the armor standing articulated, to the left of the sagging doorway. "Oh!" she said. "He's the one who—"

Chester tapped the armor with a tentacle so that the hollow metal rang.

"Oh," the princess repeated, but with understanding. "It's empty."

"It's the armor I wore—when you saw me," Dennis explained.

"But how did you. . . ?" Aria began, pausing at her husband's broad smile.

"You wanted to see where I came from," Dennis said. He was proud that what he could now demonstrate would amaze even a princess familiar with Rakastava's sophistication. "Mirror, show us Emath."

The glass clouded and cleared, above the sun-struck crystal beauty of Emath Palace. The pendant on Aria's breast spun more swiftly, as if it were trying to match the dazzling scene in the mirror.

"Oh . . ." the princess breathed. From the way she looked aside to him, Dennis knew that in her heart she'd doubted until now his tales of the palace in which he'd been raised.

"Closer," Dennis ordered. "Show us the village."

The mirror's point of view shifted down, toward the shingled roofs and half-timbered houses that had grown up around the palace and the prosperity of community Hale ruled. A twelve-foot demon of smoke and orange flames turned to face them.

Aria started but did not cry out. Dennis had his sword drawn a hand's breadth before intellect over-ruled reflex. The demon was not *here*. . . .

Two men in orange livery were entering a shop. The demon followed them as far as the door, bending to stare within as it gripped the jamb with either hand. No one else was visible on the street, though faces peered furtively through upper-floor shutters.

After a moment, the liverymen returned. Both were laughing as one dropped coins into the fat purse on his belt. They walked around the corner, the hulking de-mon behind them. Only when the trio was out of sight did other citizens appear cautiously from doorways.

"That's where you lived?" Aria asked, as careful as she could be to keep the distaste out of her voice.

"That isn't where I lived," Dennis said, his hand still playing with the pommel of his sword. "It's—what's become of the place in which I lived.

"Show me my father!" he added harshly.

The mirrored scene tilted dizzyingly through angles and the walls of the palace. It settled on King Hale, staring from a balcony out at the harbor. There was trash and litter on the floor with him. Beyond the double doors into the royal suite was a wrack of garbage and clothing left where it had been cast aside. Hale's cheeks were sunken; there were dark rings around his eyes.

As Dennis watched, his father took a drink from the squat green bottle in his right hand; but there was no life in his face, even at that.

"Enough!" Dennis shouted.

He didn't have to ask to see the throne room. He knew what—and who—he would find there.

Aria leaned softly against his arm. "Can you show me Rakastava, Dennis?" she asked, as though she were unaware of the tumbling fury in the mind of the man who loved her.

Dennis took a shuddering breath. "Mirror, show us King Conall," he directed, as willing as she to get his mind away from what was happening in Emath.

Conall was on his throne in the assembly hall, watching what seemed to be a dramatic performance by a score of costumed actors. A hundred or so other citizens watched with their king.

Pointless, but harmless; and a further reminder of Parol on Emath's throne.

"Do you want to see your own room?" Dennis said, forcing his mouth into a smile. The mirror responded to his intent before he stated it as an order—clearing and freezing again on the gold and white chamber in which he had watched Aria bathe.

As he'd intended, that sight and its memories rushed all grimmer thoughts from Dennis' mind.

Aria grinned. "You watched me—didn't you?" she said.

Dennis nodded, his eyes on the mirrored scene. A smile of embarrassment played with his lips.

Aria nestled closer to him. "You have a beautiful body, my husband," she whispered. "Perfectly beautiful."

"Ah," said Dennis. "Is there something else you'd like to see? Anything?"

"I'd seen nothing of the world before you came, Dennis," Aria replied honestly. "This—hut—is as wonderful and new as anything else could be. But . . ."

She looked over to the suit of armor. "I don't understand how you came to me beneath the city. Your armor was here—and there aren't any steps down to Rakastava's cavern except the staircase that was locked behind me and, and Gannon."

"Mirror, show us the cavern," Dennis directed with a

smile. "Now, we may not be able to see anything there, because the light faded when I'd killed the—"

But there *was* light. The water flickered with a clinging, gray phosphorescence like the rich sea beyond Emath harbor. The long shape of Rakastava, headless and still, was a line of shadow . . . but beyond it, where the water was deeper—

"Closer!" Dennis ordered.

In the water, the woman that was not a woman waved her human arms.

"Have you come to me, Prince Dennis," said the sea hag, "to pay your father's debt?"

Dennis stared transfixed.

"Dennis?" said Aria in concern.

"Dennis!" cried Chester in fear.

The sea hag extended her arms through the mirror and grasped Dennis around the waist. At the last instant he tried to cling to the mirror's frame, but the creature's inexorable grip pulled him away from the bronze as easily as a starfish opens clams.

The great maw gaped. For a moment the youth dangled above it. Then the arms released him and he fell, into the gullet of bone and blood-red tissue.

The sea hag closed her mouth. The lovely girl-face smiled. An arm waved up to Aria and Chester.

And with the slow certainty of lava moving, the sea hag sank out of sight.

In Malbawn's hut, the mirror cleared and its surface turned to glass again. Only then did the princess begin to scream.

CHAPTER 55

"No!" Aria cried. She turned away from the mirrored image of her horrified face and kicked the nearest object—a cow's thighbone. It rolled; but the bone was past hurt, and the open toe of Aria's gilt sandal gave her foot no protection.

"No," Aria repeated, but the word was a gasp of pain.

"It is not good to be angry at a hard fate," Chester said.

"How can you *say* that?" the princess demanded. "Chester, I've only known him for a week, but you've been with him all his life. Wasn't he your friend? Don't you care about him?"

"Do not be heartsore over a matter when its course comes to a halt," the robot said, quoting again—but there was a tone of appraisal in his voice that Dennis would have recognized if he had heard it.

"I . . ." Aria said.

She started to wring her hands, but will and royal training restrained her. Instead she walked into the sunlight, stepping with measured precision and using the pain jabbing her right foot as a reminder to control herself.

"Chester," she said, facing the bright meadow. "Is there no way that we can get him back?"

Cows watched her, their jaws moving side to side. Their ears snapped audibly as they flicked at insects.

"There is a way you can get him back, Princess," the robot behind her said.

Aria spun onto him, beautiful and imperious. "Then what is it?" she demanded. "What can I do?"

"The sea hag likes pretty things," Chester said softly.

The tip of one tentacle touched or did not quite touch the pendant spinning unsupported between the princess' breasts. "It might be that if you went to the sea beneath Rakastava with all your jewelry . . . and with your lute to summon the sea hag, for your voice is a pretty thing as well, Princess. . . . It might be that she would come, and—who can say what might happen then. . . ?"

CHAPTER 56

"Oh," murmured Dalquin. The pleasant, middle-aged man had become King's Champion by default when Gannon vacated the position. He adjusted the lens of his lantern to concentrate the beam and throw it farther.

Even so, the lantern could scarcely hint at the size of Rakastava's half-submerged corpse. "Oh . . ." Dalquin repeated.

"Aria, I wish you wouldn't insist on coming down here," said King Conall. He could *feel* the size of the cavern, but though he craned his neck in an attempt to see the ceiling, darkness hid all the boundaries.

Aria remembered the morning Rakastava blazed like incandescent steel and the light of the creature's body glared from dripping stone. Dennis had stood before her then, his sword drawn and his armor in harsh silhouette against the monster which would have her life if it could. . . .

"Father, I didn't ask you to come here with me," Aria said. Her voice was as cold and hard as the sword which saved her that morning. "Go back, and I'll join you when I'm finished."

Conall looked doubtfully at the cloak which he and Dalquin had arranged on the coping under Aria's direction. Lowering his voice a trifle (though Dalquin was politely distant and the huge room drank voices anyway), the king said, "Is it because you and, ah, Dennis are having a problem? Believe me, dearest, you mustn't be concerned about a little awkwardness early in a mar—"

"Father!" Aria snapped. "I appreciate your helping me, but it's time now for you to go."

"I . . . well, whatever you want, dearest. . . . But I do wish—" Conall looked at his daughter directly for the first time since they'd entered the cavern beneath the city he ruled "—that you'd at least keep the lantern."

"Thank you, father," Aria said, "but I'll do this as I've planned."

Clutching her lute, she watched the backs of the men who retreated to the bright upper world of the city. Just before they disappeared up the stairs, Aria heard Dalquin say, "Just where *is* Prince Dennis, anyway? I haven't seen him. . . ."

Blinking back tears, Aria seated herself cross-legged on the coping beside the half-folded cloak and tuned her lute with practiced fingers. With the lantern gone, the glow of her spinning pendant was enough to cast faint shadows onto the mother-of-pearl and exotic woods inlaying the sound chamber.

But the sea was beginning to hint at gray light also.

Aria began to sing, her fingers plucking the strings with perfect, plangent timing in her own accompaniment. The words were ancient, older than the settlement of Earth by men:

> *The dead are gone and with them we cannot speak;*
> *The living are here and ought to have our love.*
> *Leaving the city gate I look ahead*

And see before me only mounds and tombs. . . .

The sea's stirring was so faint that at first it could have been driven onto the water by the lute-strings themselves. But it brightened; and, with a motion so gentle that the water didn't rush over the coping, the sea hag surfaced.

The woman-face looked at the princess. Aria sat transfixed. For a moment, she felt that she was looking at herself reflected in a frost-etched mirror.

"Sing," said the sea hag; and when the creature spoke, all semblance to humanity was lost forever.

Aria struck a chord:

In the white aspens, sad winds sing
Their long murmuring kills my heart with grief.

"Why have you come to me, Princess of Rakastava's City?" the sea hag asked. Its voice was as hollow as the cavern in which it and Aria were the only living things.

"Give me my lover, sea hag," Aria said. "Return my Dennis to me." Her fingers drew a melodious arpeggio from the lute strings. Her heart was filled with terror and blue ice.

The sea hag laughed, its great mouth gaping to pour out notes that filled the cavern as the roars of Rakastava had filled it—before Dennis and his sword ended the roaring forever.

"You will not have your lover, woman," the sea hag said. "He is mine by a bargain older than his soul."

Aria lifted the chain from her neck. The pendant followed the metal links as though there were a physical connection between them and the carven crystals, each nested at the heart of the next larger.

"I will bargain with you, then," Aria said. "Give me a sight of my husband, my lover, and I will give you this."

The sea hag sighed like the wind driving through a

mountain gorge. "Give it to me, then," the creature said. "Throw it to me. . . ."

The bauble was an heirloom from the days of Earth's first human settlement. It had been as much a part of her life as Chester was to Dennis.

Aria obeyed without hesitation.

The sea hag caught the chain in one "human" hand. For a moment, the crystal dangled in the air.

The creature's real mouth opened; the face and the hand smeared into the scaly visage of the monster that they only decorated; and the pendant dropped into the bone-ribbed gape.

Dennis rose out of the sea hag's mouth.

Aria couldn't see how he was being lifted. Dennis wore the same clothes that he had when the creature snatched him from her side, and his sword still hung in its sheath . . . but there was no expression on his face, and no light in his eyes.

"Sea hag!" Aria cried. She flipped back the top of the cloak folded beside her. All her jewelry lay there, gold and crystal and pieces of ancient work with fiery hearts as bright as stars. "All that you see here is yours—if you let my Dennis go."

The creature sighed again. Dennis began to move forward—slide forward, motionless himself but resting on a translucent membrane like the stomach of a starfish belched out to digest what the creature could not swallow whole.

Dennis was as rigid as a statue until he reached the stone coping. Then, like a man moving in his sleep, he took one hesitant step—and another—to stand on solid ground. He blinked, raising a hand to rub his eyes.

Aria would have embraced him, but she couldn't move—couldn't *speak*.

"I accept your bargain, Princess Aria," said the sea hag.

The flattened membrane spread, extending still further. It covered the jewelry, the gold and things far more precious . . . covered the cloak. . . .

Flowed over the Princess Aria and drew her back into the open maw—with her lute, and with all the things she had *meant* to offer in trade to the sea hag.

Dennis turned. His eyes were trying to focus on a reality he had left utterly from the moment in which the sea hag engulfed him. He could hear Chester's tentacles clicking on the stone stairs, coming to greet his master's return, but there was something moving on the phosphorescent sea, and Dennis was sure that it must be important.

"Who is it?" he called. "Who are you?"

But the sea hag and her treasures had submerged so softly that not even the slap of waves on the stone answered Dennis' cries.

CHAPTER 57

"But how could she *do* that?" Dennis muttered, sitting on the coping with his face in his hands. He'd suspected that the ripples in the sea were—something wrong. If he'd just rushed them, perhaps with his sword he could have . . .

Done little or nothing, to be logical. The sea hag had been in water too deep for Dennis to reach the creature, much less for him to use his blade effectively.

"She *can't* have thought I'd want her to do that, to sacrifice herself."

"One never knows the heart of a woman," Chester said smugly, "any more than one knows the sky."

Dennis looked up sharply. The phosphorescence was fading from the water, but there was still enough light for him to peer at his companion as though there were something to be read in the metallic countenance.

"Did you put her up to this?" he demanded. "Did *you* tell her to throw herself away, Chester?"

"Master . . ." the robot replied with an unexpected hesitation. "There were questions that she asked me,

the Princess Aria. I answered those questions . . . and
now you are back with me, as I would wish if my
makers had permitted me to wish."

Dennis' face grew very still. Then he nodded and
hugged the robot's smooth body to him.

"It's not what I'd have wanted, Chester," he whispered. "But it's all right. It's all right." He paused. "So
long as we get her back."

"It may be, Dennis," Chester said in a meek voice,
"that you will wish to slay the sea hag after the Princess Aria is returned to you."

The youth straightened to look at his companion,
though he could barely make out the robot's shape. "I
don't care about killing it, Chester," he said. "So long
as it gives me back my Aria—and leaves us alone."

"Do not trust your enemy," Chester quoted, "lest his
heart contrive your destruction."

Dennis got up. His companion's tentacle curled into
his palm and led the way through darkness toward the
stairs. It struck him forcibly that Chester was showing
more initiative than his human builders, so many gen-
erations ago, might have intended.

"All right, Chester," he said aloud. "Maybe we'll
finish the thing for good and all, if that's what you think
we must do. But first, we must free my Aria. . . ."

CHAPTER 58

"Prince Dennis," Conall said as he and Dalquin quickened their stride to keep up with the younger, taller man. "I don't mean to intrude, but *really* I must know what has happened to my daughter."

"Sir," said Dennis, "she's no longer here, through no will of my own. And Chester and I are going to get her back immediately."

The youth knew he was being uncommunicative not so much because time was short, but because he didn't want to tell Conall what had befallen the princess. Conall would blame Dennis—

And Dennis already blamed himself, whatever Chester or reason might say.

Even reason admitted that if Aria had never met a vagabond named Dennis, she wouldn't be in the sea hag's gullet now.

"Yes, but—" said Conall, looking about him in awkward concern. The cattle byres were clean, as everything in Rakastava was clean: but the warm, animal odor of cows still hung in the air.

"Open," Dennis said to the wall. Direct sunlight drew wordless gasps from the two citizens of Rakastava, though Conall and Dalquin had seen the sun before.

Had seen the sun several times during their lives, in fact.

Dennis strode onto the cow path, knowing that Conall would not follow with his questioning.

"Do not be called, 'the rude one,' Dennis," Chester said, "because of your disregard for others."

Dennis turned. "Sir," he said, "I—"

His tongue touched his lips, and he remembered the salty taste of Aria's blood. "I love your daughter. I will have her back from, from where she is. On my life, I promise you."

He bowed, hoping the king didn't realize that in Dennis' mind, the forfeit of his life was at least as probable as the success he'd promised. His duty to courtesy done, Dennis and Chester continued down the trail.

Behind them, they heard Dalquin saying, "Now Dennis is a good lad and a brave one, sir. He'll not let your daughter come to any harm."

Around a corner of the path, Dennis shook his head sadly. If only *he* could be so confident.

"What if the sea hag stays deep in the sea, Chester?" he asked. "It doesn't matter that we can—go to her through the mirror if we, if I drown before . . ."

"It is not to the sea hag that we will go, Dennis," the robot replied calmly, "but to its life, which is on the Banned Island beyond the jaws of Emath Harbor."

"You mean the hag will be on the Banned Island," Dennis said, half in question as he tried to make sense of Chester's words.

"The creature may be there and may not," Chester explained with a note of exasperation. "But its life is on the island, and it will come to its life when you hold that in your hands."

Dennis frowned. "Chester, how can the sea hag's life be separate from her?" he asked.

"Because she is not really alive, Dennis."

"That can't be!" Dennis said with unintended firmness.

"Am I alive, Dennis?"

"Of course you are!"

"Then the sea hag is alive, Dennis; but her life is on the Banned Island."

The pasture was bright and a friend to Dennis by now, all the things Rakastava was not. Some of the differences—the way the grass tickled and could cut; the insects that buzzed and sometimes stabbed; the excessive heat when the sun was full in the sky—were discomforts and bad from any logical standpoint, but . . .

But life wasn't a sterile endeavor, and life wasn't truly possible in an environment as sterile as that of Rakastava.

"We won't stay in Rakastava," Dennis said aloud. "In the city. We'll go back to Emath or build a house in this pasture or something."

"After you have slain the sea hag, Dennis," Chester reminded. "And first, it is to Mother Grimes and not Malbawn's mirror that we must go."

Dennis loosened his sword in its scabbard. "She's dead, isn't she, Chester?" he asked, remembering the way his companion had let him enter Mother Grimes' house unwarned—because he had not asked for advice as he should have done.

"She is dead, Dennis," the robot agreed. "But her baton is there where you left it, and you will need it now."

Dennis stopped in the tall grass. "I said I didn't want anything to do with that."

"Do not squander the little you have when there is no one else to support you," Chester quoted sharply.

"Chester, I *saw* what that, that *stick* did to you," the youth pleaded. "I don't want to touch it. Look, my sword is good enough."

He drew the long blade, as though sunlight dancing on the metal were an argument.

"Dennis," the robot said gently, "on the island, the sea hag will try to stop you. She will send out things that are of her and not of life; and for those you might trust your sword, though it is my mind that the sword would fail you."

Dennis swallowed. "But—" he began.

"But the sea hag has still greater powers," Chester continued, ignoring his master's interruption. "She will send things that have the semblance of persons . . . but it may be that she will send the persons themselves. If she does that, Dennis, and you trust your sword . . . you will wish it was on yourself instead that you had used your blade."

Dennis closed his eyes for a moment, trying to shut out the vision he had just seen—Aria falling in two parts, a shocked look on her face as she died; and blood, so much blood. . . .

"Right," he said. "Let's go find the baton."

CHAPTER 59

Dennis expected Mother Grimes' house to look more weathered, but essentially the way it had been when he glanced back at it after hacking his way clear.

"Oh . . ." he murmured in distaste and horror when he saw the reality. "Oh. I should have known."

The "house" *was* Mother Grimes, a chitinous shell to draw in the unwary. Dead, Mother Grimes decayed as quickly as her sons had rotted where Dennis left their corpses sprawled in the grass.

The roof had fallen in; the upper portions of the walls were bare and white. The layer of flesh which had pretended to be wood and brick and stone was now slumped onto the ground as a pond of thick green fluid in which maggots swam and feasted.

Dennis stared at what he had seen and walked into, thinking it was a house. He nibbled at his lower lip, wondering what kind of deceptions he would face on the Banned Island.

"The baton is here, Dennis," Chester said from a short distance away. One tentacle pointed to the ground, where the object had fallen when Dennis hurled it away from him. "Do you wish that I should carry it?"

The youth shivered in the sunlight.

"No," he said in a firm voice. "I'll carry it, Chester. It's part of my duty, I think."

The robot didn't respond directly, but Dennis thought he read approval in the expressionless features.

CHAPTER 60

When they reached Malbawn's hut, Dennis' sweat-sticky skin prickled all over from grass-cuts and nervousness. The shade of the sagging roof was comforting.

Chester wasn't unlatching the pieces of star-metal armor so that Dennis could put it on. The youth gestured toward the suit and said, "Ah, won't I. . . ?"

"The armor will be of no use to you today, Dennis," Chester said. There was no compromise in his tone, though he added, "You may wear it if you wish, to shield your fear if not your body."

"No, I don't need that," Dennis said coldly. Chester's calculated insult had frozen away the nervous flutterings that nibbled Dennis' mind the way insects and itching had worked on his skin in the pasture.

Chester touched Dennis' wrist with a tentacle, then withdrew it. "He whose good character makes him gentle," the robot said, "is master of his own fate."

Dennis took his right hand from the pommel of his sword and rubbed the robot's carapace, the way he'd done for friendship and reassurance all his life.

"I'm frightened, Chester," he said quietly. "But I'll be all right. What do we do now?"

"It is now that we must go to the Banned Island, Dennis," the robot replied.

Dennis opened his mouth to give the order, but the mirror was already shifting and clearing on—

A sight as striking, and as clearly artificial, as the glitter of Emath Palace.

The Banned Island rose out of the sea like a poplar spiking upward from a close-mown lawn. There was a forest fringe at the island's base, and that in itself was a hint of unnatural power.

The jungle, as dense and green as that of the hinterland beyond Emath Village, grew down to the tide line. There was no raised corniche to protect the vegetation from waves tossed high by storms, yet some of the trees visible were centuries old.

Dennis licked his dry lips, remembering Hale the Fisherman, wrapped in storm and certain doom when he first met the creature to whom he bargained an unborn son.

The sea hag ruled the Banned Island; and she ruled also the tempests which would have devastated it.

Beyond the jungle was a spire of porous rock, reddish-brown and probably laterite like the stone of the Emath headlands. The spire was five or six hundred feet high, tall enough to dwarf the greatest of the forest giants at its feet.

Even in the mirror's shrunken and foreshortened view, Dennis could see that the rock's crumbling surface made the spire impossible to climb. It was little more than a vertical gravel pile, with no hand- or foothold that would take a human's weight.

A circular glass staircase was built along—or grew from—one side of the rock. Emath Palace was all facets and lines, while this staircase seemed to have dripped down like icicles. All its parts were smooth and rounded, but they spread in a baroque profusion of landings and balconies buttressed to the spire by shining cantilevers.

The top of the spire was covered with a dome of smooth crystal.

Dennis drew his sword, gripping the hilt firmly to prevent his hand from trembling. "Closer," he ordered, and the mirrored vision swooped down obediently.

Dennis still couldn't see through the glass dome. It reflected the sky and, he realized with a jolt of fear, showed him and Chester distorted in the curves of the surface. Memory of the sea hag's arms extending for him raised the youth's voice an octave as he shouted, "Back! Take me away from the dome!"

The companions' viewpoint flip-flopped in two sudden stages. The island was a thorn sticking out of the steel-gray sea, visible mostly for the ring of froth its margin scraped from the gentle surf.

Dennis took a deep breath. He had no reason to suppose the dome's reflection was as dangerous as his instinct had told him . . . but he was willing to trust instinct when it told him to fear anything connected with the sea hag.

"Chester," he said in a controlled voice, "is the sea hag beneath the dome?"

"The life of the sea hag is there, Dennis, that is so," Chester agreed.

"Then that's where we—" Dennis began, but Chester interrupted him by continuing, "But the mirror will not take us beneath the dome."

"Eh?"

"The mirror will carry us only within the dome's surface, where we will stay so long as the sea hag wishes, or for eternity; and eternity will end first, it is my belief."

"Then how are we to—" Dennis blazed; and caught himself, because he was venting anger instead of thinking or even asking for help. He didn't need Chester to tell him the answer, not if he thought for himself.

"The mirror will set us on the shore of the island," Dennis said formally. His face wore the smile that calm had returned to him. "From the shore we will climb the stairs to the dome, where we will take the sea hag's life, be it in her body or apart from it."

"Her life is not in her body, Dennis," Chester said with equal calm.

"And we will release the Princess Aria," Dennis continued. "As she released me."

"So we shall do," the robot said. "If you are as bold as you showed yourself in Rakastava, Dennis; and if you are as wise as you are bold."

"Mirror, show us the shoreline," Dennis ordered. And, as their viewpoint rushed down like a funnel's sides sloping to the throat, the companions stepped forward onto a shore of coarse red shingle crumbled from the island's rock.

The sea lapped Dennis' feet. He looked around him and jumped in surprise at what he hadn't seen through the mirror because of the angle. "Chester!" he blurted. "There's a boat here on the shore!"

"Why should there not be a boat, Dennis?" the robot replied coolly.

Dennis ran his hand over the sun-cracked wood of the gunwale. It was ordinary enough, a net-tending skiff like the one in which his father had made his lonely journeys; but it was properly drawn onto the shore, not cast up by a storm surge, and this was—

"But Chester, no boats can land on the Banned Island. Anyone who tries founders in a storm or, or—"

"Or is drawn down by the sea hag, that may be," Chester said, completing the thought. "But the choice is the choice of the sea hag; and the sea hag may choose to allow a landing."

"Well, it doesn't concern us," Dennis said; but it concerned him very much to know who might be on the island, with him and with the sea hag.

He couldn't see the stairs because of the foliage overhanging the narrow beach. A faint path—bruised leaves and twigs broken here and there—led into the vegetation.

To himself and to Chester, he said, "We'll find the sea hag's life. And we'll trade it to her for Aria. And then we'll leave."

"The crocodile is merciless, Dennis. There is no truce with it."

Dennis shrugged his shoulders.

The sea hag had bargained and had kept her bargains. However dangerous it might be to let the creature live, Dennis knew in his heart that he would keep any bargain he made with her.

He could look at his father and see what came of trying to cheat.

Careful not to let the baton in his left hand brush him when he swung his arms, Dennis strode forward.

CHAPTER 61

The undergrowth caught at them in its familiar way. Dennis could have cut his path broadly with a few swipes of his sword: his thick, practiced wrists driving the star-metal edge would lop down anything smaller than a full-grown tree. But . . . once past the jungle's sunlit fringe, Dennis could walk without a real struggle.

The jungle and its denizens had been friends to him. The birds that hooted away in explosions of brilliant color were a reminder of the life and beauty in the world. The lizards counselled patience with their rigid bodies and bright, darting eyes.

And even the bark and leaves had a delicate architecture which Dennis realized was beyond the ability of men—or the sea hag—to duplicate.

So instead of slashing his way through the jungle, he stepped with care; twisting free of thorns if he hadn't dodged them in time; accepting that his clothes would be torn by the time he reached his destination—but that torn clothes wouldn't matter, whether he survived the day or did not survive.

Dennis had proved he could kill. If he chose to prove that he spared life wherever possible, then that was nobody's business but his own.

"A wise man avoids harming others so that he not be harmed himself," Chester quoted from behind him.

Dennis laughed. "No, it's not because of that, Chester," he said. "What I do to this bush or that lizard doesn't affect how the sea hag treats me—or whether a limb falls down and knocks my brains out. But it makes *me* feel good, so that's reason enough."

And in the back of his mind, Dennis prayed (despite his words) that someone was keeping a tally; that someone was saying, *Well, this is a good boy. We'll free his wife and make sure that he isn't killed or horribly maimed. . . .*

Something crashed through the woods toward them.

The canopy was very dense, choking the ferns and bushes of the undergrowth with lack of sunlight. Nothing to hinder a swordstroke.

Dennis' eyes were wide and his mouth was half open. His left arm held the baton to the side where it wouldn't interfere if he slashed; and his sword, with an edge like whispering death, was poised to let the life out of any opponent at all.

Dennis' mother burst from behind a screen of ferns.

Selda's face still wore the remnants of cosmetics, streaked by hard use and the tears of fright she was still shedding. She stumbled over a root and fell, ten feet from Dennis; but she didn't see her son until she tried to get up—and from her scream, she didn't recognize Dennis even then.

"M . . . mother?" Dennis said.

Selda peered through the mat of her disarranged hair. It had grown out several inches since the last time she'd dyed it, leaving the roots a mixture of gray and mousy brown against the fading orange nearer the tips. Dennis recognized the dress as one of her favorites, rose pink with a bright green sash.

After a week in Rakastava, he also knew that the colors made an ugly combination with each other and with his mother's ruddy complexion.

"Oh thank goodness, Dennis, you're here to save me!" Selda said. She tried to struggle to her feet, but she seemed to have twisted her ankle in falling. "I fled here to escape Parol. It—it's been terrible since you've been gone!"

Selda stretched out a hand to her son. Instead of stepping forward to lift her, Dennis stood transfixed. His tongue licked his lips, but his mouth was too dry for that to help.

It *had* to be his mother, but—

Shocked, fearful again at his lack of response, Selda lifted herself and hobbled forward. "Dennis? Darling?" she said. "Why are you—"

"Don't come closer!" Dennis screamed. His sword lifted of its own volition. He remembered the way it sheared through Mother Grimes' body, the way the blood sprayed him and the walls as she fell. . . .

"Dennis!" Selda cried in horror, staggering toward her son with both hands out and a look of disbelief on her worn, familiar face.

Dennis thrust with sudden instinct and practiced skill, his body blending into the motion of his arm.

His left arm. The baton's white tip touched and flicked away from Selda's fingers as Dennis stepped away.

It wasn't Selda standing before him. It wasn't even anything alive.

A thing of sputtering wires, like a sculptor's armature on which to smear clay as the first stage of casting a human statue.

A statue of Queen Selda, perhaps; but the wires were featureless, fleshless. All they had was the spit and sparkle of lightning coursing through them, clothing them in blue haze and whispering menace.

"Oh . . ." Dennis murmured.

The creature now stood naked and quiescent before

him. If he'd used his sword on it, he'd have received a blast like the one Rakastava had used to stun Chester as they battled in the cavern.

Dennis looked back at his companion.

"It will not harm you now, Dennis," Chester assured him. "It is a part of the sea hag, but you have drawn its will to injure you."

"But it's a machine. It isn't *alive!*"

"The sea hag is not alive, Dennis," the robot repeated.

"I think I see the staircase through the trees, Chester," the youth said, trying to get his pulse under control. He moved on, giving the thing of wires a wide berth.

It followed them; but Chester said nothing, so Dennis said nothing further.

The staircase was only a glint. Its base was hidden beneath the creepers which used the structure as support to mount toward the sky; but something had broken through the mass of greenery in the past few days, trampling down the vines and leaving foliage to yellow as its torn tips starved.

Dennis touched his left index finger to a handrail that looked as though it had been spun by two sources which dripped molten glass in opposing circles. He rubbed it, noticing the friction. His fingertip felt hot instead of gliding along the surface as it would on the walls of Emath Palace.

"A long way up," Dennis murmured as he started to climb. He'd have to be careful not to slip on the glass treads, but he no longer regretted not having a hand free to grip the rail.

Chester's tentacles click-*click*ed along with Dennis, sounding just as they had in childhood in the halls of Emath Palace; and behind both of them, the wire creature paced. Where its feet touched the vegetation, juices sizzled and the green leaves turned black.

The glass tower was built in slanted bands along the side of the rock. The stairs themselves twisted and rose more sharply than the structure that enclosed them, treads meeting "floor supports" at acute angles and increasing the sense of unease with which Dennis climbed higher.

Dennis paused frequently, not so much because he was tired but for safety's sake. His eyes drew down instinctively after a few minutes of climbing the steep, quickly turning stairs; and whatever danger he faced would come from above him.

He wasn't—he didn't think he needed to be—in a hurry. By stopping for a moment and getting his breath, he was also able to shake away the mesmerizing numbness induced by the helical staircase.

At first when Dennis looked out, he could see nothing but jungle through the arches of the latticework tower. As he mounted higher, flashes of sea foam and brilliantly blue water became visible through the leaves. Then, when he guessed he was halfway up (though the spiral of light turned blue by the way it wicked down through the glass stairs gave him no certain measure), his eyes caught a glint beyond the sea.

"That is the palace, Dennis," Chester said in answer to the question his master hadn't asked. "It is Emath that you see."

"Well, we'll . . ." the youth muttered. He wasn't sure how he wanted to end the sentence. "When we're done here, we'll. . . . Well, that doesn't matter until we're done here."

A door creaked open above them.

The star-metal sword was much lighter than a steel blade of equal size, but it still had considerable weight and leverage. Dennis' arm tired, so that the point dipped slowly as he climbed. Twice already it had ticked against the higher treads, sparking without harm to either metal or the glass.

At the sound of the door, adrenalin lifted Dennis' arm and blade as though he were perfectly fresh. He thought of waiting for further motion above—but from where he stood, he couldn't see anything except the bottom of stair-treads.

Dennis rushed the sound, trusting Chester to cover his back.

A man had come out of a door of wood and strap-iron, set into the rock. The door opened onto a landing, half a turn of the staircase above where Dennis had climbed when he heard the sound; and the landing itself spread into a broad, icy balcony which overlooked the sea. The man stood, squeezing the rail of twisted glass with his broad, powerful hands when Dennis burst onto the landing.

"Father!" Dennis gasped. His blade wavered.

"Dennis?" the man said. "Dennis! My prayers were answered!"

King Hale's face was gray; he looked thinner than Dennis remembered him being, even in the last days before Hale was due to pay his debt to the sea hag. His right hand trembled as he held it out toward Dennis— half in greeting, half to ward off a shocking apparition.

The sword trembled in Dennis' hand also.

"Son?" Hale said. "Parol exiled me here—he's made his own bargain with the sea hag. Are you here to free me?"

He started forward, stepping doubtfully.

"No!" Dennis shouted. "You're not my father!"

"Oh, son," Hale whispered. The old man—older than his years, now; older than Dennis had ever dreamed his strong, hot tempered father could look—fell to his knees.

For a moment Hale pressed his hands to his face. Then he lowered them and said, "Dennis, I can understand why you'd feel that way. A true father would never have made the bargain I did. But—"

He started to rise again, his eyes imploring and one of his work-roughened hands reaching out toward Dennis "—can't you find it in your heart to forgive me now, my son?"

His father had never hugged him. Dennis looked at

the open arms and pleading expression, feeling all the years of hurt and fear and anger melt out of his heart. He sheathed his sword and stepped forward.

Behind Dennis, a spark went *tsk*! across two wires of the manikin which had followed him.

Dennis hadn't dropped the baton because he hadn't remembered it. He'd been a boy again, offered the affection he'd always hoped—and never received—from his father. The white end touched King Hale's forehead—

And there was no King Hale: only a clear sack, man-shaped and filled with bubbling, yellowish fluid. The sack was featureless, as the wire thing had been; but it rose from its knees, the membrane folding and bulging like human skin, and stood with its lumpish arms at its side.

Trembling as though he stood in an arctic wind, Dennis stepped back from the creature—the construct—which he'd almost embraced. He drew his sword and, after a moment's consideration, sheathed it again.

Chester had been right: the sword would be no help to him here.

"Chester," the youth whispered, "I *knew* that wasn't really my father. I knew it mustn't be, but . . ."

"You did not know, Dennis," the robot said gently. "Your father could be here. Even I can not tell truth from image in this place that is the sea hag's place."

"Chester, do people do what they want to do, even when they know they mustn't? Do other people. . .?"

"People see what they hope to see, Dennis," Chester replied, stroking his master's shoulders. "People know what they wish to know, and they act on that truth which they create for themselves. And it may be . . ." but here the robot's voice grew so soft that Dennis was not sure of the words he was hearing ". . . that they are happier to live lies."

Dennis looked out over the sea, sun-struck and faceted with choppy waves. He was higher than he'd ever been before, even in the tallest of the palace towers.

The brilliant openness of everything before—and below—
the balcony gave him a touch of vertigo.

"All right," he said under his breath. "There's a long
way yet to go."

He was not surprised when the thing of fluid shuffled
along behind them, following the thing of wire. The
foot membranes squelched as they settled on each tread.
Bubbles continued to rise through the yellow fluid.

Dennis knew he must be nearing the dome, because
the jungle was very far below when he leaned out and
looked. If he turned his head to peer upward, he saw
nothing but sky and the sun-dazzling eave molding of
the tower's next layer above.

Dennis was breathing quickly now. Tired from the
climb, he was sure, but—nervous also. Very nervous.

He looked at Chester. "Do you have any wisdom for
an old pupil, my friend?" he asked jokingly.

"Do not undertake any task and then carry it out
badly," the robot obediently quoted.

The youth's wry smile became a real one. "We won't
do it badly," he said, squeezing the tentacle Chester
offered him. "We'll do it right."

If it kills me, his mind added.

Three steps higher, and Dennis saw the stairs meet a
floor of rainbow glass. There was no door at the top,
only a rectangular slot.

Through the slot, Dennis could see his own distorted
features reflected from the concave inner surface of the
dome which covered the spire of rock.

"There'll be something waiting right there for us,"
Dennis said musingly. "Ready to get us as soon as our
heads come over the edge of the floor."

"Do you wish me to go before you, Dennis?" Chester
asked.

Dennis thought . . . Thought of Chester flying through
the air, struck by Malduanan's leg as he lunged to save
his master's life; Chester wreathed in blue fire, his

limbs flailing wildly as he blocked the lightning bolt Rakastava meant for Dennis.

Chester crumbling into rust, struck by the baton as Dennis dangled helplessly from the ceiling that was part of Mother Grimes.

"No," he said quietly. "Thank you, Chester. But this one's mine."

He poised, then rushed up the remaining stairs with the robot behind him.

CHAPTER 62

Nothing attacked as they burst out onto the smooth glass floor.

Aria ran toward them from the large pavilion beneath the center of the dome.

"Oh, Dennis!" she called as her slippers twinkled over the mirroring floor. "Oh my love, you've won!"

The glass above Dennis had a pebbled appearance. Its outer surface was beaded with water wrung from low clouds and the wind-lifted spray. The youth glanced up, saw himself shrunken and foreshortened; and looked back with a hard expression at what seemed to be his wife.

The only structure within the dome was the one from which Aria had come, a flat-roofed circle or ornamented marble columns. The pavilion was reflected from the concave dome to the floor and back again—hundreds of times—in a rosette, like the pattern of reality glimpsed through a bee's eye.

And in every image, a distorted princess scuttled to meet an equally monstrous youth.

305

"Wait!" Dennis shouted. His right hand touched his sword hilt—snatched itself away as intellect overcame instinct—and patted back, though without drawing the weapon.

Aria paused with a look of amazement on her face. "Darling?" she said. Then, "Ooh! What are those?"

The manikins had shuffled up the last of the staircase. They hissed and bubbled softly, their faceless visages turned toward Dennis like the eyes of retainers in Emath Palace.

"What are *you*?" Dennis said harshly. "Just like them, aren't you? One more trick."

Aria's face jerked back as though Dennis had slapped her. "What do you mean?" she said. "I— Oh. Did you lose your memory when the sea hag held you? I'm your wife, darling. You've saved me from the sea hag."

She stepped toward Dennis again with a radiant expression and her arms spread wide.

"*Wait!*" Dennis screamed. He thrust the baton out in front of him to ward away the princess. "You're not really Aria!"

"Dennis?" Aria said in bewilderment. "Of course I'm Aria. You've reached the heart of the sea hag's power, and she's surrendered me to get you to leave. There's a boat on the shore that we can take wherever we please."

Dennis' mouth was dry. The baton was shaking so badly that he clasped his right hand over his left to control it. "I don't think you're really Aria," he said, enunciating very carefully. "I think you're another, another sending from the sea hag, like, like those."

He nodded toward the manikins with an awkward twitch of his head, but he couldn't bring himself to take his eyes away from Aria—what looked to them to be Aria.

"Those *things*?" Aria said in horror and amazement. "Dennis, are you all—"

"Now, I'm going to touch you with the—with this," Dennis said firmly. He stared at the end of the baton, so that the princess's figure blurred beyond it. "It won't hurt you if you, if you're Aria. . . ."

"It will just turn me into something like—*them*," the woman said with icy unconcern. "Very well, Dennis. I was willing to forfeit my life to save yours. I just didn't realize that you'd be the one to destroy me yourself."

"No, it's not like that!" the youth said desperately.

"Dennis," Aria said. He met her eyes.

In tones as precise as if she were cutting them out of stone, she went on, "If your heart has so little love in it that you can't tell me from *those* things, then go ahead—strike me with your weapon. But if you do that . . ."

The look Aria gave him was by turns pitying and hurt. "But if you do that," she repeated, "you and I are through forever. I can't love a man who trusts me so little."

Dennis' heart froze and shrank away from him, until there seemed to be nothing in his chest but a mote as frigid as the dust between the stars.

"The fiend overcomes the wise man through cunning," Chester murmured.

"The woman I love wouldn't have offered that choice," Dennis said quietly. "It remains to be seen whether I loved a real woman or a woman my mind imagined."

The baton darted out. At the last instant, the princess tried to dodge past and embrace him—but Dennis had a warrior's eye and a swordsman's hand. The baton's white tip brushed Aria's cheek; and it wasn't Aria, just a thing of gray-white metal that creaked as its outstretched arms settled back against its sides.

Even on this manikin there was no hint of a face. The metal was smooth, not molded into features. It wasn't polished enough to reflect the iron certainty of Dennis' stare.

"Where now do we go, Chester?" Dennis whispered as he watched the thing that was not Aria and felt his heart start to beat again.

"The life of the sea hag is within the pavilion, Dennis," the robot said.

"Then we will go into the pavilion," the youth said. His voice still lacked emotion, but the color was beginning to return to his cheeks.

Holding the baton ready, Dennis and Chester walked deliberately into the pillared structure. The feet of the manikins followed with a muted spat!/*squelch*/click!

There were two rows of pillars—the inner circuit offset from the outer one, equal in number but slimmer; so delicate, in fact, that they looked scarcely able to stand, much less support part of the roof's weight.

The columns were porcelain, not marble; colored and patterned, but glass like the dome and staircase up to it.

The center of the pavilion was sunken. Dennis took the steps down to a surface three feet below the floor on which the pillars rested. Within that, a shaft thirty feet in diameter that seemed to drop to Hell or the center of the Earth, whichever was farther.

Machinery was built into the waist-high wall: dials and gauges, buttons and levers; plates that were nothing until someone touched them in the correct way so that they became—anything at all.

The apparatus didn't frighten Dennis now, the way he'd been frightened by similar artifacts when he saw them for the first time in the Wizard Serdic's laboratory; but he didn't understand them, and the machines weren't anything he particularly *wanted* to understand.

In an alcove set across the shaft from Dennis, a crystal egg spun in the air.

He thought at first glimpse that it was Aria's pendant—fear made his heart leap—but Chester said, "That is the sea hag's life, Dennis. Take it and she will bargain with you."

The circular walkway was broad enough for the youth to walk counter-clockwise around it without need to fear the shaft gaping to his left—but it made him uneasy nonetheless. Chester walked behind him—and the three manikins, non-hand in non-hand, followed, the thing of metal in the center.

Dennis swallowed; but they could do him no harm. Chester had said so. . . .

Dennis reached for the globe spinning unsupported in the alcove. The shaft gave a great sigh that ruffled the youth's garments and echoed throughout the dome.

Crisply, as though he had practiced the action and his heart was not hammering in his breast, Dennis dropped the baton on the floor and seized the crystal in both hands. It fought him for a moment, but his grip tightened—

And mastered it.

He stepped to the edge of the shaft and looked down.

The shaft was no longer bottomless. Water winked in it, no farther down than the sea was beneath the dome; and in the water was a blob of color that could only be the sea hag.

CHAPTER 63

"I have your life!" Dennis shouted, cringing inside himself for the deep, thundering echoes of his own voice.

The water and the thing within it rose higher, driving the air ahead of it with another pistoning sigh.

"I will bargain for my life, King Dennis," said the gape that was the sea hag's throat—glimpsed from above, and hinting at a depth equal to that of the shaft before the creature entered it. "I will make you King of Emath, and all in Emath will obey you as they did your father under our bargain."

"Return Aria to me unharmed," Dennis said, suddenly exultant to realize that he *had* won, that he controlled the sea hag as surely as her storm and threats had ruled Hale the Fisherman on that day before Dennis was conceived. "Leave us alone and I'll return your life to you."

The sea hag laughed. It was rising closer, so that for the moment when the real mouth closed, the face and torso of a human female smiled and waved at Dennis.

"Dennis, son of Hale," said the creature in a voice of mocking thunder. "Dennis, liar's son! You will bargain and try to cheat me, boy."

"I will keep my word, sea hag," Dennis said.

He raised his left fist over his head. "And this too, I promise: if you do not return my Aria at once, I will shatter what I hold as if it were an egg."

The sea hag rose higher yet, almost to the level of the walkway. Its mouth opened.

Aria slid up to her husband's side on the translucent membrane that had freed Dennis in the cavern.

Dennis reached out his free hand. "D-darling?" he said. Aria's eyes were blank.

Her arm felt cool, but it was human flesh—and it warmed to Dennis' touch.

"Return my life, Dennis!" said the sea hag.

The water in the shaft was receding, leaving a salt tang behind. The creature's voice deepened with echoes as the sea hag plunged as swiftly as it had risen.

"Dennis?" Aria murmured. She moved her head and took a cautious step to prove that her legs still worked. "Dennis? Is it really you?"

Return my life . . . echoed in the dome and in Dennis' memory.

He squeezed Aria's shoulder to indicate that he wasn't leaving her; and he stepped toward the alcove from which he had wrenched the crystal.

"Do not trust your enemy, lest you die cursing!" said Chester.

"Dennis," said Aria in concern for which she didn't know enough to have a reason. "Are you going to. . .?"

"Return my life!" thundered the deep organ-note of the sea hag's voice.

"What the sea hag does is her business!" Dennis shouted over his shoulder to his companions, through the reverberating echoes. "I'll keep my word!"

He turned. The three manikins stood between him

and the alcove. Each extended its right arm toward him.

"What. . . ?" Dennis said. His head twitched as he started to glance back at Chester—and caught himself, unwilling to look away from the manikins.

"They are of the sea hag, Dennis," said the robot behind him. "Give them the crystal."

Return my life . . . said the echoes.

"We control them now, you and I," Chester said. "I have asked them to return the life to their maker."

Dennis stretched out his left hand, with the crystal which glowed and quivered and sometimes seemed to whisper to his bones.

The manikins didn't have hands, but the lumps which illusion had clothed with the semblance of hands now reached out together and took the fragile crystal. They moved with a delicacy which belied their appearance, touching neither Dennis nor one another as they gripped the object with balanced pressure.

The hairs on the back of Dennis' arm prickled as the sparkling wires brushed close—but the youth didn't move until the crystal was firmly in the joined grip of the manikins.

Dennis looked at the featureless voids; and for just an instant, he thought he saw Aria smiling at him again from the blank metal that had mimicked her.

But that was illusion, and it was gone before Dennis could be sure it had existed at all. He stepped away.

The manikins moved forward in jerky unison.

"Watch out!" Dennis said, reaching to block Aria behind him; but she slipped into the crook of his elbow and encircled his waist with her own soft arm.

The manikins ignored them. Holding the crystal before them, they stepped; and stepped; and—

"*Return my life!*"

—stepped again, into the shaft together.

"The sea hag has what it demanded, Dennis," said

Chester in a metallic shout through the echoes. "Now we must go, and quickly."

"What's going to hap—" Aria said as she and Dennis, arm in arm, followed the robot up the steps to the main floor.

Water splashed, far below.

"—pen?"

Blue lightning flashed and sparkled up the shaft.

"Run faster," Chester said. One of his tentacles snaked out to support Dennis as the youth's foot slipped on smooth glass. "The acid will mix smoothly with water, but when it touches the sea hag—"

Dennis paused, passing Aria ahead of him into the narrow stairwell. The shaft belched yellow-green vapor—

And the dazzling white glare of magnesium burning in the shaft made the interior of the dome blaze as though the sun had come down from the heavens. The pavilion's porcelain columns shattered from the reflected heat.

Dennis plunged down the staircase. Aria was well ahead of him. Barefoot: she'd kicked off her slippers and was bouncing down, hitting only each third or fourth of the wedge-shaped steps. Dennis gripped the central rail and followed, knowing that the worst which could happen if he fell was that he'd be bruised or break some bones.

Gobbets of molten glass were rained past the arched openings like the first breath of a volcanic eruption. If Dennis and his companions didn't get off the Banned Island soon, he was pretty sure that they would melt; or burn; or smother.

Dennis thought of the creature which told him it was Aria and which demanded that he enter its embrace. At least death would have been quick when the arms encircling him blazed sun-bright.

The rock spire shook. Bits of laterite flaked off the stairwell's inner face, pattering down the steps beside the fleeing companions. The air filled with a roar too

great to be called a sound. Dennis wasn't sure whether
it came from the fire, the sea hag—

Or the core of the planet.

Dennis spun around the balcony where he'd found
the manikin which looked like his father. A loud *crack!*
broke the omnipresent thunder. He didn't look back.

He didn't have to. Two lines split their way down the
outer surface of the stairwell—ribbons of irregular thickness, dancing with the light they spilled out in an
iridescent variety of wavelengths.

Then the stairwell's multi-arched exterior slipped in
an increasing rush: crumbling, chanting glassy hymns to
the wind, and painting all the world nearby in a dazzling rainbow coruscance.

Faster, Dennis' mind whispered.

There was no reason to speak the word aloud. Aria
already took ten steps to his nine, and Chester deliberately slowed his pace to keep from getting too far ahead
of his human companions.

They were down among the trees, now. The trunks
of the nearest were waving, their leaves and branches
stripped away by the tons of glass which had cascaded
through them moments before.

Birds spun and squawked in the air in colorful confusion. An occasional lizard clung to an island of bark on a
stripped trunk, its eyes wide and its throat-pouch
fluttering.

Something thumped from the top of the spire. Again
Dennis refused to look behind him, but the sun dimmed
as it tried to shine through the cloud of gas and debris
which puffed out of the shaft.

They were among the creepers, now, very close to
the ground. Dennis saw bright, fresh blood on a step.
His heart jumped. Aria's foot, spiked by a thorn—but
she continued to bound forward in a wave of blond hair,
ignoring her hurt and the chance of hurting herself
again.

Dennis would have drawn his sword when he hit the

ground, but there was already a flurry of vegetation in the direction of the shore. Chester stalked ahead on four limbs, spinning the tips of the other four like cutting blades. Foliage and small stems disintegrated.

Dennis lifted Aria in both arms and ran after the robot. He was saving her bare feet from further harm; and he was holding her close, because he loved her, would always love her, from the Cariad's magic or Aria's own, and they might not have very long to live.

The top of the laterite spire pulverized itself in a staggering blast. A second explosion took a bite off what remained, pelting the leaf canopy with pebbles and whipping the sea to momentary foam as the companions reached the shore.

Aria squirmed out of Dennis' grasp and set her shoulder against the boat's gunwale to push it off even before he did. Chester pushed as well, but the narrow curves of his tentacles ground deep in the shingle as the robot put strain on them.

It was Dennis' boots and the flexing of his powerful calf muscles that broke the keel's grip on the land and kept it jouncing and sliding down to the water.

Chester and Aria slipped over the weathered gunwale. Dennis continued to stride forward, knee-deep in the water, as he pushed the fishing boat ahead of him.

Another explosion spattered bits of rock. The chunks were too light to hurt seriously, but they flew hard enough to sting.

"It is time that you come aboard with us, Dennis," Chester said.

"No, I want to get—" Dennis insisted, and the last of the sentence drowned in the sea when he stepped off the island's underwater edge—as abrupt as had been the spire pointing up into heaven.

Chester's tentacle, prepared for the event, looped under the youth's armpits and lifted him aboard spluttering. "Small advice, if heeded, can prevent great harm, Dennis," the robot chided.

A deeper explosion shook the Banned Island. Nothing more flew from the truncated spire, but the sea lifted in a swell that flattened the chop as it expanded from the shore. The boat rocked.

Dennis settled onto the center thwart and took the oars. He looked over his shoulder and his destination, then began stroking. He tried to remember the motions he had watched his father make so many times.

In the stern sat Aria, her hands demurely in her lap. She seemed none the worse for being swallowed down by the sea hag. The nested pendant spun merrily between her breasts.

Aria combed a hand through her loose hair, lifting out a bit of twig. "Where are we going, darling?" she asked. A faint tremor in her voice warned Dennis that reaction was beginning to catch up with the princess now that she'd time to rest.

"We're going to Emath, my love," Dennis said. He glanced over his shoulder again. "We're going to my home."

In a softer voice he added, "Maybe it's still my home."

CHAPTER 64

The sea was calm, and there was very little current along this stretch of coast . . . but there was some, and that was enough to throw off an oarsman as totally inexperienced as Dennis was. He realized before he'd pulled half way that the boat was drifting north of the the north headland.

Unless they got help from a passing vessel, they were going to land at the foot of the jungle instead of rowing into Emath Harbor directly.

"There ought to be other boats out, Chester," the youth said doubtfully as he rested his oars for a moment. "At least ordinary traffic, even if nobody put out to see what was happening to the Banned Island."

His palms were calloused, but the oar-looms stressed the skin in a pattern different from that of a swordhilt or any other work he had done with his hands. He was going to have some bad blisters soon. . . .

"It may be," said Chester, "that Parol does not permit citizens to leave Emath, for fear that none would return to be ruled by him."

Dennis had shifted his sword so that it didn't interfere with his clumsy attempts to row. He touched the pommel and said, "It may be that I will have questions to discuss with Parol—before I put him out of Emath for good and all."

Their boat grounded at the base of the corniche, the ten-foot cliff which waves had sliced from the side of the continent. The rock was porous—an easy climb up to the level of the jungle, even without the help Chester gave Dennis' boots and Aria's bare feet.

Flowers bloomed with a saffron pungence. When a creature hooted from the far depths of the jungle, Dennis smiled as though he'd been greeted by a friend.

"We—go through this?" Aria asked. Her glance indicated the profusion of flowers and broad leaves around them, filling the clifftop.

"Oh!" Dennis said, startled out of his reverie. None of the immediate stems and creepers were thorny, and the ground would open out as soon as they got within the jungle's sunlit margin, but . . .

"Here," he said, grasping his sword. "I'll cut—"

"No need," Aria said, touching his arm with a smile. She pushed forward, into the mass of foliage which gave before her.

"You really love this, don't you," she added without looking over her shoulder.

"The, the jungle?" Dennis said. He put his arm around the princess's shoulders and hugged her, then stepped past. "Here, I'll lead."

Dennis walked on, handing aside whippy twigs so that they didn't snap back at Aria. "It was the first time I was on my own—"

He paused, smiled, and reached back for the tentacle he was correctly sure that Chester would be ready to curl into his hand.

"On my own with Chester," he corrected himself. "And that brought me many things, most importantly you, my love."

"It brought you to yourself, Dennis," the robot said. "Is not that also of importance?"

"Important to me," Aria said with a smile in her voice, joining her hand briefly with Dennis and Chester before they all separated to get on with the business of moving through heavy cover.

One of the dragons roared from the perimeter of Emath Village.

"You know," Dennis said, "I think that was a bad idea to begin with. Cutting the village off from the, from everything but the sea, really."

He loosened the sword in its scabbard, thinking of the way he had crept—and scuttled—across the perimeter only weeks before.

"It'll be different from now on," Dennis muttered under his breath.

CHAPTER 65

The vegetation surrounding the magical perimeter formed a hostile wall.

Nets of vine and brambles cloaked sword-shaped leaves whose tips would spike all the way to an unwary man's shin-bone. Ants with mandibles like wire-cutters patrolled paths through the foliage. The bees which frequented the blossoms rose when the companions approached. They buzzed and hovered, flexing their abdomens under them to point their stings forward.

Dennis paused. "I thought it was all a nightmare," he mused aloud. "What I remembered from the first night in the jungle. Along with the, with the ghost in my dream. But this *is* the way I remembered it."

"Wizard's work?" Aria asked.

"I don't think it's—" Dennis said.

"Wizard's work imposed on the land, Princess," Chester said flatly. "And the land responding, as all things respond to hostility. 'He who loves his neighbor, finds a family around him.' "

The dragons on guard had heard them talking. One of the beasts snuffled close to the invisible barrier and began to scratch with its foreclaws. Its body was a wall of black scales which blocked the rare opening through the leaves.

The dragons' breath, redolent of the fish they were fed and not wholly unpleasant to Dennis after so many years in a fishing community, oozed heavily through the foliage.

Dennis drew his sword. "All right," he said, eyeing the bees with the caution they deserved. "Let's go."

He brought his star-metal blade up in a curve that sheared a mass of briars as though they were cobweb, then made the second cut which turned the slice into a pathway. Chester moved ahead of the youth, pushing aside the sliced vegetation whose thorns could do him no harm.

It was as though they'd planned the maneuver; and perhaps they had, during the battles they'd fought together since leaving Emath. Chester waited; Dennis slashed the rest of the way through the barrier—

And Aria's white mantilla snapped once, twice, overhead, startling back the insects which were preparing to buzz down in attack.

Both dragons roared as the companions pushed toward them through the jungle wall. Dennis, in the lead again, was laughing in exultation.

They'd shrunk. These guard-beasts weren't as large as the pair that had chased him when Dennis fled Emath.

He flicked his sword at the nearer dragon. It snatched at the blade—and snatched back its injured foreleg with a yelp.

Dennis slapped the beast's snout with the flat of his weapon. "Chester!" the youth cried. "These aren't the same dragons. Has Parol replaced the old ones with these little fellows?"

Chester was raised to his full height on four limbs, spinning the others above him to weave a false silvery bulk that kept back the other guard-beast.

"They are not so great as Malbawn and Malduanan, Dennis," the robot said, advancing through dust that was ankle-deep on the humans. The three companions were within the dragons' perimeter by now. "Nor yet so great as Rakastava . . . but they are the beasts that have guarded Emath for all your life."

The dragon which had cut itself on Dennis' sword made another lunge at him. Dennis shifted his arm slightly. The beast blatted and scrambled back, pricked between the nostrils by the star-metal point.

In sudden determination, the injured guard-beast rushed its fellow from the side and knocked it down. The pair of dragons began to bellow and claw one another, rolling across the perimeter in a huge cloud of the dust they had pulverized during their years of pacing.

Dennis and his companions began to step with care and reasonable quickness across the remainder of the trackway. It struck the youth that you could be very brave and very well armed—and still be crushed to death by a couple of dragons battling in frustrated fury.

"Fortune goes as fate commands," Chester called, over the dragons' roars; but the beasts were flopping and snarling in the opposite direction, and the three of them could spring the last yards into Emath Village if they had to. . . .

Dennis looked toward Emath, taking his eyes off the dragons for the first time since he'd slashed his way into the perimeter they patrolled. The streets, roofs and windows were full of people who stared back at him.

Somebody shouted, "It's Dennis! It's the prince!"

Thugs in orange tried to struggle through the crowd to get to the speaker.

At the head of the central street which led from the palace to the perimeter was a line of men in Parol's

orange livery. They were supported by a pair of demons whose hair of smoke and flame billowed as high as
the nearest eaves.

Rifkin stood in the middle of them; even fatter than
Dennis remembered him, and carrying a polished black
staff as tall as he was.

"Go away!" shouted the ex-butler.

"Rifkin, who are you to tell me to do anything?"
Dennis replied. Only ten feet separated them, but those
within Emath were treating the perimeter as a physical
barrier.

"Get away from here!" Rifkin shouted back. "Whoever you are, you're not wanted in Emath!"

He gestured with his staff of office. The two demons
bent toward Dennis. Their rippling bodies breathed
with the soft, sucking sound of flames.

"Chester," Dennis said quietly. He was well aware
that his boots were still sunken in the dust of the
perimeter, and that the dragons might rush back at any
moment. "How may we kill these demons?"

"The demons cannot be killed, Dennis," the robot
explained, "because they are but images, as empty as
the features of those with whom the sea hag greeted
you on the island."

"That'll do," Dennis muttered.

Before he could act, Aria stepped closer to one of the
demons and waved her mantilla in its insubstantial face.
"Begone!" she cried. "Out of the prince's way!"

The huge figure quivered like a picture projected on
smoke when the breeze blows. Then it was gone. Rifkin
jumped back, and Aria began to laugh like mocking
silver bells.

Dennis strode forward. There were twenty liveried
guards, all of them armed, and Aria's scrap of lace
wouldn't stop a sword-cut. The remaining demon floated
toward him, hot and dry and blurring the youth's vision
of Rifkin as if through a fiery screen.

If Dennis could take out the leader of Parol's men with his first stroke, perhaps the rest would—

"All hail Prince Dennis!" boomed a voice from the crowd. The same voice, Ramos' voice—and Hale's old friend raised high both of the guards who had gone to silence him.

Ramos' great calloused hands were locked on each guard's right wrist. One of the men still waggled his sword vainly.

It acted as a banner to rally the people of Emath Village against their orange-clad oppressors.

A roofing tile struck down a guard, but the rush by hundreds of citizens was too sudden and overwhelming for further missiles to be necessary. The second demon vanished, an empty phantasm which left behind no trace of its passage.

Rifkin dropped his staff. He jumped backward, away from the mob—and bumped into Dennis, who scarcely had time to turn his sword and avoid cutting the ex-butler apart by accident. Rifkin saw what he'd done and screamed, plunging back the way he'd fled. He was starting to tear off his orange tunic, as though that could save him.

It did give the people a useful idea, though. As Dennis and his companions stepped into Emath, the mob began to wave flags of orange fabric as they shouted, "Hail Prince Dennis!"

Ramos had gotten rid of his two captives. He swept his arms around Dennis—still bigger than the youth and far too careless of the drawn sword. One of Chester's tentacles whisked the blade aside to avoid disaster.

"I never thought you'd return, lad," the old man blurted. "I thought that little swine Parol had made away with you."

"None of his doing," Dennis said, hugging Ramos hard with his left arm. "Are—are my parents. . .?"

"He's got them in the palace," Ramos said. Even

though their heads were close together, they both had to raise their voices to be heard over the mob.

"To the palace!" somebody cried, taking up the words.

"King Dennis to the palace!" hundreds of throats replied in a building chant. The crowd surged back down the street, parting to let Dennis and his companions through to its head.

"*King Dennis!*" the people roared.

CHAPTER 66

Chester walked in front of them, his glittering tentacles providing a breathing space for the others without threatening the members of the friendly mob.

"How many more guards are there, Ramos?" Dennis asked. The old man strode at his right side as Aria did at his left.

"No more," Ramos replied. "Parol must have sent them all out when he realized that it was you coming."

Dennis looked around in amazement. "Twenty men couldn't force their rule on Emath," he protested.

"Fear can force its rule on any number of men, Dennis," said Chester before Ramos could respond.

Some of the ex-guards, disarmed and stripped to underwear or less, were skulking along at the edges of the crowd. Those who met Dennis' eyes looked away in fear . . . but they were more afraid not to be a part of the event.

Part of the triumphal return of Prince Dennis to the palace in which he'd been born and raised.

Dennis sheathed his sword. It had won him a princess for wife, but now he realized that he might never *need* the star-metal blade again. There were accounts yet to settle with Parol—

But Parol wouldn't fight him with swords. Of that he could be certain.

The palace was a garden of pure light refracted in sprays of color. It didn't look large to Dennis, now that he'd stood at the glowering foot of Rakastava.

But it was just as beautiful as he remembered it being; and it was his home.

The doors of the main entrance hung ajar. The arch in front of them was covered with what looked like cobwebs—except that the strands were each as thick as a man's little finger.

Dennis looked up the palace facade. Other openings—windows, doors onto balconies; everything large enough to pass an adult—were similarly blocked.

"Chester, is there some sort of trick?" Dennis asked in puzzlement. "Will—lightning strike me when I cut the cords or something like that?"

The tip of one of Chester's tentacles hovered close to the webbing, looking for all the world like a male spider gingerly approaching the lair of a possible mate.

"There is no trick, Dennis," he said. "It may be that Parol thinks you will not be able to cut the web; and it may be that Parol has no better way to prevent you, however long he thinks this obstacle will delay you."

"Not very long," Dennis murmured, drawing his sword again after all.

The mob had stopped, whispering at the web's uncanniness. The glitter of the weapon threw them back fractionally, each row shifting a body's breadth toward the rear—bumping into the row behind it and shifting again.

Dennis swept the blade down. The edge that had taken off Rakastava's heads found the web no hindrance, though the strands parted like heavy wire.

Dennis stepped into Emath Palace. He felt as though he'd been gone a lifetime.

The pillared hall to the throne room smelled sour. Aria's nose wrinkled instinctively, though she quickly blanked her face and glanced over to see whether Dennis had noticed her expression.

He had, but he couldn't blame her. The palace had the odor of a snake den.

The mob stopped outside. A glance behind him showed Dennis a block of doubtful faces staring through the doors, past the remnants of webbing.

He forced a smile at them. They couldn't help. And he couldn't blame them for being afraid.

"The first thing we'll do . . ." Dennis said quietly to his companions. His boots and Ramos' thudded on the crystal, while Chester's many limbs clicked a subtle counterpoint. Aria walked in silence, a cloud of warmth at Dennis' side and in his mind.

". . . is to air the place out and get it back to normal."

"Come in, wanderer!" called a high, nervous voice from the throne room. "Come into my sanctum!"

The door-leaves were of mother-of-pearl. Once there would have been an attendant here to control the flow of petitioners seeking King Hale.

But Hale was gone; the attendants were gone; and the doors were ajar. Dennis pushed the leaves fully open, using his left hand and right foot.

"Put up your sword!" the voice screamed from the dim interior.

"I don't need a sword for you, Parol," Dennis said, sheathing the weapon with a single smooth motion.

Usually the point caught on the scabbard lip, or the blade bound halfway down. Not this time.

Dennis had seen in the mirror the drapes of painted sailcloth with which Parol had covered the throne room. Until he entered the chamber, he hadn't appreciated how cramped and oppressive the place became with all its scintillant crystal hidden.

"Only Dennis may enter!" the voice cried. "I warn you!"

Ribbons of sooty flame rose to either side of the throne, barely illuminating the figure seated there to eyes adapted to the sun outdoors.

Dennis gripped the edge of one of the sailcloth hangings and pulled.

"What are you doing?" the voice demanded.

Something cracked above. A broad sheet of canvas billowed and rushed down with fragments of flimsy scaffolding. Rainbow light filled the back wall and the throne room.

Dennis' parents knelt at the foot of the throne. They were bound and gagged. The creature behind them was squat, black, and vaguely man-shaped, though even in the brighter light it had no more features than the sea hag's manikins.

The sword it held was long enough to lie across the throats of Hale and Selda together.

CHAPTER 67

Parol giggled from two mouths, his own and that of the great-eyed creature clinging to his shoulder.

"The tarsier," Dennis muttered under his breath, remembering the little beast whose ugliness had struck him the day he entered the wizard's apartments. It had been in a glass bubble, then, like all the other creatures he'd thought were dead. . . .

"So . . ." said Parol. "We have an impasse, do we not. A situation not as either of us would wish it, Dennis."

The hood was flopped over much of Parol's face, but what wasn't covered had aged the way soft wood ages at the tide-line: gray and wrinkled so deeply that the skin seemed to be cracking down to the bone. . . .

"I want nothing of yours, Parol," Dennis said steadily, looking past the imploring grimaces of his parents. "You can leave with everything of yours. Everything of, of your predecessor, too. But you have to leave."

The tarsier chittered something.

The black figure—its color was an absence of light,

not a shade of its own—tugged at Selda's faded hair, raising her chin and baring her neck more obviously to his blade.

"Must I, boy?" Parol whispered. "I've learned things, you see. I'm very p-powerful. . . ."

His glance darted around the room as he spoke, falling on the sunlit wall, on the eyes of the youth facing him. The lie stuck in Parol's throat and choked off his voice.

"Give it up—" Dennis said, but the tarsier was whispering into Parol's ear.

"No!" the wizard cried from the throne. "No," in a lower voice, nervous but seductive, "we'll game for it, Dennis, we'll *game* for Emath. That's fair, isn't it?"

His eyes flicked around, never lighting for long, never comfortable where they lighted.

"What sort of a game?" Dennis asked quietly.

Chester was quoting some warning from the doorway, but this was between the two of them, boy-prince and boy-wizard as they had been when Dennis left Emath. . . .

Parol stood up. The base of the throne raised him three steps above the crystal floor, but he still seemed to have shrunk within his robes since Dennis saw him last.

"You will ask me questions," Parol said in a sing-song voice as though he were repeating the words from rote. The tarsier's mouth was working, but if it was making sounds they were too soft to be heard at any distance from Parol's shoulder.

"You will ask me three questions, any questions you please . . . and if I fail to answer them, all three of them, then I will leave. And you will be Prince of Emath, Dennis the Wanderer."

Parol began to giggle again. His cowl had fallen back and his face looked like a dead man's.

"You will be prince," the wizard resumed, his voice still quivering with humor or hysteria. "But if I suc-

ceed, little Dennis— then I will have your life. That's a
fair offer, isn't it?"

Stark terror flashed from Parol's eyes. *"Isn't it?"*

"That's not a fair bargain," Dennis said as his mind
raced, sure there was a catch somewhere in the offer.
"Exile for exile: whoever loses, leaves Emath forever."

"You know I'll never be safe here while you live!"
Parol blazed. "Look at them out there!"

His arm gestured toward the door and the hall beyond
which the citizens of Emath watched. *"Look* at them!"

The tarsier chittered again, audible but not words.

Parol shivered and closed his eyes. His wrist had
looked skeletal when it shot from beneath the sleeve of
his robe.

"No, Dennis, no," the wizard said with his voice
composed. He opened his eyes. "I offer you two lives
for a life. That's fair, isn't it, don't you think that's fair?"

Selda whimpered through her gag.

Dennis walked to a covered portion of the wall and
deliberately ripped down more of the canvas. Flecks of
paint fluttered away from the hangings as they fell.

There wasn't a better choice. There wasn't another
choice at all.

He turned again to the throne.

"All right, Parol," he said. The false flames still hung
in the air, but the prismatic wash of sunlight through
the walls had faded them to vague shimmers.

"Swear on your soul, Dennis!" the one-time apprentice demanded. "Swear that I may have your life if I
succeed!"

"I swear that on my soul!" Dennis shouted back,
unable to control his voice in the tension. "Now are
you ready, or shall I tear your heart out with my
hands, for all your false bogeys?"

But he knew there was nothing false about the black
creature which delicately brushed its machete against
the throats of Hale and Selda, as if it were stropping the
blade.

"Ask," Parol said simply. His eyes were wide open.

It was easy to find a question whose answer Parol couldn't know. "Where is the sea hag?"

The tarsier whispered.

Parol cried, "Dead!" but when his ears took in the words his tongue had uttered, all the blood drained from his face and his hands began to tremble.

"Oh . . ." someone whispered, Aria or Ramos or Dennis himself.

"Who is it claimed the Princess Aria unless a champion should save her?"

As the tarsier whispered, Parol lurched down one of the three steps on which the throne stood.

"Rakastava," the wizard shouted, "and you slew Rakastava too, Dennis, but you won't escape me!"

Dennis couldn't think for terror. Fear for Aria and his parents, fear for the folk of Emath Village who were his folk and his responsibility since he led them in revolt. Fear of failure—

But not fear for himself, because all that had been burned out of him when he dreamed in the jungle.

And that was his question, the answer the tarsier couldn't know because it had never happened outside of Dennis' mind.

"To whom did I tell a story in my dreams the night I left Emath, Parol?"

Parol stepped to the crystal floor, shouting the words of his tarsier familiar, "Serdic! Serdic! And I have your—"

The apprentice's hand was stretched out to deliver the bolt of flame to which Dennis' oath had bound him. Something formed in the air behind him.

"—life!"

The arms of the Wizard Serdic closed about the pasty boy who had been his apprentice. Parol had spoken the name that closed the bargain Serdic offered Dennis in the rain-soaked jungle.

The flesh had slumped away from Serdic's hands and the right side of his face, but half his smile remained; and the scribbling of fungus across it.

The tarsier tried to leap clear, but one of the wizard's bony hands caught it in the air. The little beast screamed, louder even than Parol—

And they disappeared, wizard and apprentice and familiar, leaving only the fetid odor of decay where they had been.

The knife clanged to the floor. The black creature had vanished, as though it never was.

"All hail King Dennis!" Ramos shouted.

Dennis turned in shocked amazement. "What?" he said. "No!"

"All hail King Dennis!" Aria cried in her clear silver voice.

"All hail King Dennis!" roared the crowd, mob no longer, as it burst into the crystal corridors that were clear at last of magic and the horrors that magic spawned.

Dennis wanted to cut his parents free, but Ramos was doing that already with a blunt-tipped bait-cutting knife. Other hands were ripping down the last of the painted cloth with which Parol had tried to blot out the sun whose light he feared.

"Look, I can't—" Dennis protested, knowing that he couldn't even hear himself with the cheerful tumult filling the room.

Aria reached for his hand, took it, and walked her husband backward up the steps to the throne.

"But I—"

"*Hail, King Dennis!*"

In the end, King Dennis raised his arms high to acknowledge the cheers of his new subjects.

THE END

THE KING OF YS
POUL AND KAREN ANDERSON

THE KING OF YS—
THE GREATEST
EPIC FANTASY
OF THIS DECADE!

by Poul and Karen Anderson

As many authors that have brought new life and meaning to Camelot and her King, so have Poul and Karen Anderson brought to life a city of legend on the coast of Brittany . . . Ys.

THE ROMAN SOLDIER BECAME A KING, AND HUSBAND TO THE NINE

In *Roma Mater*, the Roman centurion Gratillonius became King of Ys, city of legend—and husband to its nine magical Queens.

A PRIEST-KING AT WAR WITH HIS GODS

In *Gallicenae*, Gratillonius consolidates his power in the name and service of Rome the Mother, and his war worsens with the senile Gods of Ys, that once blessed city.

HE MUST MARRY HIS DAUGHTER—OR WATCH AS HIS KINGDOM IS DESTROYED

In *Dahut* the final demands of the gods were made clear: that Gratillonius wed his own daughter . . . and as a result of his defying that divine ultimatum, the consequent destruction of Ys itself.

THE STUNNING CLIMAX

In *The Dog and the Wolf*, the once and future king strives first to save the remnant of the Ysans from utter destruction—then use them to save civilization itself, as the light that once was Rome flickers out, and barbarian night descends upon the world. In the progress, Gratillonius, once a Roman centurion and King of Ys, will become King Grallon of Brittany, and give rise to a legend that will ring down the corridors of time!

BAEN FANTASY

Baen Books is happy to announce a new line devoted exclusively to the publication of fantasy. As with Baen Science Fiction, our aim is that every novel will exhibit genuine literary merit—but only in the context of powerful story values, idea-driven plotlines, and internal plausibility. Here are some of the first offerings in our new line:

THE KING OF YS—*THE GREATEST EPIC FANTASY OF THIS DECADE!*
by Poul and Karen Anderson

ROMA MATER, **Book I**
Before there was an England there was Roma Mater. Before King Arthur, the King of Ys . . . Ys, daughter of Carthage on the coast of Brittany, ruled by the magic of The Nine and the might of the King, their Husband. How The Nine conspired with their gods to bring him to them, though he belonged to Mithras and to Rome, is only the beginning of the story . . .
65602-3 $3.95

GALLICENAE, **Book II**
Gratillonius is the great and noble King of Ys, a city of legend that treated with Rome as an equal—and lived on after Rome had fallen. This is the story of his nine queens, and penetrates to the very heart of the legend.
65342-3 $3.95

***DAHUT*, Book III**
Dahut is the daughter of the King, Gratillonius, and her story is one of mythic power . . . and ancient evil. The senile gods of Ys have decreed that Dahut must become a Queen of the Christ-cursed city of Ys while her father still lives.   65371-7 $3.95

***THE DOG AND THE WOLF*, Book IV**
Gratillonius, the once and future King, strives first to save the surviving remnant of the Ysans from utter destruction, and then to save civilization itself as barbarian night extinguishes the last flickers of the light that once was Rome!   65391-1 $4.50

ANDERSON, POUL
THE BROKEN SWORD
Come with us now to 11th-century Scandinavia, when Christianity is beginning to replace the old religon, but the Old Gods still have power, and men are still oppressed by the folk of the Faerie.
                                               65382-2 $2.95

ASIRE, NANCY
TWILIGHT'S KINGDOMS
For centuries, two nearly-immortal races—the Krotahnya, followers of Light, and the Leishoranya, servants of Darkness—have been at war, struggling for final control of a world that belongs to neither. "The novel-length debut of an important new talent . . . I enthusiastically recommend it."—C.J. Cherryh
                                               65362-8 $3.50

BROWN, MARY
THE UNLIKELY ONES
Thing is a young girl who hides behind a mask; her companions include a crow, a toad, a goldfish, and a

kitten. Only the Dragon of the Black Mountain can restore them to health and happiness—but the questers must total seven to have a chance of success. "An imaginative and charming book."—*USA Today*. "You've got a winner here . . ."—Anne McCaffrey.

65361-X $3.95

DAVIDSON, AVRAM and DAVIS, GRANIA
MARCO POLO AND THE SLEEPING BEAUTY
Held by bonds of gracious but involuntary servitude in the court of Kublai Khan for ten years, the Polos—Marco, his father Niccolo, and his uncle Maffeo—want to go home. But first they must complete one simple task: bring the Khan the secret of immortality!

65372-5 $3.50

EMERY, CLAYTON
TALES OF ROBIN HOOD
Deep within Sherwood Forest, Robin Hood and his band have founded an entire community, but they must be always alert against those who would destroy them: Sir Guy de Gisborne, Maid Marion's ex-fiance and Robin's sworn enemy; the sorceress Taragal, who summons a demon boar to attack them; and even King Richard the Lion-Hearted, who orders Robin and his men to come and serve his will in London. And who is the false Hood whose men rape, pillage and burn in Robin's name?

65397-0 $3.50

AB HUGH, DAFYDD
HEROING
A down-on-her-luck female adventurer, a would-be boy hero, and a world-weary priest looking for new faith are comrades on a quest for the World's Dream.

65344-X $3.50

HEROES IN HELL

created by Janet Morris

The greatest heroes of history meet the greatest names of science fiction—and each other!—in the greatest meganovel of them all! (Consult "The Whole Baen Catalog" for the complete listing of HEROES IN HELL.)

MORRIS, JANET & GREGORY BENFORD,
C.J. CHERRYH, ROBERT SILVERBERG, more!
ANGELS IN HELL (Vol. VII)
Gilgamesh returns for blood; Marilyn Monroe kisses the Devil; Stalin rewrites the Bible; and Altos, the unfallen Angel, drops in on Napoleon and Marie with good news: Marie will be elevated to heaven, no strings attached! Such a deal! (So why is Napoleon crying?)   65360-1 $3.50

MORRIS, JANET, & LYNN ABBEY, NANCY ASIRE,
C. J. CHERRYH, DAVID DRAKE, BILL KERBY,
CHRIS MORRIS, more.
MASTERS IN HELL (Vol. VIII)
Feel the heat as the newest installment of the infernally popular HEROES IN HELL® series roars its way into your heart! This is Hell—where you'll find Sir Francis Burton, Copernicus, Lee Harvey Oswald, J. Edgar Hoover, Napoleon, Andropov, and other masters and would-be masters of their fate.
                                   65379-2 $3.50

REAVES, MICHAEL
THE BURNING REALM
A gripping chronicle of the struggle between human magicians and the very *in*human Chthons with their

demon masters. All want total control over the whirling fragments of what once was Earth, before the Necromancer unleashed the cataclysm that tore the world apart. "A fast-paced blend of fantasy, martial arts, and unforgettable landscapes."—Barbara Hambly   65386-5 $3.50

EMPIRE OF THE EAST
by Fred Saberhagen

THE BROKEN LANDS, Book I
A masterful blend of high technology and high sorcery; a unique adventure in a world on the brink of ultimate change; a world where magic rules—and science struggles to live again! "The work of a master."
—*The Magazine of Fantasy & Science Fiction*
65380-6 $2.95

THE BLACK MOUNTAINS, Book II
East meets West in bloody conflict on a world where magic rules, but technology is revolting! "A fine mix of fantasy and science fiction, action and speculation."
—Roger Zelazny   65390-3 $2.75

ARDNEH'S WORLD, Book III
The gripping climax of the "Empire of the East" series. "Ranks favorably with Tolkien. Exceptional in sheer unbridled zest and imaginative sweep."
—*School Library Journal*   65404-7 $2.95

SPRINGER, NANCY
CHANCE—AND OTHER GESTURES OF THE HAND OF FATE
Chance is a low-born forester who falls in love with

the lovely Princess Halimeda—but the story begins when Halimeda's brother discovers Chance's feelings toward the Princess. It's a story of power and jealousy, taking place in the mysterious Wirral forest, whose inhabitants are not at all human . . .

65337-7 $3.50

THE HEX WITCH OF SELDOM (hardcover)
The King, the Sorceress, the Trickster, the Virgin, the Priest . . . together they form the Circle of Twelve, the primal human archetypes whose powers are manifest in us all. Young Bobbi Yandro, can speak with them at will—and when she becomes the mistress of a horse who is more than a horse, events sweep her into the very hands of the Twelve . . .

65389-X $15.95

Have You Missed?

DRAKE, DAVID
At Any Price
Hammer's Slammers are back—and Baen Books has them!
Now the 23rd-century armored division faces its deadliest
enemies ever: aliens who *teleport* into combat.
55978-8 $3.50

DRAKE, DAVID
Hammer's Slammers
A special *expanded* edition of the book that began the
legend of Colonel Alois Hammer. Now the toughest, mean-
est mercs who ever killed for a dollar or wrecked a world
for pay have come home—to Baen Books—and they've
brought a secret weapon: "The Tank Lords," a brand-new
short novel, included in this special Baen edition of *Hammer's Slammers*. **65632-5 $3.50**

DRAKE, DAVID
Lacey and His Friends
In Jed Lacey's time the United States computers scan
every citizen, every hour of the day. When crime is de-
tected, it's Lacey's turn. There are a few things worse than
having him come after you, but they're not survivable
either. But things aren't really that bad—not for Lacey and
his friends. By the author of *Hammer's Slammers* and *At
Any Price*. **65593-0 $3.50**

**CARD, ORSON SCOTT; DRAKE, DAVID;
& BUJOLD, LOIS McMASTER**
(edited by Elizabeth Mitchell)
Free Lancers (Alien Stars, Vol. IV)
Three short novels about mercenary soldiers—never be-
fore in print! Card's hero leads a ragtag group of scientific
refugees to sanctuary in Utah; Drake contributes a new
"Hammer's Slammers" story; Bujold tells a new tale of
Miles Vorkosigan, hero of *The Warrior's Apprentice*.
65352-0 $2.95

DRAKE, DAVID
Birds of Prey

The time: 262 A.D. The place: Imperial Rome. There had never been a greater empire, but now it is dying. Everywhere its armies are in retreat, and what had been civilization seethes with riots and bizarre cults. Against the imminent fall of the Long Night stands Aulus Perennius, an Imperial secret agent as tough and ruthless as the age in which he lives. But he stands alone—until a traveller from Earth's far future recruits him for a mission so strange it cannot be disclosed.

55912-5 (trade paper) $7.95
55909-5 (hardcover) $14.95

DRAKE, DAVID
Ranks of Bronze

Disguised alien traders bought captured Roman soldiers on the slave market because they needed troops who could win battles without high-tech weaponry. The leigionaires provided victories, smashing barbarian armies with the swords, javelins, and discipline that had won a world. But the worlds on which they now fought were strange ones, and the spoils of victory did not include freedom. If the legionaires went home, it would be through the use of the beam weapons and force screens of their ruthless alien owners. It's been 2000 years—and now they want to go home.   65568-X $3.50

DRAKE, DAVID, & WAGNER, KARL EDWARD
Killer

Vonones and Lycon capture wild animals to sell for bloodsport in ancient Rome. A vicious animal sold to them by a trader turns out to be more than they bargained for—it is the sole survivor of the crash of an alien spacecraft. Possessed of intelligence nearly human, it has two goals in life: to breed and to kill.

55931-1 $2.95

DAVID DRAKE

"Drake has distinguished himself as the master of the mercenary sf novel."—*Rave Reviews*